"I'd say you need me, Dr. Logan. You need me real bad."

Ryan had never seen a pair of eyes that could manage to look so innocent and so not…at the same time.

And hiring Maddie Kincaid to be his assistant was a plan that made sense. On the surface.

But…

"I know what you're thinking. You're worried about us being together in the house for too long. That I might start getting ideas."

"No, it's not that."

She half laughed, half sighed. He told himself that she was sitting too far away for him to feel her breath on his face. That the last thing he wanted was to feel her breath on his face.

She went on. "After what I've been through, marriage is the last thing on my mind. Trust me."

He did.

Oh, hell. It wasn't *her* he didn't trust….

Dear Reader,

"In like a lion, out like a lamb." That's what they say about March, right? Well, there are no meek and mild lambs among this month's Intimate Moments heroines, that's for sure! In *Saving Dr. Ryan*, Karen Templeton begins a new miniseries, THE MEN OF MAYES COUNTY, while telling the story of a roadside delivery—yes, the baby kind—that leads to an improbable romance. Maddie Kincaid starts out looking like the one who needs saving, but it's really Dr. Ryan Logan who's in need of rescue.

We continue our trio of FAMILY SECRETS prequels with *The Phoenix Encounter* by Linda Castillo. Follow the secret-agent hero deep under cover—and watch as he rediscovers a love he'd thought was dead. But where do they go from there? Nina Bruhns tells a story of repentance, forgiveness and passion in *Sins of the Father*, while Eileen Wilks offers up tangled family ties and a seemingly insoluble dilemma in *Midnight Choices*. For Wendy Rosnau's heroine, there's only *One Way Out* as she chooses between being her lover's mistress—or his wife. Finally, Jenna Mills' heroine becomes *The Perfect Target*. She meets the seemingly perfect man, then has to decide whether he represents safety—or danger.

The excitement never flags—and there will be more next month, too. So don't miss a single Silhouette Intimate Moments title, because this is the line where you'll find the best and most exciting romance reading around.

Enjoy!

Leslie J. Wainger
Executive Senior Editor

Please address questions and book requests to:
Silhouette Reader Service
U.S.: 3010 Walden Ave., P.O. Box 1325, Buffalo, NY 14269
Canadian: P.O. Box 609, Fort Erie, Ont. L2A 5X3

KAREN TEMPLETON
Saving Dr. Ryan

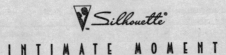

Silhouette®

INTIMATE MOMENTS™

Published by Silhouette Books

America's Publisher of Contemporary Romance

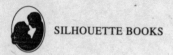 SILHOUETTE BOOKS

ISBN 0-373-27277-4

SAVING DR. RYAN

Visit Silhouette at www.eHarlequin.com

Printed in U.S.A.

Books by Karen Templeton

Silhouette Intimate Moments

Anything for His Children #978
Anything for Her Marriage #1006
Everything but a Husband #1050
Runaway Bridesmaid #1066
†*Plain-Jane Princess* #1096
†*Honky-Tonk Cinderella* #1120
What a Man's Gotta Do #1195
**Saving Dr. Ryan* #1207

Silhouette Yours Truly

Wedding Daze
Wedding Belle
Wedding? Impossible!

†How To Marry a Monarch
**The Men of Mayes County
*Weddings, Inc.

KAREN TEMPLETON,

a Waldenbooks bestselling author and RITA® Award
nominee, is the mother of five sons and living proof that
romance and dirty diapers are not mutually exclusive
terms. An Easterner transplanted to Albuquerque, New
Mexico, she spends far too much time trying to coax her
garden to yield roses and produce something resembling
a lawn, all the while fantasizing about a weekend alone
with her husband. Or at least an uninterrupted conversation.

She loves to hear from readers, who may reach her by
writing c/o Silhouette Books, 300 E. 42nd St., New York,
NY 10017, or online at www.karentempleton.com.

To country doctors everywhere,
whose selflessness epitomizes the best in human nature.

Acknowledgments

To Oana Nisipeanu, M.D.,
who answered my medical "hows?";
to Kelli Garcia,
for giving me a virtual peek
inside a small-town doctor's office;
to Debrah Morris and Linda Goodnight,
for being my "tour guides"
to Northeastern Oklahoma and for making me fall in
love with that part of the world, sight unseen;
to JoAnn Weatherly,
for answering my questions about geriatric hip fractures.
Any goofs are mine, not theirs.

Chapter 1

"Keep your shirt on! I'm coming, I'm coming...*dammit!*"

His big toe now throbbing, Ryan Logan continued down the dark stairs in his stockinged feet, all the while fumbling with the buttons to the flannel shirt he'd dragged on over his tee at the doorbell's first shriek. He yawned so widely his jaw popped: he hadn't gotten to bed but two hours ago, at three-thirty. Which meant his blood wasn't yet moving fast enough to ward off the damp, late September chill that permeated the old house. Judging from the rain still battering the roof, there'd be no sunrise.

He'd no sooner plowed one hand through his hopeless hair when the bell blatted again. On a muttered curse, he yanked open the front door: the two little kids standing on the porch jumped a mile. Ryan's heart twisted—the pipsqueaks were soaked through, the boy's dark eyes glittering in terror and excitement underneath a fringe of scraggly bangs. Pale fingers gripped closed a stringless, nothing-colored hooded sweatshirt, his other hand hanging on for dear life to the shivering little blonde beside him. Ryan had never seen either of them before.

The boy stumbled backward a little, taking the girl with him. His eyes went wide and his mouth sagged open, but nothing came out. It dawned on Ryan how scary he must look.

"It's okay, son," he said, squatting down. Wasn't anything he could do about the bed-head, but he could at least reduce his six-foot-two frame into something less intimidating. He lifted his voice just enough to be heard over the rain pummeling the porch overhang. "What is it?"

"You the doctor?"

"Sure am."

The trembling child glanced back into the rain-drenched darkness, then at Ryan, still warily.

"Mama said to come."

With a nod, Ryan leaned over to grab his boots off the mat by the door. He was wide-awake now: odd hour calls came with the territory when the closest hospital was forty-five minutes away.

Both floor and kids flinched when Ryan stomped his foot firmly inside the first boot. "Sorry," he said, sparing them both a quick smile. The boy couldn't have been more than five or six, his sister—Ryan assumed—maybe three or so.

"She said to hurry," the boy said.

Ryan shoved on the other boot, grabbed his denim jacket off the stand by the front door and shrugged into it. "Where is your mama?" he asked, clamping his broad-brimmed hat on his head with one hand, snatching his black bag off the hall table with the other.

A beanpole arm flailed out. "D-down there. In the car." The bright eyes glanced back at him over a chin quivering from both emotion and the raw autumn chill, Ryan guessed. "She said to tell you the b-baby's comin'."

Oh, Lord.

Ryan dropped the bag back on the table and pulled the dripping children inside. He took a precious moment to crouch in front of them again, gently squeezing the boy's shoulder, smiling into the little girl's huge, frightened eyes. "Stay right here," he softly commanded, then bolted out into the driving rain before the boy had a chance to protest.

* * *

The steering wheel bit into Maddie Kincaid's palms as she choked back a bitter scream. Despite the piercing, damp cold inside the old Impala, sweat drenched her flannel nightgown underneath her car coat. The pains had come on so sudden, her only thought had been to get out, get help. She hadn't even bothered to put on socks—if she could've bent over to begin with—and now her feet felt like Popsicles inside her canvas slip-ons.

The pain crested, passed. On a deep, panicky sigh, she leaned her head on the back of the seat, determined not to cry, even though it was highly unlikely anybody'd hear her over the hammering rain and wind. She'd never meant to send Noah and Katie Grace out in the storm, but they'd been gone before she could stop them. At least she'd remembered seeing the office sign in front of the slightly dilapidated, two-story house when she'd passed it yesterday. Something to be grateful for, at least.

But—a blast of wind plastered another layer of leaves to the windshield—what if nobody was home? What if she had to deliver this baby herself, right here, and take care of two other children besides?

Something like a laugh tried to well up in her throat. Just when you think things can't possibly get any worse…

"Oh, God, oh, God, oh God," she whimpered, rolling her head back and forth, only to suck in a sharp breath when the next pain began clawing its way through her belly. Her labor with the first two had been nothing like this. Especially Noah's. All that walking, *trying* to get things moving—

The scream escaped this time as fire blazed through her crotch. She tried to get on top of the contraction, to focus her breathing, as the searing pain obliterated everything but itself—

The car door flew open, sending chilled air and wet leaves swirling inside; a large male hand landed on her rock-hard belly, provoking a little yelp. She glanced over, registering little more than pale eyes, a hard-set mouth and prickly cheeks, all shadowed by a cowboy hat. "Where're my kids?" she managed through clenched teeth.

"Inside. Safe."

"Alone?" Fear surged through her, more intense even than the contractions. "They're scared to death of bein' in a strange place by themselves! They're—"

"Fine," the man said quietly. "How far apart are they?" His voice was gentle, low. Totally lost on her. Sheets of water drummed relentlessly into the mud by the car, on the Impala's hood and roof, irritating her no end. She realized the man's hand still rested on her distended belly.

"I hope to heck this means you're the doctor."

"Looks like this is your lucky day, ma'am." He removed his hand; she glanced over, saw he was squatting by the open car door. Rain streamed off his hat brim. "So." Patience weighted the single word. "How far apart—?"

"I don't know," she bit out. "Constant, seems like."

"Can you walk?"

"You think I'd've let my kids out in this rain if I could?"

No sooner were the words out than a pair of strong arms slipped around her, lifting her up and out of the car. With a little cry, Maddie tucked her head against the solid, firesmoke-scented chest, trying to avoid the pelting rain. The doctor cocooned her inside his jacket as best he could, plopped his hat on her head, then gently shifted her in his arms to slam the car door shut.

"Hang on," he shouted over the din. "I'm gonna get you to the house as fast as possible, okay?"

Huddled underneath the coat, the precariously angled hat, Maddie nodded weakly, the pain mercifully subsiding for the minute or so it took for the trek to the house, set back from the road maybe a hundred feet or so.

But only for a minute. The instant they got inside, another contraction vised every muscle from her ribs to her knees. She bit her lip to keep from screaming in front of her babies, standing wide-eyed in the old-fashioned vestibule as the doctor swept her past them and down a narrow hallway. She was barely aware of the children's sneakers beating a tattoo against the bare wood floor as they followed, Noah asking her over and over if she was all right.

"I'm fine, sugar," she managed, somehow, even though she couldn't see him. Still, she winced a little as the doctor lowered her onto the edge of a bed covered in a heavily textured bedspread, flinching in the sudden flash of a bedside lamp being turned on.

"You feel like pushing yet?"

She shook her head.

"Good. Means we got a minute."

He helped her out of her coat, then disappeared. Seconds later, he was back with a pile of linens, what looked like some shirts or something, and his black bag, which he thunked onto the nightstand. Noah and Katie Grace stood rooted to the spot a few feet away, Katie with her thumb in her mouth. Water dripped from both their heads, had turned Noah's gray sweatshirt—two sizes too big, but she'd found it for next to nothing at some yard sale—nearly black. Maddie moaned and struggled to get up. "They're all wet—"

Another pain slammed into her, grabbing her breath. She doubled up, falling onto her side into the bed, mortified and aggravated and plain scared out of her wits. Her eyes clamped shut, but a tear or two still escaped. Through her nightgown sleeve, she felt a warm, steady touch, which she had to admit did calm her some.

"I'll take care of it," the doctor said. "You just concentrate on having this baby, you hear?" She managed a nod, the bedspread rough against her cheek. "Good. Water break yet?"

"Uh-uh."

"Here—" A thick, white towel appeared in her line of sight. "In case it does while I'm tending to the kids."

Maddie struggled to protest, but her body had other ideas. The next few minutes were reduced to disjointed impressions—a radiator clanking, rain slashing against the window, wet clothes plopping on the floor as the doctor soothed her frightened children. The fact that nobody had appeared to help him out. Like a wife or housekeeper. Or something.

Suddenly she felt a painless but decisive sensation in her lower belly, like a pin pricking a balloon; she barely managed to stuff the towel between her legs to catch the gush of warm liquid. She swiped at a tear trickling down the side of her nose, hating the thought of a stranger taking care of her children. Of her. That she had no choice in the matter.

More fluid seeped into the towel with the next contraction. Maddie only half watched, silently panting, as the doctor wrapped her children in warm blankets, settling them into an overstuffed armchair in the corner of the room, close to the sizzling radiator.

She heard the change in his voice, knew he'd seen.

"You two just snuggle up for a bit while I check out your mama. All right?"

"Yes, sir," she heard from Noah, and relief trickled through her. He tended to be skittish around most men these days. Especially ones as big as Dr. Logan. Not that Maddie could blame him for that, she supposed.

Again, the doctor vanished, reappearing maybe a minute later. He fussed with something or other nearby, then turned to her, his thick, damp hair a dull gold in the weak light. He raked one hand through it, raising a field of curved spikes on the top of his head.

"I put the kids' clothes in the dryer," he said, his gaze snagging on the towel indelicately wadded between her legs, which for some reason provoked a low chuckle.

Maddie squeezed shut her eyes, breathed through the next wave of pain. "What's so blamed funny?"

"My timing, looks like." He grabbed another towel, replacing the first one. She opened her eyes to catch his nod in approval as he briefly inspected it, tossed it into a plastic tub. "Fluid's clear. Good sign. Now let's see what's what."

The next few minutes passed in a blur as the doctor palmed her belly, pronounced the baby in the correct position, then prepared both the bed and her for the birth. All the while, his face remained expressionless, his manner calm, efficient, unembarrassed, even when he helped her remove her soaked panties. Several pillows now at her back, Maddie watched him fish his stethoscope and a blood pressure cuff from his bag, noted how his height was offset by a kind of wiriness, that his movements were sure and graceful. She began to relax, at least enough to say, "You know, I don't normally let a man remove my underwear without getting his name first."

"Logan," the doctor said, amusement—she hoped—making his mouth twitch. "Ryan Logan. The degrees are up in my office." He jerked his head to the right. "On the other side of that wall." She saw his attention flicker briefly to the kids, both of them already out like lights, Noah snoring softly. Dr. Logan looked back at her, barely smiling. "Looks like they're down for the count."

She nodded, licked her lips. Figured she may as well preempt the first round of questions. "I didn't do that to him."

"I didn't figure you had. You want some water?"

Maddie nodded again; Dr. Logan poured a glass of water, handed it to her. "Just a sip, now—"

"I know, I know."

She sipped, handed him back the glass, catching the compassion in his expression. And a boatload of questions, waiting off to the side. He picked up a cordless phone, punched a number into it. "Calling for reinforcements," he explained. "The midwife. How far along are you?"

"I think I'm about three weeks early—"

He frowned, then spoke to the person on the other end. "Hey, Ivy, got a surprise delivery about to happen over here, was wondering if you'd... Uh-huh." He laughed softly, etching creases at the corners of his eyes, then sobered. "Small, from what I can tell. Early, a bit. But the head's engaged, she's a multip... No, I haven't. Thought I'd wait for you to do that." He turned to Maddie, his expression unreadable. "Third baby?"

"Uh-huh."

"How long you been in labor?"

She opened her mouth to answer, only to be strangled by another pain. Dr. Logan leaned over to massage her shoulder, his kindness adding yet another layer of achiness to the twenty worries already suffocating her.

"Yeah, they're real strong," he said quietly into the phone, his eyes locked with hers, silently coaching her through the contraction. "And she's got that look on her face…. No, not yet, but I wouldn't wait, if I were you. Membranes ruptured, maybe ten minutes ago? I doubt she's gonna have a long second phase. Yep, door's unlocked."

He disconnected the phone, set it on the nightstand. When the pain subsided, she noticed the severely dipped brows, the firm mouth turned down at the corners.

"Okay, let's back up here a second—you *think* you're three weeks early?"

She didn't miss the edge to the question. "Yes."

"Labor came on quick then, I take it?"

"An hour ago, maybe…*ooooh!*"

Without thinking, she grabbed his hand with the next contraction, squeezing shut her eyes, swallowing down the howl threatening to strangle her. She felt Dr. Logan's free hand cradle her hard belly, the other warm and steady under the pressure of her fingers. Floating over the pain, his voice eased her through the contraction.

"Minute and a half. Good." She looked up, grateful to see his expression had softened some. He was younger than she'd at first thought, she realized with a bit of a start. A lot younger. Mid-thirties, maybe. Weren't country doctors all supposed to have white hair and potbellies?

The bed creaked a little when he eased himself onto the edge. Not looking at her face, he pushed back her nightgown sleeve, strapped the blood pressure cuff to her arm. "By the way, I'm not in the habit of removing a woman's underpants without knowing her name, either." A pair of wire-rimmed glasses appeared from his pocket; he snapped them open before settling them into place. "So," he said, pumping up the cuff. "You are?"

"Miserable."

He smiled a little, squeezing the bulb until she thought she'd lose the circulation in her fingers, frowning slightly as the needle hitched, dropped. "Pressure's a bit high, Miserable."

"Might have something to do with my bein' a little stressed at the moment."

He grunted. Strong, smooth fingers slipped around her wrist. He focused on his watch. "New in town?"

"You could say that. And my name's Maddie. Maddie Kincaid."

"And…is there a Mr. Kincaid?"

The wedding ring had been one of the first things hocked, not that it had brought much. Still, Maddie found it interesting he wasn't making assumptions one way or the other. "Not anymore—oh, *Lordy!*"

"You ready to push?" she thought she heard the doctor say, but since she already was, the question seemed moot.

Ryan grabbed a set of disposable latex gloves from his bag and snapped them on. So much for waiting for Ivy to do the internal. Yes, he was the doctor, but he was also a stranger. And this gal didn't need any more on her plate right now, that was for damn sure. But she shouldn't be pushing before he knew if she was fully dilated or not.

"Sorry," he said, slipping down the sheet. "I really need to—"

"It's okay." Marbled knuckles gripped the sheet as she panted out, "But it's not every man I'd let do this on the first date."

Biting back a smile, Ryan quickly examined her, relieved to find all systems go. And her blood pressure wasn't dangerously high, just enough to bear watching. Not that deliveries made him nervous—he'd done his fair share over the past ten years—but he wasn't real excited about doing an out-of-hospital birth with an underweight woman, three weeks early—she thought—whose case he didn't know.

"You can go ahead and push now," he said, leaving the sheet up and peeling off the gloves.

"Like you've got any say in it," she got out, just before her face contorted again. But not with pain this time. With determination.

Ryan wriggled into a fresh pair of gloves, deciding against asking her if she wanted to get the kids up. They were zonked, nobody needed the distraction right now, and if she'd wanted them up, he had no doubt she would have made her wishes known.

Three pushes later, the baby's head crowned. No surprise there.

"Pant, Maddie, pant! Don't push, you hear me? Pant the baby out…yeah, like that, good. Baby's real small…the idea is to birth it, not launch it into orbit."

For a split second, her startled gaze met his and she looked as though she might laugh…only another surge diverted her attention.

"Pant, honey! That's right, that's a girl… Good, good… okay…here we go…!"

He steeled himself for her screams…but they never came. One of his patients had likened giving birth to squeezing a cannonball through the eye of a needle, an image which had pretty much burned itself into his mind. Maddie Kincaid, however, either had the highest pain threshold known to womankind or was possessed of a will Ryan decided he did not ever want to tangle with.

Two blinks later, a tiny, perfectly shaped head slid out, the cord loosely wrapped around the baby's neck. Ryan easily untwisted it, helping the little thing to rotate before easing first one shoulder, then the other, out from underneath the pubic bone, then presented Maddie Kincaid with her new daughter—five and half pounds, tops, of flailing determination, red and wrinkled and bald, but with a set of lungs capable of waking the dead in three counties.

With a sound that was equal parts laugh and sob, Maddie thrust out her arms. "Give her to me! Is she okay? She must be okay if she's cryin' like that, right?"

"She's fine," Ryan said, trying to ignore the strange, burning tightness in the back of his throat that assailed him every time he delivered a baby. He quickly suctioned the perfect little nose and mouth, wrapped little missy in a clean towel and laid her on Maddie's stomach. He should probably get to the Apgar scoring, but God knows millions of healthy babies had been born over the years without being graded like eggs the minute they were born.

"You're a peanut, but you're a real perky little peanut," he said softly, rubbing the tiny thing's back through the towel. Then he looked at the skinny, scrappy woman who'd just produced the now-quieter infant squirming in her arms, and something inside just melted, like when your muscles get all tense but you don't even realize it until someone tells you to relax. "You done good, Mama. Shoot, you didn't even work up a good sweat."

Silver eyes, full of delight and mischief, briefly tangled with his. "Widest pelvis in the lower forty-eight," she said, her grin eclipsing the entire lower half of her face.

And the thought came, *This is no ordinary woman.*

A moment later, in a flutter of skirts and long salt-and-pepper hair, Ivy Gardner burst into the room, took one look at the situation and said, "Figured you'd get the fun part, leave the cleanin' up to me!" Except then the two-hundred-pound woman, her hair barely caught up in a couple of silver clips, swept over to the bed. "I'm Ivy, honey," she said to Maddie, her expression softening at the sight of the baby. "Oh…wouldja look at this cutie-pie?" She let out a loud cackle. "Boy or girl?"

"A girl. Amy Rose."

Ivy grinned. "Amy. *Beloved.*"

"That's right."

But Ivy had already turned her attention to other matters, massaging Maddie's abdomen to facilitate the expulsion of the placenta, all the while cooing to the new baby and praising her mama.

Ryan left them to it. Ivy Gardner had delivered more than five hundred babies in the last twenty-five years, had never lost a one. Or a mother, either. And right now, he figured his patient could use some mothering herself.

His heart did a slow, painful turn in his chest as he peeled off his gloves, staring out the window. The rain had stopped, he realized, the sky pinking up some in the east.

And Ryan found himself beset with the strangest feeling that his life had just changed somehow.

He glanced over at the two children, stirring from sleep on

the chair. It plumb tore him up, seeing those three—now four—in the condition they were in. What had brought Maddie here, with two small children and as pregnant as she was? She didn't look like she was much more than a kid herself, although he supposed she was at least twenty or so. Except for the mud on the bottoms of their jeans, the kids' clothes had been clean enough, but they were worn, probably secondhand, the little girl wearing her brother's hand-me-downs, he guessed.

His gaze drifted back to Maddie. Scraps of light brown hair, the color unremarkable, grazed her cheeks and neck, the shoulders of her faded nightgown. Paper-thin, freckled skin stretched across prominent cheekbones, a high forehead, a straight nose. When she spoke or laughed, her voice was rusty. When she gave a person one of her direct looks, it was like staring into a bank of storm clouds.

And those storm-cloud eyes clearly said, "I'm more than life has ever given me a chance to be."

Right now, those eyes were fastened on her newborn child, the harsh angles of her too-thin face aglow with the rush of new-mother love. Born too soon, the infant wasn't quite "done" yet, but he was sure Maddie didn't see the wrinkled, ruddy skin, the bit of hair plastered to the head with vernix, the little face all smushed up like a dried apple. The infant yawned, and Maddie giggled.

"You're a funny-looking little thing," she whispered, and Ryan almost laughed out loud.

"Mama?"

Ryan turned in time to catch another sleepy yawn. Noah's hair had pretty much dried by now, sticking up all over his head in a mass of little horns. Ryan could relate.

"Hey, grasshopper," he said, scooping the child off the chair, blanket and all. "Come meet your new sister."

For an instant, the child cuddled against his chest. Too sleepy to protest, probably. He smelled sweet. Clean. Whatever was going on in Maddie Kincaid's life, she'd given her children baths last night. An effort which had probably brought on the premature labor.

Ryan set the child, still huddled under his blanket, on the bed at Maddie's knees. The boy rubbed his eyes, yawned again. Then frowned. "Another *girl?*"

"Oh, now, hush up," Maddie said over a weary, but relieved, laugh, as Ryan deposited an owl-eyed, silent Katie next to her brother. "There's nothing wrong with girls, silly billy—"

"Good Lord!" Ivy peeled the back of the blanket from the boy's shoulder. "What on earth do you have on?"

"Their clothes were all wet," Ryan said, "so I stuck 'em in the dryer. Figured they'd be okay in my shirts for a little bit." Ivy lifted eyebrows at him. Ryan shook his head—*don't ask.*

But Noah was busy angling his head at his sister, his brow beetled. "You *positive* she's a girl? 'Cause she sure don't look like one."

Maddie reached up and ruffled his hair. "Yes, baby, I'm sure. If you don't believe me, you just go on ahead and ask the doctor."

"You think maybe Daddy might've liked her better'n Katie Grace an' me?"

The room went so silent, you could hear the muted thumping of the dryer, clear out in the pantry. Standing at the foot of the bed, his arms crossed, Ryan didn't move, not reacting when Ivy's gaze shot to his. But he saw the flush leap into Maddie's translucent, speckled cheeks, and anger suddenly knifed through him as he remembered the scars he'd seen on the child's back. They'd been old, healed up for some months, but they hadn't been the result of any accident.

Maddie blinked several times, then swallowed, obviously trying to figure out what to say. With her free hand, she reached up, drew her firstborn down onto her chest to place a fierce kiss in all those spikes. "Doesn't matter now, baby. Only thing you have to remember now is how much *I* like you and Katie. And I love all three of you with all my heart, forever and ever and ever. You hear me?"

Ryan's eyes burned. How many times had his own mother, gone now nearly twenty years, said the same thing to one or the other of her three sons? Except then Noah, as kids will, switched the conversation to more practical matters by announcing he was hungry.

Ivy beamed. Feedin' and birthin'—the woman was in her element now. "Well, I just bet you are, sweetie. And Mama, too." She turned questioning brown eyes on Ryan. "I didn't figure you'd have anything decent in that kitchen of yours to make breakfast, so I brought my own fixin's, if that's all right."

He feigned a hurt expression. "I'm not a barbarian, Ivy. There's eggs. I think. And coffee."

"Oh, well, then," Ivy said on a huff. "As if you could give a nursing mother coffee, for goodness' sake. Not to mention children." Elbows pumping, full skirt flapping around her calves—this one had mirrors and embroidery all over the bottom tier—Ivy sailed toward the bedroom door, turning back when she hit the doorframe.

"Noah and…Katie, right?" The kids turned to her with synchronized nods. Ivy held out her hand. "Let's go see if your clothes are dry yet before you trip in those T-shirts. Then you can help me make pancakes."

Two pairs of questioning eyes turned to their mother. Katie's thumb popped into her mouth.

"It's okay," Maddie said with a smile. "You go on, now."

They went. Maddie at once sank back into the pillows, letting out a sigh as her eyes drifted shut. Worn out from the strain of pretending, would be his guess. As if reading his mind, she said quietly, "It's been a long time since they've had pancakes." She opened her eyes, but didn't move. "I'm very grateful to you. And Ivy. But we best be on our way as soon as I can move, before they get spoiled."

Ryan grabbed the footboard, a scowl digging into his forehead. "Giving the kids a good breakfast is hardly spoiling them. And unless you can assure me you've got someone to help you out for the next few days, you're not going anywhere until I say it's okay."

A pointed little chin, only marginally bigger than her son's, reared up. "It was an easy birth. And I was up after the other two in a few hours."

"By choice?"

He was actually startled to see tears well up in those gray eyes. She looked away, busying herself with unbuttoning her gown to put the baby to breast. A flush of self-consciousness stung Ryan's cheeks as he watched Maddie help her new daughter find the nipple. Why he should be reacting at all made no sense. He'd watched dozens of mothers nurse their babies. Hell, how long had it been since nakedness had meant anything more to him than anatomy?

The alert, hungry infant hit pay dirt almost at once; Maddie's soft laughter glittered with love and momentary surcease from her worries, and something inside Ryan warmed a little more…and made him feel as if he needed to justify his presence in the room.

"Tired?" he asked.

Maddie shook her head. The fingers of her left hand—graceful, short-nailed—stroked her baby's cheek. "No."

"It's not a sign of weakness to admit you're tired after having just given birth, Maddie."

Her mouth stretched thin. "I'm fine."

"Okay, you're fine. Feel like talking, then?"

After a moment, she said, "Answering questions, you mean?"

"A stranger gives birth in my house, you might say I'm curious. And concerned."

Pride flashed in those silvery eyes. "I'll pay you for delivering the baby."

"I'd bet my life on it. But that's not what I want to know."

Again, he saw the tears, figured she'd do just about anything to keep them from falling. "I could say it's none of your business."

Ryan tried real hard to squelch the exasperation this woman seemed determined to stir to life inside him. "You made it my business when you showed up here in labor. You're at least twenty pounds underweight. So forgive me for taking my job seriously, but I want to know why. You're blamed lucky the baby's as fit as she is, but it won't do you or her any good to neglect yourself any more than you already have. Did you even have any prenatal care?''

Maddie stared hard at the baby, her mouth set. With her free hand, she swept a hank of straggly hair off her face; it fell right back. ''This is my third child. I know how to take care of myself.'' She looked up at Ryan. ''I don't smoke or drink, if that's what you're thinking, and I ate as well as I could. I never have weighed more than a hundred ten pounds, even when—''

She stopped, cleared her throat, fingering the baby's cheek.

Ryan let out a ragged sigh, deciding a cup of coffee sounded real good, right about now. ''I'm not judging you, Maddie,'' he said, and she snorted her disbelief. ''I'm not. I just wonder how you're going to take care of yourself. And your children.''

After a moment, she said, ''I'll get by.''

He folded his arms. ''You know, why didn't you just go ahead and have the baby in the car?''

Her mouth twisted. ''There wasn't room.'' A beat or two passed before she added, ''I don't like being beholden to people.''

''I gathered that much,'' he said, then waited until she looked at him. ''But it looks to me like you haven't got a whole lotta choice in the matter right now. All I want you to worry about for the next few days is feeding that new daughter of yours and getting your strength back.''

The eyes sparked, like the flash of sword-steel. ''I don't need—''

He stared her down. She got quiet, but her embarrassment pricked his heart when she palmed away a tear. ''We're strangers to you. Why should you feel obligated to take care of us?''

Ryan suddenly felt hard pressed not to strangle the woman. Moving as cautiously as his brother Cal might with an unbroken colt, he eased around the bed and sat on its edge, leaning over so she had no choice but to meet his gaze. ''Let's get one thing clear, right now. Obligation doesn't have a blamed thing to do with this. Like it or not, you and your daughter are now my patients, because I took an oath a long time ago that won't allow me to see the situation any other way. Got that?'' She hitched one shoulder, her mouth quirked. ''Good. At least we got that settled.'' He leaned over, grabbed a clipboard and blank chart off the nightstand. ''So let's make it official. Full name?''

''Madelyn Mae Kincaid.''

''Age?''

''Twenty-four.''

''Is that the truth?''

She blew out a breath. ''You can check my driver's license if you don't believe me. Which is in my coat pocket with my change purse.''

So she was a few years older than he'd thought. Still awfully damn young to be a mother three times over, though.

''Address?''

Her resultant silence gave him no choice but to look over. She was frowning down at the baby. ''Maddie?''

After a moment, she met his gaze. ''I guess I don't have one, just at the moment. Well, unless you count the Double Arrow.''

The Double Arrow. His brother Hank's place. Wasn't the Hilton—hell, it wasn't even a Motel 6—but she'd been safe there, at least. However, even cheap motels ate up money at a good clip. Money he suspected she didn't have. ''Where were you before?''

''Arkansas. Little Rock.'' She made a face. ''We moved there from Fayetteville after Noah was born...'' Something in her expression led Ryan to believe there was more, but then she said, ''I came here to find my husband's great-uncle. Maybe you know him? Ned McAllister?''

''Ned? You're kidding? He's kin to you?''

''Like I said, by marriage. I...we've never actually met.'' Then she paled even more, if that was possible. ''Oh, no...he didn't die or anything, did he?''

Ryan let out a soft laugh. ''Ned? I imagine that old buzzard'll outlive me. But his bones aren't as strong as they used to be. Broke his hip last week, so he's in the hospital over in Claremore. Which is where he'll be for some time, at least until he's finished up his physical therapy.''

"Oh!" With that one word, Ryan could see Maddie's last shred of hope vaporize. She looked down at the baby, her hand trembling when she stroked the infant's cheek. "He never had a phone—well, I suppose you know that—and all I had was a P.O. box for an address. I knew I was taking a chance, just coming on out here like this, but there was absolutely nobody else...."

Pride and panic were a helluva combination, weren't they?

The baby had fallen asleep. Ryan leaned over and gently removed her from Maddie's arms, making sure to keep the infant well swaddled in the double receiving blankets Ivy had brought, even though the heat had taken the chill off the house by now. She was diapered, too—Ryan always kept packages of disposables in his office to accommodate his littler patients. And their sometimes forgetful mothers.

He sure did have a soft spot for the babies, he admitted to himself as he smiled at little Amy Rose, giving Mama a chance to regain control. Shoot, giving *himself* a chance to quash a feeling akin to hitting a patch of black ice.

Lucky thing for him he was real good at steering out of the skids.

"I've got some clothes for her, back at the motel," Maddie said on a shaky breath. He glanced over at her, imagining how ticked she'd be if she had any idea how worn out she looked, lying there against the pillows. "I guess I kinda forgot them, once the pains hit."

Ryan felt one side of his mouth lift. "Understandable."

Maddie stayed quiet for a moment, her attention fixed on the baby, then let out a sigh. "Before you ask...my husband's dead."

Somehow, he wasn't surprised. "I'm sorry."

"So am I, but not for the usual reasons."

He couldn't quite decide if that was regret or anger flickering at the edges of her words. Maybe a bit of both.

"He leave you broke?"

Her laugh was humorless. And her lack of verbal response told him this was not a topic currently open for discussion.

What kind of man left his wife and children this bad off?

If Maddie Kincaid had started having babies at nineteen, it was highly doubtful she had much in the way of education or skills. What she did have was three little kids. And more courage than most men he knew. But here she was, in a strange town, the only person she knew in it medically incarcerated for the foreseeable future. And even so, what on earth good would Ned McCallister do her? Not only was the ornery old man the least likely candidate to take on a woman with three small children, but there was no way Maddie and her kids could live in that shack of his.

What they had here was a crisis situation, no doubt about it. And Ryan had the sinking feeling that somehow, he had been the one appointed to handle said crisis.

From the kitchen emanated the aroma of pancakes and coffee, Ivy's commanding voice chattering to the children. A few hardy birds, oblivious to the fact that summer was over, chirped and twittered outside the window as the sun burned off what was left of the storm. Needing to move, to be doing something, Ryan laid the baby down in the bassinet he'd retrieved from his office before the delivery. There had to be an answer here. One that wouldn't make his head hurt.

"Your folks still around?"

After a moment, she said, "I already told you. There's nobody."

Don't get overly involved with your patients. How many times had Ryan's instructors drummed those words into his head? But if he didn't believe healing was less about procedures and medicines and biological function, and more about giving a damn about the human beings who put themselves in his care, then those pieces of paper up on his wall in the other room meant squat.

Of course, not many people understood that, any more than they understood that personal sacrifice came with the territory.

Nor did Ryan understand quite what was happening here. Yes, he cared about his patients. All of them. Even old Miss

Hightower, whose contrariness Ryan had long since attributed to a simple fear of growing old, of being alone. But this was different. Something about this one struck a personal chord way down deep, way past the day-to-day caring he dispensed, along with the occasional antibiotic and common sense advice, to his other patients.

It had been a long, long time since anything had shaken him up the way this situation was threatening to. He didn't know what he was going to do about it—about Maddie—but he sure as hell knew he didn't like it, not one little bit.

He patted the edge of the bassinet, twice, then started backing toward the doorway. "I think I'll just go see what's keeping Ivy in the kitchen, then go get myself cleaned up," he said, wondering why the hell he felt so skittish in his own house.

Chapter 2

Maddie frowned at the doorway for some time after Dr. Logan's departure. Despite his going on about her not leaving until he said it was okay, she was getting a real strong feeling he wasn't all that comfortable with the idea. Although she guessed his reaction had less to do with her personally than it did with his just not being real used to having houseguests.

That's what she was going to go with, anyway.

Crossing her arms over her wobbly belly, she surveyed her surroundings for the first time. Which provoked another strong feeling—that Dr. Logan was not someone overly concerned with his environment. Oh, she supposed the faded floral wallpaper, the coordinating murky drapes and dark-stained wood trim bordering the windows might've been okay, forty or fifty years ago. But if it hadn't been for the sunlight glittering and dancing across the room, it would be downright depressing in here. And wasn't that a shame? Far as she was concerned, everybody deserved a home that was cheerful and inviting. Especially someone as nice as Dr. Logan.

Not that it was any of her business.

On a sigh, Maddie carefully snuggled down on her side, watching her new daughter snoozing in the bassinet by the bed. She ached some from the couple of stitches she'd had to have, but not badly. Although she could feel the adrenaline that had been keeping her going the past couple of days quickly draining away. The baby scrunched up her tiny face in her sleep, pooching out her mouth, then giving one of those fluttery little gas smiles. Maddie smiled, too, skimming one finger over the itty-bitty furrowed brow. Maybe after a bath, Amy Rose would start looking more like a human baby—

Just like that, a fresh wave of worry washed over her. Maddie rolled onto her back, her hands pressed to her eyes, wishing like heck she could just let her mind go blank for a little while, even though she knew full well that things weren't going to change simply because she didn't want to think about them.

All right, so she supposed necessity sometimes made a person confuse hope with reality, but still, it had been silly counting on being able to stay with Jimmy's Uncle Ned. But what on earth was she going to do? She had fifty dollars to her name, twenty-four of which would go for the motel room. There was little point in going back to Arkansas, since she no longer had a home or knew anybody who could help her there. Which meant she had to stay here in Haven.

If she did that, she could apply for assistance in Oklahoma…but who knew how long that would take to kick in? Or how much it would be?

Or, if she got a job, which she wouldn't be able to do for a few weeks at least, what was she going to do with the kids? How could she possibly afford full-time day care for the two younger ones, part-time for Noah while he was in school, on the kind of salary she was likely to get?

She could maybe sell the car, get a few hundred bucks for it…but if she did that, how would she get around? Where were they going to live?

What if they tried to take her children away?

Maddie's chest got all tight, like she couldn't get enough air in her lungs: no matter how hard she tried to fit the pieces of what was left of her life together, they simply refused to go. For all intents and purposes, she and her babies were homeless.

Homeless.

Her hand flew to her mouth, but not fast enough to block the small cry of despair that escaped. It just seemed so blamed *unfair.* She wasn't stupid. Or helpless. And heaven knew, she wasn't lazy. Yet here she was, so far up the creek, she couldn't even remember the feel of the paddle in her hands.

Everything that could be sold had been, to pay bills, to pay off Jimmy's debts. All they had were the few things in the trunk of the car—some household items, a couple of the kids' favorite toys, some odds and ends she couldn't even recall at the moment—and the two mangy looking suitcases filled with clothes so worn, Goodwill probably wouldn't even take them. Take them *back.*

A silent tear, then another, raced down her cheek: you know you've reached rock-bottom when you can't even afford Wal-Mart.

Approaching footsteps and whispered conversation galvanized her into hurriedly wiping her eyes on the hem of the Downy-scented sheet, then gingerly pulling herself upright. Even when her hormones weren't all goofy, Maddie was a person who cried at the drop of a hat, feeling things deeply as she did. Jimmy had hated it with a purple passion, but that's just the way she was. A second or two later, Ivy ushered in the children, Noah grinning over a bedtray heaped with pancakes, sausage, eggs, milk, juice.

"Look what we brung you, Mama!"

Maddie's vision went fuzzy all over again when she caught sight of her son's great big old grin, how bright his eyes were. Up until a few months ago, he'd been as likely to get into mischief as the next little boy—too smart for his own good, she'd been inclined to think on those days when he'd seemed hell-bent on driving her completely up the wall. She hadn't fully realized until this moment how much she'd give to have a reason to fuss at him again, for him to feel confident enough to test his limits. And hers.

And look at Katie Grace! The polar opposite of her rambunctious brother, who'd play quietly by herself for hours and hardly ever complained about anything, even Maddie's quiet little baby doll was smiling.

Some color had leeched back into their cheeks, too. Noah's, especially. He'd always been fair-skinned, like she was, but he'd gotten so pale these past few months she was afraid people would start asking her if he was sick.

"Ivy says you gotta eat it all," Noah pronounced, the whole lot nearly spilling in his zeal to get it settled over her lap.

Oh, my. It was more food than they'd seen since they left Little Rock two days ago. More than she'd seen at one time in months.

"We'll share," she said to Noah, who had settled on the bed to study his baby sister, butt in the air, chin resting in his palms. Katie crawled up beside Maddie, snuggling against her side.

"Oh, they already ate," Ivy said, helping to arrange pillows behind Maddie's back. She grinned down at Noah. "For such a little thing, he can sure pack it away. Five pancakes, two pieces of sausage, and two glasses of juice. And sweetie pie here got down a whole pancake and a piece of sausage."

The first bite of pancake stuck in Maddie's throat: she'd been doing well to be sure they got peanut butter sandwiches every morning.

And every night.

A strong, comforting hand landed on her shoulder. "You're here now," Ivy said gently. "You and your babies are safe, you hear?"

She nodded, swallowed. But the tears came anyway.

A second later, she was engulfed by warmth and kindness like she hadn't known since her foster mother's house. In fact, Ivy reminded Maddie a bit of Grace Idlewild, who'd done her level best to give Maddie some stability in her life, who'd made her believe you could accomplish just about anything with hard work and determination.

But right now, she didn't need to be thinking about things

she couldn't change, so she decided to take what comfort she could against Ivy's formidable bosom, barely hearing the midwife's explaining away Maddie's tears to her other babies as something that some ladies go through after they have a baby, that's all, and they weren't to think another thing about it.

Then Ivy scooped Maddie's new daughter into her arms. "You eat. I'll get her cleaned up in the kitchen, where it's nice and warm. Ryan told me you've got some clothes for her back at the Double Arrow, but I always bring a little undershirt and sacque with me, just in case. Come on, you two—let's let Mama finish up her breakfast in peace."

Then they were gone, leaving Maddie alone with more food than she could eat in three meals and more worries than any one person should have to deal with in one lifetime.

Ivy had changed the radio station on him.

A frown bit into Ryan's forehead as he walked into the warm, coffee-and-pancake scented kitchen, his hair still damp from his shower. Country music whined softly from the small radio on the windowsill; except for those times he needed to keep an ear out for the weather, he usually kept it on the classical station out of Tulsa, a habit inherited from his mother. Living alone had its definite advantages. Like being able to count on the radio station staying set where you left it.

Not to mention being able to cross your own kitchen floor without dodging three other bodies. Generally Ryan considered himself pretty mellow, but he tended to get ornery when confronted with an obstacle course between him and his morning coffee. In fact, he nearly tripped over Noah, who for some reason decided to back up just as Ryan got behind him to reach for the coffee pot. Ryan grabbed the kid's shoulders to keep them both upright; the boy jerked his head up, his eyes big, growing bigger still as Ryan scowled down at him. He hadn't meant to, it was just that between his not being able to figure out what to do about Maddie and her kids and his caffeine withdrawal…

Oh, hell.

Ryan quickly rearranged his features into a smile, but the
damage had been done: Noah dashed back to Ivy's side like
a frightened pup, glancing just once over his shoulder at Ryan
before returning his full attention to Ivy.

"What's that?" the kid asked, pointing to the baby's
tummy.

The midwife held the nearly naked baby in a secure football
grip, suspended over the pockmarked porcelain sink as she
gently sponged off the little head. "That's her umbilical cord,
honey," Ivy said, patting the baby dry with a towel, then
launching into a detailed description of placentas and umbilical cords that apparently fascinated Noah. For at least two
seconds. Then having apparently recovered from his close encounter with the bogeyman, he wandered over to the back
door and looked out into the large backyard. There wasn't
anything that would be of any interest to children, Ryan didn't
think—a bunch of overgrown oaks and maples, a badly ne-
glected rose garden, a wooden shed—but Noah timidly asked
if he and Katie Grace could go outside anyway. Ryan said he
didn't see why not, since the sun had come out, burning away
at least some of the moisture from the leaf-strewn, fading
grass.

The children—and his first cup of coffee—gone, Ryan
poured himself another mug, then leaned against the counter,
squinting against the sunlight slashing through the curtainless,
mullioned backdoor window as he watched Ivy in action. Little Amy Rose Kincaid, less than two hours old, was wide-
awake, her dark eyes intent on Ivy's face as the midwife
dressed the infant in a miniscule T-shirt, booties and a plain
yellow sacque with a drawstring bottom. The baby stared at
her so hard, she nearly went cross-eyed. Ivy laughed.

"Looks like she's trying to figure me out."

"Tell her there's a hundred bucks in it for her if she does."

Ivy rolled her eyes, then said, "Probably wondering what
I did with her mama. Isn't that right, precious?" She swaddled
the baby up in a receiving blanket, scooped her up onto her
shoulder. "Bet she's gonna be a sleeper. Her Apgar was fine,
by the way," she added, then scowled at Ryan. "Probably

better than yours would be right now. That your third cup of coffee?"

"Second." He frowned. "You keeping track?"

"Well, shoot, boy, somebody's got to. You've got some nerve, you know that, lecturing people about their diets when you still eat like a college kid yourself. And a dumb college kid, at that."

He shrugged. Took another swallow. "A doctor's prerogative."

"Foolishness, more like." She nodded toward the stove, ancient when Ryan had first seen it as a kid, more than twenty-five years ago. But it still worked. Apparently. Since he'd broken down and gotten a microwave last year, he avoided the thing almost as much as he did paperwork. "Go on," Ivy urged. "There's some sausage and scrambled eggs left. I'd make you pancakes, but I've got my hands full right now."

No point in arguing. Not that he wasn't hungry. It just seemed cruel to give his stomach something it wasn't going to get on a regular basis. But he grabbed a stoneware plate from the drainer, his heavy socks snagging on the wooden floor as he lumbered over to the stove, where he piled on a half dozen links, God knows how many eggs. A lot.

"And get yourself some juice, too," Ivy commanded. "I don't suppose I need to tell you about antioxidants."

Ryan got the juice, sloshing it over onto the eroded Formica counter when he tipped the pitcher a half inch too far. Ivy clucked—Ivy clucked a lot—then wiped up the spill one-handed.

"When you gonna get yourself a housekeeper, is what I want to know."

With a groan, Ryan sank down onto a kitchen chair, some fancy Victorian press-back number Suzanne had picked out when they were still engaged. He shoveled in a bite of egg before replying. "For one thing, I don't need to be tripping over some stranger in my own kitchen every morning." Noah's dark, frightened eyes flashed through his memory, making him frown. Harder. "And for another, what am I supposed to pay her with? My charm?"

"Oh, Lord. Then you would be in trouble."

Ryan shrugged, took a swig of coffee, downed another forkful of egg.

"Of course, you could get yourself a wife instead, you know."

Yeah, well, he'd figured that was coming. "You applyin' for the job?"

"Don't be fresh."

He almost grinned. The caffeine must be kicking in. Not to mention the food. After a gulp of the juice, he said, "Anyway, if I don't have the money or the charm for a housekeeper, how in tarnation am I supposed to take care of a wife?"

Of course, both of them knew the problem went much deeper than that, although Ivy had flat-out told Ryan his objections were nothing but bunk more times than he'd care to remember. For some reason, though, judging from her squinty eyes—which meant she was more carefully considering her response than she was normally prone to do—this was apparently not going to be one of those times. He'd no sooner breathed an inward sigh of relief, however, when she slammed into him from another angle.

"Well, I don't suppose I can do much to shake the stranger-in-your-kitchen business," she said. "But there's no earthly reason you should be having money problems, and you know it. You got enough patients to keep three doctors busy, and most of those who don't pay private have insurance or Medicare or something. The house is free and clear, you don't have any dependents and you went to school on scholarship, so there's no school loans to pay back. So what gives?"

"Criminy, Ivy!" So much for his better mood. Still chewing, Ryan lifted his bleary gaze to hers. How other folks survived morning conversations was beyond him. "What lit your fire this morning?"

With a loud sigh, she dropped onto the chair opposite him, rubbing the baby's back. "I'm worried about you, is all. Figured that fell to me when your mama died. She'd be all over your case, and you know it.''

This, he didn't need. On top of having people cluttering up his kitchen, a woman he didn't quite know what to do with in his guest room and a practice that kept him running ragged but close to the poverty line at the same time, Ivy's reminding him about his mother was just one straw too many.

Yes, Mary Logan certainly would be on his case. Not to mention his brothers' as well. When it came to getting their acts together, lifewise and lovewise, all three of her sons seemed to have struck out. And for a woman who'd preached the family unit as the bedrock of civilization the way she did—and lived it, to boot—her sons' disastrous records would have sent her to her grave, if cancer hadn't done the job first when Hank and Cal were still in their teens.

The family had drifted apart after her death, like a solar system without its sun. Not so much physically—all three of them were right there in Haven—but emotionally. And Big Hank, their father, hadn't seemed to know how to bind up the wounds, either. Had too many of his own to tend to, would be Ryan's guess. Wounds from which he never fully recovered. The old man simply faded into himself, little by little, quietly dying in his sleep five years after his wife's passing.

Mama would have given them all hell, if not the back of her hand, for giving in like that. For giving up. And Ivy, who'd been Mary's best friend, had simply taken up their mother's cause. One day, Ryan supposed, he'd appreciate it.

One day. Not this morning. Not when the events of the last few hours seemed hell-bent on rattling him to kingdom come.

So he impaled a sausage, waved it at her. ''Do me a favor, Ivy—stick to midwifery. Which reminds me…the Lewis baby turned yet?''

''Yesterday, thank you, so no, I don't need you, and you're changing the subject.''

He stuffed the whole sausage in his mouth, mumbled, ''Damn straight,'' around it.

Ivy let out a little sigh of her own, shifted the dozing infant to a more secure position on her shoulder. "You know she's got to stay here, don't you?"

His plate clean, Ryan kicked back the last of his juice, got up to carry his dishes to the sink. "I'm hardly going to turn the woman and her kids out, Ivy."

"I know that. But I figured you'd probably try to find someplace else for her to stay."

He shook his head, washing up his few dishes, then started in on the griddle and skillet. "No. At least not for the next week or so. I want to keep an eye on her. And the baby."

"And then?"

Yeah, well, that was what was making the eggs and sausage do somersaults in his stomach, wasn't it? "I don't know. She tell you she's kin to Ned McAllister?"

Ivy heavy brows lifted. "No. How?"

"Her husband's great-uncle."

She angled her head. "And her husband is…?"

"Dead." Ryan took a moment to let some of the anger burn off, then said, "Jerk left her with nothing."

"Oh…that poor thing."

Ryan turned to Ivy, wiping his hands in a dishtowel. "You saw the scars?"

Ivy sighed. "The father?"

"According to Maddie. I see no reason not to believe her."

That was worth several seconds' clucking. "Life's thrown some real curve balls at that young woman."

Ryan couldn't disagree there. He glanced up at the clock, grabbed his jacket from where he'd dumped it earlier over the back of the kitchen chair.

"Where you goin'?"

"Over to Hank's to pick up whatever Maddie's left in her room."

"Think he'll be up for a visitor this early?"

"Ask me if I care," Ryan said, punching one arm through his jacket sleeve. "I've got office hours starting at eight-thirty, and I figure Ms. Kincaid just might like her clothes before six o'clock this evening."

* * *

Hank greeted him barechested and scowling, his jeans un-snapped. A toothbrush dangled out of his mouth; comb tracks sliced his dark, wet hair. Eighteen months older, two inches taller and twenty-five pounds heavier than Ryan, Hank Logan was what some folks might call "imposing." Others bypassed niceties and went straight for "scary." And with good reason. Nothing pretty about that mug of his, that was for damn sure, every feature sharp, uncompromising, anchored by a twice-broken nose that made a person think real carefully before disagreeing with him. Everything about Hank Logan said, "Don't mess," and most folks didn't.

Which led a lot of people to wondering what on earth had possessed the guy to buy a beat-up, run-down, sorry-assed old motel and go into the *hospitality* business.

Hank had been a cop in Dallas, up until a couple years ago, when his fiancée had died in a convenience store robbery gone to hell. And so had Hank. The force shrinks had finally convinced him he needed to take some time off before facing the world again with a gun strapped to his hip. So Hank had come home on a six-month leave. But, while Ryan had his practice, and Cal, their youngest brother, the family horse farm to look after, Hank had been suddenly left with nothing.

Until this motel.

He never got back to Dallas.

Hank took one look at Ryan and swore, the effect somehow not all that intimidating around a mouth full of toothpaste suds. "She had the baby?"

"I won't even ask you how you figured that out."

"Hell, Ry—" Hank ducked back inside his apartment adjacent to the office, a hellhole if ever there was one, and strode back to the bathroom. Ryan followed, shutting the door behind him. As usual, some opera singer was holding forth from the CD player.

"She was in her ninth month," Hank was saying over the sound of running water and an emotionally distraught soprano. "Her car's not here this morning. And you are. Doesn't take a genius."

Ryan, however, hadn't really heard that last part, fascinated—in a ghoulish kind of way—with the state of his brother's apartment. The only refined thing about it *was* the music. While none of the Logan brothers would win any housekeeping awards, from the looks, and smell, of things, Hank seemed determined to see just how bad his place could get before it ignited from spontaneous combustion. Layers of dirty clothes, moldering fast food containers as far as the eye could see, dishes stacked like drunken acrobats in the sink— the place redefined *dump*.

"For cryin' out loud, Hank—why don't you pay Cherise an extra fifty bucks to clean up in here once a week?"

From the bathroom, he heard spitting and rinsing, before Hank reappeared, laconically buttoning up a denim shirt. Dry heat hummed from a vent under the no-color drapes, teasing the hems. "I do. She comes tomorrow."

"I take that back. Make it a hundred. And remind me to make sure her tetanus shots are up to date."

Hank grunted.

"And how'd you know Maddie Kincaid was in her ninth month, anyway?"

His brother had let his cop-short hair grow out—a lot—but he still moved with a kind of taut awareness, as if he expected the bad guys to pop out from behind his Murphy bed. His eyes as dark as Ryan's were light, Hank tossed his brother a glance as he rifled through a pile of clothes on an ugly up-holstered chair, looking for something. "I asked. She said three weeks yet."

Lord. Hank had probably frightened her into labor. "The baby had other ideas."

Hank found what he was looking for—a belt—and threaded it through his jeans. "How'd she find you?" He dug in his pocket for a stick of gum, a habit taken up after Ryan finally convinced him to give up smoking. The wrapper drifted to the floor after he poked the gum into his mouth.

"I have no idea. She and the kids just showed up."

"Huh. You take her to the hospital?"

"I was doing well to get in position in time to catch the baby. That's why I'm here. To get their things."

Hank nodded, snatching a spare set of keys off a hook by his door. He grabbed a leather jacket from the back of a dinette chair and opened the door to the biting cold.

They walked the short distance in silence, gravel crunching underfoot, their breath frosted in front of their faces. Hands rammed in his pockets, Ryan glanced around. You couldn't exactly say Hank'd been singlehandedly restoring the place to its former *glory*, since that was a word one would never have associated with the Double Arrow, even in its heyday. But he was definitely restoring it, shingle by shingle. A dozen single-room units out front, a half dozen two- and three-room cottages down by what the previous owners generously called a "lake." The single rooms were pretty much done; Ryan imagined it would take another year, maybe two, before the cottages were ready for occupants. At least, the two-footed variety.

It was a pretty spot, actually, especially this time of year with the ashes and maples doing their fall color thing. With a little effort—okay, a lot of effort—Hank could turn the motel into someplace folks might actually want to stay.

The scrape of a key in a lock caught Ryan's attention; they stepped inside Unit 12, Ryan breathing a silent sigh of relief that the room seemed—and smelled—clean. A little strong on the Pine-Sol, but that was okay. Calling the county health authorities on his own brother wasn't high on his list. Especially as Hank could still probably beat the crap out of him, if he had a mind to.

The twin beds were both undone, a denim jumper and blouse neatly laid across the back of the desk chair. One suitcase was open on the metal-and-strap rack, the contents still more or less intact. Ryan quickly gathered the few stray items, including a plastic soap case and toothbrush from the bathroom sink, haphazardly folding the clothing before stuffing everything into the open case, then clicking it shut. Even without really looking, though, he could tell the clothes were worn and faded. For a woman with such intense pride, her predicament must be eating her alive.

Ryan hauled the cases out to the truck, Hank meandering

wordlessly behind. To tell the truth, none of the brothers had much to say to each other anymore. Which was a shame, he supposed, since they'd been close as kids, even though they'd tormented each other like any normal siblings.

Hank stood with his arms crossed, the stiff breeze messing with his hair. "Now what do you suppose makes a woman that pregnant up and leave wherever she was?"

Ryan settled the cases in the truck bed, turned back to his brother. Little had caught Hank's interest since his return, other than this rat-trap. But damned if Ryan didn't catch a whiff of genuine intrigue about Maddie Kincaid.

"Desperation," he said simply. "Husband's dead, she's got no money from what I can tell. And her only living relative is here."

"Yeah? Who?"

"Ned."

Black brows shot straight up. "McAllister?"

"Yep."

"Damn. She really is havin' a bad string of luck, isn't she?"

"To put it mildly." Ryan pulled his wallet out of his back pocket, fished out a twenty and a five. "Let me settle up for her room."

But Hank shook his head. "Forget it. In fact, if she needs a place to stay—"

"No," Ryan said, too quickly, tucking the bills back into his wallet. "I need to keep an eye on her. And the baby, you know."

Hank gave a nod, then a sigh. "Pretty thing," he said, which just about surprised the life out of Ryan. Far as he knew, it had been a long time since Hank had noticed a woman. Much less mentioned one. And that he'd notice this one, in her ninth month, skinny as a rail, with two other kids to boot…well, it didn't make a whole lot of sense, and Ryan wasn't about to figure out why it bothered him, but maybe it meant Hank was coming back to life.

Which was a good thing, right?

"I suppose she'd clean up okay," Ryan said nonchalantly, climbing behind the wheel.

Hank's long, craggy face actually split into a grin. A *grin*. A grin the likes of which Ryan hadn't seen for longer than he cared to remember.

He gunned the truck to life, more irritable than he had any right or reason to feel.

Chapter 3

Ivy and the kids rushed out the back door just as Ryan pulled up, the midwife going on about taking the kids with her on her rounds, she'd just been waiting for Ryan to get back so Maddie wouldn't be alone. And that she'd updated Maddie's chart, it was on his desk, everything looked real good.

Then they were gone in a blur of dust and engine growls—Ivy's battle-scarred Ford pickup had a good five years on Ryan's—leaving Ryan with a fresh pot of coffee and profound relief that Ivy'd taken the kids away for a bit. Keeping an ear out for Maddie and Amy Rose was one thing; watching two little kids while seeing to his patients was something else. He'd lost his last nurse/receptionist to marriage and a move to New Mexico not a month ago, had yet to replace her. Sometimes he had a temp in to help, but he usually found it less problematic in the long run to wing it on his own. His paperwork was suffering some, but he told himself he'd catch up, one of these days. Years.

Ryan got himself another cup of coffee and wended his way toward the haphazardly connected group of four rooms that made up his office. The house sat on a double-sized corner lot, three blocks from the center of town. Back in the twenties, a back parlor and summer porch had been converted into an office/exam room and waiting room with its own entrance. Later on, somebody got the bright idea to build a breezeway linking the original office to the detached garage, which had served double duty ever since as auxiliary exam and file rooms.

The layout didn't make a lick of sense, architecturally speaking, but it suited Ryan's purpose well enough. And that was all that mattered.

He'd peeked into the waiting room on his way to Maddie's room: no one yet. Good. He only had a handful of actual appointments today, but every fall, soon as school started, there were the usual rash of coughs and colds, not to mention the playground boo-boos and football injuries. About due for the first round of strep, too, he imagined.

The door to the back bedroom was slightly ajar; Ryan slowly shouldered it open, saw that Maddie was asleep. He'd intended on just setting the suitcases down and getting out of there, except one of the cases wasn't as flat on the bottom as he'd thought so that it fell over onto the wooden floor with a *bang!* loud enough to set him back five years.

Maddie twisted around in the bed, her eyes soft and unfocused. The room smelled of sunshine on clean linens, the sweet scent of newborn baby. An odd sensation that managed to be vague and sharp at the same time sliced through him as a stray shaft of sunlight grazed the top of her head, turning her dull brown hair a rich, golden color. And she had on one of his shirts, he noticed, that blue plaid that had gotten all soft, just the way he liked it.

"One problem with this hotel," he said, his throat suddenly dry, "is the lousy room service."

Maddie smiled, slowly and lazily, and his heart just hopped right up into that dry throat. "Hardly," she said in that scratchy little voice of hers, before carefully pushing herself upright. Her just-washed hair was all feathery and soft around a scrubbed face, making her look more than ever like a child.

Only not.

She yawned, then nodded toward the cases. "Thanks."

"No problem." He shifted, hooking his thumbs into his jeans pockets. Told himself he was the doctor, he had a right to be there. "Sorry to wake you."

Her eyes had gone a smoky-blue. From the colors in the shirt, he supposed. "S'okay," she said, only then she must've noticed he was staring at the shirt, because she looked down at it, then back up at him, blushing a little. "Ivy said you wouldn't mind if I borrowed this until I got my things."

"I don't," he said, because oddly enough, he really didn't. Only then she laced her hands around her knees through the bedclothes, and smiled, and damned if something inside him didn't just melt all to hell.

Ryan cleared his throat. "How're you feeling?"

"Like I just gave birth. Other than that, not too bad."

"Any light-headedness?"

"Uh-uh."

"Bleeding's normal?"

"Seems so to me, and Ivy said it was, too. I'm cramping some, but I guess that's to be expected."

Ryan folded his arms across his chest, grateful to be back on solid ground again. "A good sign, actually."

"What they don't tell you is the pain doesn't quit once the baby's born."

"You want a Tylenol or something?"

But she shook her head, just as he figured she would.

"You don't have to tough it out, you know."

A thin smile stretched across her lips. "Yes, I do."

Not knowing what to say to that, Ryan walked over to the bassinet, grinning down at the ruddy-faced little girl asleep inside. "She kind of grows on you, doesn't she?"

This time, Maddie's laugh was full and rich. "Takes after her mama, I guess."

Despite the lack of self-pity in her words, they perturbed him nonetheless. "You're not red and wrinkled, Maddie," was the only thing he could think of to say, which was at least worth another laugh.

"No, I suppose not. But I'm no beauty, either. Not like

Katie Grace. I imagine I'm gonna have to beat the boys off with sticks by the time she's ten.''

Amy Rose began to stir, making little "feed me" noises. Ryan gathered up the baby with an ease fine-honed from handling other people's babies for so many years, talking silliness to her as he checked her diaper—no meconium yet, but he imagined that would pass with the next feed—then carried her to her mother. But he didn't give Maddie her baby right away, using the infant as an excuse to bide his time until he figured out what to say.

Damn. He was no good at this kind of thing. But there was no way he could let her self-deprecation pass, either.

"Don't sell yourself short," he said, which earned him a puzzled look. "We never see ourselves the way others do, you know."

"Oh," was all she said, then reached for her daughter, a tiny crease settling between naturally arched brows. Her hair slithered over her shoulders in a hundred glistening layers as she spoke softly to her baby. Her scent surrounded him, shook him, a combination of shampoo, his own clean shirt and…her. Somehow, inexplicably, whatever it was that would enable little Amy able to pick her own mama out of a hundred other nursing mothers, Ryan picked up on, too.

She undid two buttons, guided her baby to a high, small breast. Ryan made himself focus on Maddie's face, again unnerved by his reaction. Not only was it unprofessional, if not downright unethical, but up until an hour or so ago, he would have thought it impossible.

He retreated to the end of the bed, leaned on the footboard. Quietly dug himself in deeper. "In fact," he said, "my brother even commented on how pretty you are."

Her head snapped up at that. "Your brother?"

"Hank. He owns the Double Arrow."

Silence followed, punctuated only by the sounds of a busily suckling baby, the hiss of heat from the radiator. Then: "Does kindness run in your family or what?" She lifted those steely eyes to his, littered with questions. And maybe a little hope. Or was that disbelief?

Ryan folded his arms across his chest. Smiled a little over the ache nudging his heart, that this woman should mistake a casual comment—not even made in her presence, for pity's sake—for kindness. "Not especially, no. What I mean to say is, none of us are any good at flattery. Well, except maybe for Cal. I mean, our mother made good and sure we could keep company in polite society without embarrassing her, but…"

Ryan caught himself, wondering how—and why—the conversation had flipflopped. But she was grinning at him, her ingenuousness trickling past his resolve. "How many of you are there?"

Oh, hell. He didn't want to go down this path, he really didn't…but he did like making her smile. Especially since he imagined there wasn't a whole lot in her life worth smiling about these days. "Three. Me and Hank—we're eighteen months apart—and Cal, the baby."

"The baby?"

"Well, to us he is. He's eight years younger than I am."

"Which probably still makes him older than me." She angled her head, making her hair glisten some more. "Right?"

Ryan stuffed his hands into his back pockets. "Well, I guess it does at that."

"And your parents?"

"Both dead."

"Oh." Her cheeks pinked. "I'm sorry."

"They were already older when they had Hank and me. Mom was in her mid-forties when Cal was born."

"Oh, my goodness!" she said, her eyes wide, then added after a moment, "Does Cal live around here, too?"

"Yep. He raises horses, out on the family farm. Well, his farm now. We all inherited when Dad passed, but Cal's in the process of buying us out."

Her expression thoughtful, Maddie shifted the baby up to her shoulder to burp her. Then she glanced around the room, and he saw something like a shadow shudder across her features. Ryan's gaze followed, sliding over the dull wallpaper and furnishings he'd never bothered to change, although he'd been planning on giving Suzanne a free hand with redecorating after they were married. Afterward, it hadn't seemed worth the bother.

"Like I said, this hotel's not all it's cracked up to be."

Her eyes lifted to his, a smile just barely tweaking up the corners of her mouth. "How'd you come by such a big place?"

"I inherited both the house and the practice from the doctor who used to live and work here." He shrugged. "I figure as long as the house isn't falling down around my ears, that's good enough."

"Spoken just like a man," she said, her gaze meeting his for a moment before dipping back to her baby, now feeding from her other side. She palmed the tiny head, smiling a little, then glanced around. "Still, there's a nice…feeling in here, you know?"

Her wistfulness clutched at his heart. Ryan checked his watch, wondering where his patients were, why they weren't coming to stop him from hanging himself.

Why—*why?*—was he pulling the desk chair over closer to the bed, straddling it backwards and plunking his butt down?

And when her brows lifted, he heard himself say, "You'll find I'm a real good listener, Maddie."

She looked down at Amy Rose, who'd fallen asleep with the nipple still in her mouth. The temptation to let some of these worries out of her brain, like relieving the pressure on a simmering pot, was nearly overwhelming. She also knew once she started, she would be hard put to hold back. Being truthful was just part of her nature. But she did not want him to feel sorry for her, either. Only she didn't see how that was to be avoided, once she told him her tale.

Except he was waiting, and she was being rude now, wasn't she?

After Maddie buttoned herself up, she lifted her knees, laying the baby against her thighs so she could watch her sleep. So she wouldn't have to look into those kind blue eyes any more than was absolutely necessary, where she knew she

would see any number of things she wouldn't want to see.
Like judgment. Or worse, pity.

She skimmed over the first part of her life, about how her
teenaged mother had given her up to the foster care system
when Maddie wasn't but three years old; how she'd been
shunted from home to home until she came to live with Joe
and Grace Idlewild as a twelve-year-old smartmouth with a
chip on her shoulder the size of a house, and how they'd been
the closest things to parents she'd ever had; how her mother
had never come back for her, and how Maddie had eventually
given up hoping she would.

And then how, against her foster parents' wishes, she'd
fallen in love at seventeen with Jimmy Kincaid, a virtual or-
phan like herself; how the boy—for he hadn't been but eighteen himself at that point—had given her to believe that, with
him, she'd have the one thing she most wanted in the whole
world, which was a life, a family, a home of her own. How
he'd had such big dreams, about being successful, about making lots of money. And how she'd let herself believe those
dreams could be hers, in large part because he'd been the first
person she'd ever met who'd *had* dreams, which had seemed
to her at the time much more enticing than determination and
hard work.

Even though she kept her eyes averted, she told the doctor
all this without shame on her part, because while she would
admit to the foolishness of youth, there had been no shame
in *being* young. Or in having dreams, even if the dreams of
her youth had been foolish.

"Except at some point..." She let out a sound that was
half sigh, half laugh. "Well, eventually I realized that Jimmy
wasn't inclined to work for any of his dreams. He just somehow expected them to happen, I guess. But no matter what,
there is no power in heaven or on earth strong enough to make
me give up my babies the way my mama did me."

The doctor's silence made her finally look over. He was
sitting backward on the straight-backed chair, his hands fisted
one on top of the other to make a pillow for his chin while
he listened, his gaze intense.

"Even if it meant staying married to an abusive man?"

"I know that's how it looks, but he wasn't always like that. When I got pregnant the first time, you never saw anybody happier than Jimmy. And even when things were rough, he was never mean to me or Noah. Not…not at first. It wasn't until I got pregnant with Katie Grace…"

The memories stung more than she'd thought they would. But she'd gotten this far, might as well see it through. Just like she had her marriage.

"Jimmy's usual method for dealing with his frustrations was to simply walk out. Which he did more and more, toward the end," she added on a sigh. "Sometimes for hours, sometimes for days."

"And this didn't bother you?"

"Sure it did. But he'd always come home eventually, all sorry for what he'd done, and he'd always have some money—and I learned early on not to question where he got it—and I wanted so hard to believe, each time, that things would be better."

Her eyes got all gritty feeling; she took a moment until the feeling passed. "I guess I took it on myself that whether the marriage survived or not was up to me. I don't feel that way anymore," she quickly added when she saw Dr. Logan's expression darken.

"What happened?" he asked quietly.

"I got pregnant a third time. I know it sounds irresponsible, but I couldn't tolerate the Pill and Jimmy hated using…you know. So I got a diaphragm from the clinic, but then Jimmy showed up out of the blue one night and maybe I didn't get it in right, I don't know…" She grasped the sleeping baby's tiny hands, smiling when the delicate little fingers automatically grasped hers. "He wanted me to get an abortion. I said no." She swallowed. "He…didn't take it too well."

"He hit you?"

Maddie nodded, staring hard at the baby, trying to block out the memory of Jimmy's anguished face afterward. "I was so…shocked, that he'd actually do that. I mean, it wasn't like this was entirely my fault, was it? So I threatened to walk out right then and there. Only he started crying, sayin' over and over how sorry he was, that it wouldn't ever happen again. I'd never seen him cry before. Maybe I shouldn't've taken him at his word, but…we'd been married for four years by then. He was the only man I'd ever loved. And everybody makes mistakes, you know?''

Again, the silence. On a deep breath, Maddie lifted her gaze to the doctor's, seeing in his eyes the one thing she'd least wanted to—that he didn't understand. "I *had* to give him another chance, don't you see? I had two children under the age of four and another on the way. And for a while, things were better. He got a real job, we were doing okay, he stuck around… Then one of his 'buddies' came up with another 'sure thing'. I tried to talk him out of it, but…well. And of course, the 'sure thing' didn't pan out, and Jimmy got more depressed than I'd ever seen him. He still had his job, but it was just on a loading dock down at the Wal-Mart, and…and I don't know. I got the feeling he just…gave up.''

By this time, she was talking more to herself than to Dr. Logan. "I didn't know what to do. How to reach him or anything. He wouldn't talk to me by that point. He stuck around more, but he wasn't really there, y'know? Anyway, he was off from work one morning, so I decided maybe it might be nice to run to the grocery store without having to drag two little kids with me. I didn't normally leave Jimmy alone with the kids, but I wasn't feeling good and the shopping still had to be done, so I said he'd have to watch the kids. I could tell he wasn't any too thrilled about it, though. When—''

She clamped her lips together, even as the tears escaped yet again.

"Maddie?"

On a deep breath, she continued, her voice trembling. "When I got home, maybe an hour later, Katie was hiding behind the couch, crying so hard she could barely catch her breath. I found Jimmy b-back in the kids' bedroom with Noah, who was screaming, screaming…" She squeezed her eyes shut, but she could feel her heartbeat in her temples. "The belt was still in Jimmy's hand."

When she opened them, she found the doctor's eyes riveted to hers, his face rigid with fury. But he didn't say a word. So she looked at the baby instead, which only tangled up her emotions even more. "How I managed not to lose the baby, I do not know, because I started yelling at Jimmy like a crazy woman, telling him to get out of my house and to never come back, that our marriage was over, that if he ever hurt one of my babies again, I would kill him. I had no idea...."

She shook her head, still disbelieving after all this time. "He took the car, eventually landing in some bar he'd never been to before, where he got stinking drunk and picked a fight with somebody he shouldn't've. Guy hit him back, Jimmy's head caught the edge of a table when he fell. By all accounts, it shouldn't've been enough to kill him...." Her stomach was shaking up a storm; she willed it to settle down.

After a moment, Dr. Logan stood and approached the bed. He didn't say anything at first, like maybe he was afraid to, but his set mouth and wrinkled brow told Maddie probably more than she wanted to know. He simply stood beside her, his hands crammed in his back pockets, watching the baby for several seconds, until his breath suddenly left him in a great rush. "And now I suppose you blame yourself for his death?"

She thought on that for a bit, then said, "Not as much as I did at first. I mean, yes, I was the one who told him to get out, but it wasn't me who told him to drive way the heck out to some bar he'd never been in before, pick a fight with a local twice his size. And it wasn't me who'd made a mess of my life, or took out my frustrations on a five-year-old child."

The side door buzzer went off, making both of them jump.

"That'll be my first victim," he said, finally looking at her. "The office is right next door, so all you have to do is thump on the wall if you need anything—"

"I'll be fine," she reassured him with a shaky smile. "You just go on now."

He touched the baby's head with two fingers, then left the room.

"Well, hey, Alden," Ryan said, coming up with a grin for the elderly man sitting in the waiting room, a grin which he then shared with Alden's Lancaster's pinchy-faced daughter Ruthanne sitting beside him, her black patent leather purse clutched tightly on top of even more tightly clutched together knees. The old man was just in for a checkup after a bout with pneumonia he'd gone through a few weeks ago. "Come on in, come on in... How're you feeling?"

But then it was as if something just shut right down inside of him, because Ryan barely heard his patient's "Not too bad, considerin'," as the pair followed him into the office, barely said two words to the old man as he checked his vitals, listened to his lungs and heart. Wasn't until he caught the odd looks the two of them were giving him that he realized he wasn't acting like his normal self.

Which might have something to do with the fact that he sure as hell wasn't feeling like his normal self.

Ryan fixed a smile to his face, dragged his bedside manner back out on display, and got through the appointment as best he could. But after they left, rather than calling in the next patient—Sadie Metcalf and her chronic psoriasis—he decided maybe he'd better take a minute to collect his thoughts.

The fifty-year-old rolling chair behind Dr. Patterson's oak desk creaked mightily when Ryan slumped down into it, his palm cradling his cheek. It wasn't as if he'd never heard stories like Maddie's before. Or borne witness to the effects of neglect, ignorance, abuse on mind and body. And it wasn't as if he hadn't been fully aware he was wading into treacherous waters, encouraging her to talk. Still, it wasn't the tale itself that had left him so shaken—she hadn't said anything he hadn't expected to hear in any case—it was the telling of it.

The way she kept that soft, raspy voice of hers steady, even though her hands trembled with the emotion brought on by freshly remembered wounds. The way she'd looked at him—

the few times she did—as if daring him to judge her. Not that she was asking for absolution for the decisions she'd made, not even those he imagined she'd be the first to admit hadn't been any too smart.

Why he should be feeling something like admiration for a woman who made no apologies for loving a man who had left her with nothing but a pile of debts and three children, he didn't know. Yet he did. She'd given that love freely, unselfishly—the illogical, irrepressible, irresistible love of youth, Ryan mused sourly. And now, even though that love had left her in a fix and a half, her pride still balked at having to ask strangers for help.

Like a stubborn child, Ryan thought, snapping upright and rubbing his eyes. A stubborn, courageous child with the soul of a woman, a woman who deserved far more than life had given her thus far.

A woman who deserved the kind of man who would put her first.

Who could offer her more than dreams.

A rap on the office door disrupted Ryan's brooding. He got up, opened the door to look down into Sadie Metcalf's puzzled smile. "Don't mean to rush you, Dr. Ryan, but Alden left some time ago…?"

"Yes, yes…sorry," Ryan said, standing aside to let Sadie in, at the same time pushing a whole bunch of thoughts he shouldn't even be having *out*.

A tiny window over the tub let in enough light for Maddie to see her reflection in the medicine cabinet over the pedestal sink, upon which she now leaned heavily, frowning at herself. The tile floor chilled the bottoms of her bare feet; she barely noticed. The shakiness from having told Dr. Logan her story had already begun to ease some, mainly because there seemed little point in dwelling on things she couldn't change. She would grieve for what she'd lost every day of her life, but her heart told her that her marriage would've died anyway, even if Jimmy hadn't. Her love for him sure had, although she'd resisted admitting that to herself for some time after the fact.

Oh, Lord, it was all too much to think about right now. She finally got around to brushing her teeth, which is why she'd come into the bathroom to begin with. When she finished, though, she squinted at her reflection, her mind wandering off in a different direction entirely.

Why on earth would anybody call her "pretty"? All she saw was a redhead complexion without the benefit of having red hair, a mouth that was no more than a slit in her face, a nose that was too long, eyes that were too wide apart. And a figure? She wouldn't know a curve if it bit her.

And, no, she was not feeling sorry for herself. Those were just the facts of the matter.

Maddie let out a sigh, then shuffled back to bed. Oh, well…if nothing else, she supposed it was still a nice ego boost to know that some man, somewhere, found her worth looking at. And since ego boosts came few and far between in her life, she figured she might as well make the most of this one. Even if it had come secondhand, like her clothes, through a source who didn't see her as a woman at all.

Which, she thought on a yawn as she felt herself drift off, she supposed was just as well, all things considered.

Ryan's last appointment of the day—removing a dozen stitches from Roy Farver's forehead where renovating his henhouse had led to a run-in with a wily two-by-four—had been gone for a half-hour or so before he heard the thumps and thuds and animated conversation that signaled Ivy's and the children's return. They burst into his office, bringing the chill with them. Both children sported brand-new jackets, Noah's navy-blue, Katie's a hot-pink bright enough to blind half the state.

"Look what Ivy buyed me, Dr. Ryan!" Noah beamed at him, apparently momentarily forgetting his apprehension. "It gots like a hunnerd pockets an' everything!" Seated at his desk, Ryan removed his glasses to peer at the kid, who was gleefully slurping down what was left of a chocolate ice-cream cone. Dots of color stained his pale cheeks over an ice-cream stuccoed chin, while bits of yellow leaves clung to his dark curls. Then Ryan's gaze shifted to Katie, who, clinging to Ivy's hand, gave him a shy, chocolate-coated smile in return. She looked down at her coat, then back up at him, her smile broadening.

"I look pretty," she said, her voice weightless as goose down.

"You sure do, sweetheart," he said, ignoring the dull ache curled up inside his chest like a dog settling in for the night. Then he waved Noah over, grabbing a tissue to wipe off the sticky little face. When he gently took the child by the arm, however, the boy flinched, the fire going right out of his eyes.

"It's okay, grasshopper…I just want to clean you up a bit. I won't hurt you."

After a moment, Noah nodded, although he still made a helluva face when Ryan tried to undo some of the damage. "Where on earth you take these kids, Ivy?"

She hadn't bothered unfurling herself from that poncho thing she wore, so he guessed she wasn't planning on staying. "Verna Madison's youngest gal's about to have her third baby, they've got four-week-old lab pups. You seen them yet? Five of 'em, gold as sunshine. And full of the devil."

"C'n I go show Mama my coat?" Noah asked between licks, completely undoing Ryan's cleanup job.

"Your mama and sister are taking a nap," he said, wondering how Maddie was going to react to Ivy's purchases. "Which they both need." At the child's crestfallen expression, he added, "You know, I've got about a million blocks out in the waiting room. Why don't you go build something to show your mama later?"

When the children had gone, Ryan stretched back in the desk chair, making it squawk. Hard to believe those were the same frightened children who'd shown up on his doorstep barely twelve hours ago. A knot formed in his chest at the thought of any child's having to feel that kind of anxiety.

He could only imagine how Maddie must feel.

He glanced up at the midwife, whose face indicated she

was thinking much the same thing. She caught his stare, blushed. "I didn't figure it would hurt them to have a treat. And the coats were half off. Last year's stock or something."

Shaking his head, Ryan leaned forward again to gather up the charts strewn across the blotter. "Looks to me as though somebody wants to be a grandma real bad."

Ivy let out a sigh. Her daughter Dawn, whom Ivy had raised on her own, had left Haven before the ink was dry on her high school diploma, going off to college, then law school. Now an attorney at some high-falutin' firm in New York City, Ivy's only child seemed determined not only to never set foot in Haven again, but to never give her mother any grandbabies, either. "Guess I've just about given up on that score. Not that I'm not proud of my daughter, but I swear I'm gonna wring her skinny little neck if she tells me one more blessed time her career's far more challenging, reliable and stimulating than raising a kid could be."

Yeah, that sounded like Dawn, who was the same age as his brother Cal. In fact, there was a time there when Ryan had thought Cal might have been a little sweet on Ivy's daughter, but that was a long time ago....

"Now, where on earth did you drift off to?" he heard Ivy ask, and he lifted his gaze to catch the amused curiosity in hers.

"Oh, nothing," he said, standing to pull a chart out of the file. "Just thinking about...stuff."

"Uh-huh. Like what to do with your houseguests?"

He slammed the file cabinet shut. "Hadn't gotten that far yet." He peered over at her, standing there with her arms tucked up under that poncho. "Although something tells me you have."

"Knowing you, you'd put the kids in sleeping bags in the downstairs bedroom with Maddie and the baby."

He frowned. "What's wrong with that?"

Ivy huffed. She was nearly as good at huffing as she was at clucking. "You know, sometimes I wonder how on earth you were smart enough to get that scholarship to med school. How're you gonna keep an eye on mama and her baby if she's down here and you're asleep upstairs? Besides, those two youngsters need their own space, and you've got those two connecting bedrooms upstairs that would be just perfect—''

"For crying out loud, Ivy—take a breath, wouldja?" Hands on hips, Ryan simply stared at her, frozen, as something damn close to fear knifed through him, as surprising in its sudden appearance as it was in its intensity. Especially as he had no idea what he could possibly be afraid of. Okay, so maybe he hadn't had any company for a while. Like forever. No reason the prospect should make him feel uneasy. And yet everything inside him whispered, *"Watch out, buster."*

"I'll go on ahead and change the beds," Ivy said, now shedding the poncho and heading out the door and, presumably, the back stairs, "if you tell me where the clean linens are." She vanished, reappeared. "You *do* have clean linens, don't you?"

"In the closet at the end of the hall. Shoot, Ivy, I'm not a throwback."

"Could've fooled me."

He no sooner got out a sigh when he felt somebody looking at him. He turned, still frowning hard enough to make Katie Grace frown back.

"You mad at us?" she asked.

Well, that just turned him to mush. He scooped the little girl up onto his hip, just like he did with every other three-year-old who came to his office. Difference was, this one wasn't going home in a few minutes. "No, sweetheart. I'm not mad at you."

Calm, blue-gray eyes linked with his for a second before a pair of tiny arms looped around his neck.

Oh, Lord. He was in trouble now.

Chapter 4

This bedroom didn't look much different from the one downstairs, Maddie thought, but it had two windows and was a little bigger. And a bit more inviting looking, but that might have been due to the warm light given off by a pair of rose-decorated lamps on either side of the bed. Before she'd left for the evening, Ivy had fed them all, then made up the double bed in fresh white linens, turning down the covers like this was some fancy hotel.

For what seemed like the thousandth time that day, tears pooled in Maddie's eyes, that strangers should be showing such concern for her and her children. But right now, her babies came first: instead of resenting how helpless she felt, she should be grateful that there were such good people in the world.

Since she wasn't an invalid, for heaven's sake, she'd put on a pair of jeans with the doctor's shirt, and was now settled with Amy Rose in an old but comfortable padded chair in the corner of the room. Noah and Katie Grace were in the adjoining room, bouncing from one twin bed to the other. Maddie had already told them three times to stop, even resorting to the time-honored threat of "Okay, but if you fall and crack your head open, don't come cryin' to me," which the kids clearly took as permission to keep jumping. So she told the doctor, who'd been in and out carrying up her cases and whatnot, that if they did crack their heads, to just add his fixing them up to her bill. He'd laughed a little at that. But in the intervening twenty minutes, there'd been plenty of giggling, but no cracked heads, so she'd begun to relax some.

About that, anyway.

Despite her kids' shenanigans, Dr. Logan seemed to get on with them real well, which she supposed wasn't any too surprising, considering what he did for a living. But there was still something about him that only confirmed her earlier conclusion that he wasn't entirely comfortable with the situation. Nothing she could put her finger on, just a feeling.

"So how many rooms does this house have, anyway?" she asked, more for something to say than anything else.

"Well, let's see," he said, leaning against the dresser flanking one wall and crossing his arms over his chest. The storm was fixing to make an encore appearance, the wind tormenting the pyracantha branches outside the house, making them scrape against the wall. "There's four rooms downstairs, not counting the office space, another six bedrooms and two baths up here."

"Goodness."

Dr. Logan smiled. "This had been Doc Patterson's childhood home. He was the youngest of nine. His parents kept adding to the original house every few years to accommodate them all."

"And nobody in the family wanted the house after the doctor died?"

"Nope. His brothers and sisters had scattered all over creation years before, their kids all have places of their own."

"What about his kids?"

"Didn't have any. Married twice, but no children."

"Oh," she said, then got quiet for a moment, rubbing the baby's back. "So it's just you in this great big place, all by yourself?"

He paused. "Yep."

From the next room came a thump loud enough to make the sleeping baby's hands flail out, followed by more giggles.

"What made you decide to become a country doctor?" she asked, because this was something she really *was* curious about.

His mouth twitched a little. "Being sick a lot as a kid, actually."

"You?"

"Yep. Allergies, recurring bronchial infections, you name it. If Doc Patterson wasn't out at our farm, I was in here, at the office. We got to be pretty good friends, he and I. Enough that, about the time I started to grow out of many of my ailments, he started taking me with him on his calls. And I began to think I wanted to follow in his footsteps." Now he grinned, full out. "Most people I knew thought I was nuts, wanting to take on a job with no benefits, long hours, and unreliable income. But there was no talking me out of it." He checked his watch. "It's getting on to eight o'clock. You want me to get the kids ready for bed?"

She opened her mouth to say, no, of course not, only to realize there was a big difference between sitting still in a chair and wrestling two wired little kids into bed. So what she said was, "I'd be very grateful."

Dr. Logan nodded, then headed into the adjoining room. Maddie decided she'd best supervise, though, so she got up and carefully moved herself and her new daughter into the kids' bedroom, where Ryan was already pawing through the smaller of the two suitcases, looking for pajamas.

"Oh, land!" Maddie nearly gasped at the rumpled sheets and every-which-way blankets and pillows on the beds. "Would you look at what you two have done to these beds! And where did you put your new coats? They better not be on the floor somewhere!"

Naturally they both flew out of the room to heaven-knew-where, appearing not ten seconds later, panting and giggling, with the coats.

Maddie set Amy Rose, who was sawing logs to beat the

band, down on one of the beds and reached out for the coats. "Give those to me." She swiped dust and dirt off first one, then the other. "Honestly, you two." But even she could tell her scolding didn't have much punch to it. "Get your tooth-brushes out of the case and go brush your teeth," she said, and to her immense relief, they did. She turned to Dr. Logan, who was now standing with a faded Barbie nightgown in one hand and a pair of worn Barney pajamas in the other. "They love those coats so much, I don't have the heart to make them give them back."

"Well, that's a good thing, Maddie Kincaid, because you'd for sure hurt Ivy's feelings if you did that. And what do you think you're doing?"

"Fixing up the bed," she said, tugging the bedcovers up on one of the beds, then rearranging the pillow. Trying to convince herself that accepting Ivy's generosity wasn't any-thing to be ashamed of. "And no, before you ask, I'm not straining anything." From the bathroom, she heard lots of giggling and spitting, followed by a shriek. Her belly pro-tested some when she straightened up.

"Noah James!" she hollered in the direction of the bath-room, "you better not be spitting toothpaste at your sister!"

"I'm not, Mama!" More giggles. On a sigh, Maddie looked over at Dr. Logan. "I guess you have a point. About the coats, I mean. It's just…"

"Tell me if the situation were reversed, you wouldn't do the same thing."

The kids came barreling out of the bathroom, their chins a slobbery mess. Maddie grabbed a tissue from the box by one of the beds, then a child. "Well, I guess you're right about that," she said, swiping the goo off Katie Grace's chin and sending her over to Dr. Logan. In the midst of cleaning off Noah, Maddie glanced over at the doctor, who was down on one bended knee in front of the tiny girl, patiently waiting while she unbuttoned her sweater herself. When the little girl got the last button undone and beamed up at him with a look that was equal parts triumph and adoration, something twisted around Maddie's heart. Something she didn't need to be dealing with right now.

Despite what she'd said about letting the doctor do this, Maddie snatched up Noah's pajamas from where Dr. Ryan had left them on the foot of the bed. "C'mere, sugar. Let me help—"

"No!" Noah swiped the garments from her hand. "I can do it!" Maddie's brows lifted: she'd been fighting for some time, without much success, to get Noah to do more things on his own. Suddenly now he's Mr. Independent? At first, Maddie figured it was just because he didn't want Katie Grace getting one up on him. But as she caught his furtive glances at Dr. Logan, she understood a little more what was going on. Thought she did, anyway. He might have let the doctor take care of him this morning, when he was too frightened and tired to do otherwise, but now that he was feeling more on top of things, caution had returned with a vengeance.

Suddenly she heard herself say, "You think there's any way I could go see Ned in a few days?"

She had no idea why that had popped out of her mouth, especially right now, or why she saw that as some sort of solution, but it had and she did. Maybe it was just a sense of *doing* something. In any case, after a second or so, Dr. Logan shrugged and said, "I don't see why not. We'll find someone to watch the kids for a couple hours and I'll take you over."

"I don't need you to take me—"

"I'm up to the hospital several times a week, anyway, checking up on my patients or doing rounds. No sense in both of us driving over there."

"Oh. Well, yes, I suppose you have a point." She licked her lips. "And if Ned says it's okay with him, I want to see his house."

Ryan frowned. "I told you, that house isn't fit for you and the kids."

He had, over supper. But she said anyway, "I know what you told me. But I think I'm perfectly capable of deciding whether his house is 'fit' or not." She sighed at his expression, then lowered her voice, keeping an eye out on the kids, who were busy drawing pictures in the condensation on the window panes. "We can't stay with you forever, we can't go back to Arkansas, I don't have any money, and the prospect of living in my car doesn't exactly thrill me. Besides, it's not like we were exactly living in a palace before. And if I was living at Ned's, then maybe he could come home to convalesce instead of going into that place you were talking about."

Fortunately, before Dr. Logan could argue with her, his cell phone rang. He unhooked it from his belt, answering it even as he shot Maddie a look that said, "This isn't over yet."

"How high's the fever, Faith?" she heard him say. "Okay, I'll be out in about forty-five minutes, if that's okay. I'll go ahead and swab him for strep while I'm there… Forget it. The weather's threatening to get nasty again. No sense dragging the boy out in the cold and the wet."

He disconnected and turned to her, looking torn. "Will you be okay…?"

"We'll be fine," she reassured him. "Hard part's over. Go."

After one final, conflicted look, he said good-night, then disappeared.

And Maddie wondered, as she watched her oldest children climb into their nice, clean beds, if Ryan Logan was so busy always taking care of everybody else, who the heck ever took care of him?

By the time Maddie'd been in Haven for two days, she'd learned one very important thing: The women in this town looked out for each other.

Aside from Ivy's in-and-outing and fussing and hovering, it seemed like every female from here to Tulsa had stopped by to drop off a casserole or a ham or clothes or baby equipment their kids had outgrown, or to just introduce herself and tell Maddie if there was anything she needed, not to be shy, just let her know.

Lord, she'd never remember all their names.

And they'd never be able to eat all this food, not in a million years.

It was getting on to dinnertime. Since Dr. Logan was at the hospital, Ivy had been there for a couple hours, so Maddie could get a shower, at least. Amy Rose had been changed and nursed and burped, and was now snoozing away in a swing with a detachable infant seat somebody had brought over yesterday, which she'd set up next to the kitchen table. Katie Grace had conked out on the sofa in the living room, but was due to wake up any minute; Noah was sitting at the table with his head resting on his folded up arms, studying his baby sister. One foot scuffed back and forth across the tile, like to drive Maddie crazy. Not that she was going to tell him to stop. Right now, she had more pressing things on her mind. Like trying to pawn off some of this food.

"Ivy, please—at least take this tuna casserole. We've already got three!"

Wrapping herself up in her poncho for the short walk back to her house, Ivy leaned over, lifted the glass top off the dish. "Who brought this one?"

"Lord knows."

Ivy carefully raised the heavy ceramic container, squinted at the lettering on the strip of masking tape. "Oh, Lord, Arliss Potts. The Methodist pastor's wife." The dish clunked back onto the counter. "Sweet lady, generous as they come, but can't cook worth spit. Throw it out, is my advice."

"How bad can it be?"

"You ever tasted tuna casserole with nutmeg in it? *And* chili powder?"

Maddie replaced the lid. Took a step back. "Oh." At Ivy's chuckle, she said, "Why doesn't somebody just, well, maybe show her some new recipes or something?"

"And hurt her feelings?"

"Well, I don't know. Seems like a huge waste of food, otherwise."

Ivy looped an arm around Maddie's shoulders and gave her a brief hug. "Food's a lot easier to come by than goodwill." She let go, cramming a floppy brimmed hat over her long, loose hair. "I've been meaning to ask…did you call Didi Meyerhauser back? About the Baptist day care co-op?"

Maddie picked at the buttons on her oversize shirt. "Oh, I don't know—I mean, leaving Noah and Katie Grace with strangers…"

"No such thing in Haven, in case you haven't figured it out by now. And Didi's got a couple spaces now that the Sommerses moved away. *And* she said she knows you can't do your part for some weeks yet, not to worry about that. But you'll wear yourself out, taking care of two little ones with a new baby. So give her a call. She might laugh you half to death, but she doesn't bite!"

Then she disappeared through the back door, a dozen or so leaves fluttering inside in her wake. Maddie started to bend over to pick them up, then remembered that probably wouldn't be such a hot idea.

"Noah, honey, would you mind picking those up for me?"

The boy moaned a little, but he did as she'd asked. When he stood up, she did bend over then, to kiss him on top of his head. He leaned into her for a moment, then pushed away to dump the leaves in the garbage.

Well. She supposed she should do something about dinner. Not that anybody expected her to, but she could at least stick one of these casseroles in the oven, so it would be ready when the doctor got home. Whenever that might be. Didn't matter. At least she'd feel like she was earning her keep a little bit, making sure he had a hot meal waiting for him.

She opened the refrigerator, frowning at the vast array of foil-covered and plastic-lidded containers smirking at her from its depths.

"Mama? I'm hungry."

Having decided against the nutmeg-chili tuna casserole in favor of—she peeked under the foil of the nearest offering— lasagna, Maddie dragged the pan out of the refrigerator, stuck it in the oven, then looked over at her child. Amazing how quickly he'd gotten used to having food whenever he wanted it. Even in two days, she could already see his face filling out some.

"Supper's in about forty-five minutes," she said, knowing he'd just had somebody's homemade oatmeal cookies and a glass of milk not a half hour ago. "Why don't you go on into Dr. Ryan's waiting room and get a book to look at? He said you could."

"But I'm *starving.*"

Maddie eyed her son, her mouth quirked. Too bad she didn't still feed the older two the way she did Amy Rose. Then she shoved a hand through her scraggly hair, the grown-out result of a not-entirely-successful beauty-school-student haircut from six months ago. "Have an apple." She pointed to the heaping fruit bowl in the center of the kitchen table, next to her dozing daughter.

Noah scrambled up onto a kitchen chair, inspecting every single apple until he found the one that spoke to him, she guessed, a shiny greeny-red MacIntosh. He plopped his fanny on the chair seat and took a bite, chewing with open-mouthed enthusiasm and a small frown as he concentrated on which spot to attack next.

Maddie smiled, then noticed the small radio on the counter; she went over and turned it on, remembering the country music she'd heard coming from the kitchen this morning. That would be nice, something familiar. Jimmy had always listened to that hard rock stuff that jangled Maddie's nerves, turned up so high sometimes, she feared for the kids' hearing. Maddie was partial to ballads, the kind of music you could dance to, all close to your man—

Maddie made a face at the classical music and went to change the station, only to decide it wouldn't kill her or anything. So she let it be.

Katie Grace wandered in, her hair a moist tangle, her thumb in her mouth. Maddie sat at the table, patted her lap for Katie to get up on it. She loved how her babies smelled when they first awakened from a nap, how soft and warm they were. She closed her eyes: her oldest was eating; her youngest asleep; her middle one cuddling on her lap. For the moment, they were in a warm house with plenty of food and fancy music playing in the background. They were safe. And one of her strengths was being able to relish those scraps of contentment that life offered.

Out of the blue, she wondered if Dr. Logan was happy with his life.

Why he wasn't married.

Neither of which were any of her business and if she knew what was good for her, she'd cut off this train of thought right now.

After that first day, she couldn't help but notice the doctor hadn't seemed much interested in conversation. Oh, he'd checked on her and Amy Rose ten times a day, it seemed, but never stayed for more than a few minutes. And the dinners they'd shared the first two nights had both been interrupted by calls, one requiring him to leave the house before he even got a chance to finish. He'd been as kind as ever, and polite, but there was definitely something missing.

Maddie told herself it was not up to her to try to figure out what that was. Besides, they weren't going to be there long. As soon as she could get up to see Jimmy's Uncle Ned—Dr. Logan said he thought maybe next week, when she could express enough milk to leave Amy Rose with Ivy for a little while, since he didn't think it was such a good idea to take an infant into the hospital if she didn't have to—everything would be fine, she was sure of it.

Who was she kidding? She wasn't sure of anything. Not that she bought for a second the doctor's protests about the condition of Ned's house. Maddie could make a home wherever she had to. But what if Ned didn't *want* her and the kids living with them?

"You think we could watch TV?" Noah asked, tugging at her shirt.

Took a second for her brain to snap back into focus. "I suppose."

"I don't know how to work it."

With a sigh, Maddie set Katie down, smiling for Amy Rose, whose mouth was all puckered in her sleep, and followed Noah into the living room, a large front room that seemed to be all windows. Like the rest of the house, the furniture was old and more than a little threadbare, the colors faded, but the chairs and sofa matched, as did the end tables and coffee table. One thing she had to say about the place—it was clean as a whistle. Neat. No clutter anywhere. It just didn't look like anybody really lived in it.

The TV was on the small side, no remote, with the off-on button cover missing. But once she got the thing going, the picture was pretty good.

"I don't know the stations here," she said, punching through the channels. Nothing much for a child to watch at six o'clock, that was for sure, especially with no cable. But then, she didn't suppose Dr. Logan watched much TV—

"There, Mama! An animal show!"

Maddie got the children settled down on the saggy cushioned sofa, then traipsed back through the old-fashioned, formal dining room toward the kitchen, letting out a little gasp of surprise when she found Dr. Logan standing there, frowning at the collection of pies, cakes and shower-cap covered paper plates heaped with every kind of cookie there was.

She'd forgotten just how tall he was.

"Where the heck did all this stuff come from?"

"Everybody and her cousin," Maddie said, telling herself there was no reason to feel jittery around him. "It's a crying shame, though. I mean, there's no way we can eat it all before it goes bad. Maybe we could give some of it away?"

The doctor nodded. He still had on his hat and coat, although it was open so he could park his hands on his hips. It must be cold out, she thought, realizing she hadn't been outside since she got here. "Let me think on this for a minute. Seems to me there's gotta be some folks who might appreciate our spreading around the wealth a little." Then he looked at her and grinned. Not a big one, but enough to make his eyes crinkle up at the corners. "Long as we make sure we don't accidentally give anything *back*. That could be disastrous."

What could be disastrous, Maddie realized, was her fluttery reaction to his grin. Not that this should be surprising, considering what was going on in her life and that he was so soft-spoken and decent. And protective. Add to that her screwy hormones, and it stood to reason she'd be feeling a little addlepated around him. Since that was *all* it was, however, she decided it wasn't worth thinking too hard about. She even laughed a little. "I made sure to take note of who gave what. So I could send thank-you notes down the road."

That got a pair of lifted brows. "Thank-you notes?"

Maddie shrugged. "My foster mother got me in the habit. It's nice to let people know you appreciate their effort, I've always felt."

He didn't seem to know what to say to that. He shrugged off his jacket, hung it up on a hook by the back door, along with his hat. "How're you feeling?" he asked, forking one hand through his thick hair.

"Pretty good," she said. "A little tired."

"Amy Rose nursing okay?"

"Like she was born to it."

That got another little smile. He twisted around to the refrigerator, grabbed the handle. "Where're the kids?"

"Watching TV." Then she blushed. "I hope that's okay, I don't want you to think we're taking over your house or anything...."

His stunned look stopped her short. "You're my guests, Maddie. You're free to go wherever you like, use whatever I have—" he finally opened the refrigerator, then groaned "—eat whatever you happen to find. What's this?" He pointed to one of the casseroles.

Maddie peered around him to see. "Arliss Potts's tuna casserole."

"Except this," he said, pulling the dish off the shelf.

"It's really that bad?"

"Maddie, I'm a bachelor. I eat anything. Anything but this."

Well, that decided it then. On a sigh, she took the casserole from him to empty it into the lined garbage can under the sink. Except he intercepted it, gently pushing her out of the way.

"What are you doing?" she asked.

"It's what I don't want you doing that's the issue here," he said, scraping the gloppy stuff into the can. "You just gave birth three days ago. I want you taking it easy."

"If I take it any easier, I'll stop functioning altogether. Besides," she went on before he could protest, "what about those peasants who squat in the fields, have their babies, then go right on with their work?"

"Those peasants aren't twenty pounds underweight and anemic."

Well. She had nothing to say to that, she supposed. The kids laughed at something on TV. Maddie wandered over to the kitchen doorway, straining to hear that they hadn't changed the channel to something too adult for them. Jimmy had let them watch anything at all, no matter how inappropriate it was for little kids. Then he'd laugh off her fussing at him, tell her to stop being such a priss—

"Your husband didn't exactly pamper you during your pregnancies, did he?"

She whirled around, a little too sharply, grabbing onto the edge of the counter to keep from losing her balance. Dr. Logan was beside her in an instant, guiding her into a chair. "Seems your body's trying to make my point for me."

"I just turned too fast, is all. I'm fine." She tried to stand; he didn't let her.

"Yes, you are. Remarkably well, in fact. Although I'm beginning to wonder about your mental faculties."

Her gaze darted to his, her heart skipping at the intensity sparking in those clear, light eyes. He bent closer, one hand on her shoulder, the other braced on the edge of the table. Close enough to feel his breath, warm and peppermint-scented, on her face; to see each individual golden hair stubbling his cheeks.

To see far more concern for her condition in those eyes than she ever had in Jimmy's. Not even at the beginning.

"You listening to me?"

Maddie blinked, which for some reason cleared her head. "Uh…yeah."

"You may feel pretty good right now, but you're not in the clear yet. So you will take it easy until either I or Ivy tell you you're okay to do more, you got that?" He abruptly straightened, leaving her feel a little like a windblown leaf plastered to the side of a house. "Now—" he walked over, grabbed a pair of pot holders "—what's in the oven?"

"Lasagne. I just put it in, though, a couple minutes ago. Thought maybe I'd make a salad to go with it, I noticed you had some stuff in the refrigerator—"

She started to get up. One look from Dr. Logan and she thought better of it.

"Salad sounds good," he said. "I can do that." He walked over to the refrigerator, his movements agile, unselfconscious. Those of a man completely unaware of how good-looking he is.

Maddie shut her eyes.

"You okay?"

She opened them again. Dr. Logan was crouched in front of the refrigerator, digging in the vegetable bin. He pulled out a head of iceberg lettuce, a cucumber, two tomatoes. The lettuce had some brown spots on it.

"I'm fine."

Which couldn't have been further from the truth, but since her not-fineness wasn't anything that either made a lick of sense or could be put into words, anyway, she figured she may as well just leave it lay.

The doctor clunked the salad stuff up onto the counter; the baby let out a startled squeal. He got to her in a stride and a half, even though Maddie was literally right there.

"She probably needs to be changed," he said. "I'll be right back."

Frowning, although she wasn't completely sure why, Maddie propped her elbow on the table, sinking her chin into her palm. Didn't seem like ten seconds had passed before the doctor returned, ten seconds more before he'd plopped a changing pad on the table and changed Amy Rose's wet diaper. Then he picked her up in those large, careful hands, grinning at her and making the silliest noises at her daughter she'd ever heard come out of a man's mouth, before handing her to Maddie.

"So how come you don't have six of these of your own?"

she asked, settling Amy in for yet another feed, only to immediately think, *Oh, Lord, there I go again.*

Maybe one day before she turned ninety she'd learn to think first, talk second. She didn't hold out a lot of hope for that, though. As the baby blithely sucked away, she lifted her gaze to see the doctor's jerky movements as he yanked down a wooden bowl from the cabinet, clattered a small wooden chopping block onto the counter. "So," he said, whacking away at the cucumber. "I hear Didi Meyerhauser called. About the day care."

She got the message.

"Ivy talked to her, not me." She looked down at the baby, smiling at the wide open eyes staring up into hers, completely trusting that her mama would always take care of her. "I'm supposed to call her back."

He dumped the pulverized cuke into the bowl, went after the hapless tomato. "It's a good setup they've got there in the church, and you won't find anyone better than Didi at running a day care." He suddenly went quiet, the kind of stillness where you know the person's not finished talking, just gathering his thoughts so he can best figure out how to say what he wants to. But before he could do so, there was a knock on the back door, followed almost immediately by the appearance of a bundle of Lord-help-me muscles and mischief in blue jeans and boots and a denim jacket. A devilish smile twinkled underneath a light brown cowboy hat, while a covered cake tote wobbled in one hand.

There was no mistaking the family resemblance.

Maddie looked around for something to cover herself up with, settled on a kitchen towel she could just barely reach from where she was sitting. Not that she was the least bit self-conscious about breast-feeding her baby, but in her experience, it made most men uncomfortable.

Although right now, the doctor seemed to be the most uncomfortable person in the room. "What in tarnation are you doing here, Cal?"

The smile stretched out over a long, strong-jawed face, revealed a double set of deeply etched dimples. And Maddie knew, the way a woman just knows these things, that Cal Logan was one of those men your mama always warned you about. If you had a mama, that is.

"In a word...Ethel." He lifted up the cake a little. "Shoved this into my hands, gave me explicit orders not to do a blessed thing until I delivered it." Except then he went to set the cake on the counter and his smile dimmed. "Looks like somebody beat me to it."

"Hell, Cal, half the county beat you to it." Dr. Ryan waved the knife in the direction of all the goodies. "And when you go, please—take something back with you."

"And risk bringin' Ethel's wrath down around my head? Not on your life." Then, while Maddie was trying to decide if Ethel was Cal's wife or what, he walked right over to her, apparently not the least bit affected by what she was doing, and thrust out a hand. "Since my brother's lived alone so long he's forgotten his manners, I'll introduce myself. Cal Logan."

Maddie shifted the baby a bit to take hold of Cal's hand, which was warm and rough. A working man's hand. "Maddie Kincaid." Behind her, she heard the kids returning to the kitchen. "Nice to meet you."

"Likewise." Then Cal lifted his head, his whole face breaking into a grin again. "And who do we have here?"

Both kids immediately scooted across the kitchen to huddle on either side of her. "My son and daughter. Noah and Katie Grace."

Cal squatted down in front of them, tipping back his cowboy hat as he introduced himself. Dr. Logan, Maddie noticed, seemed to be chopping up his lettuce with more enthusiasm than the job required, especially as there was no need to *chop* lettuce to begin with. A second later, she heard a squeal of delight as Cal produced a quarter from behind Noah's ear.

"Do it to me," Katie breathed, and Cal obliged.

And the doctor chopped.

Then Maddie finished up Amy Rose's feed, surprised when Cal grabbed a receiving blanket from off the table, slung it over his shoulder, and reached for the baby to burp her. So while he patted Amy Rose's back—well, pounded, was more like it—and Maddie discreetly pulled herself back together, she and Cal made small talk for a minute or two, like there was nothing strange at all about her and the kids being there in the doctor's kitchen, until Cal said he needed to be going, he'd just come into town to do Ethel's bidding, at which point Maddie, who didn't know how not to be hospitable, never mind that this wasn't her house, asked him why he didn't just stay for dinner, seeing as they had so much?

Amy Rose's belch was the only thing to pierce the heavy silence.

When it was obvious that nobody was going to second Maddie's offer, Cal said, "Thanks, but I really need to get back. Got a mare about to foal, so I need to stick close to home."

Maddie looked at Dr. Logan, still expecting him to protest or say something, but he seemed to be too busy glowering.

"Another time," she said, getting up to take Amy back from Cal and put her back in the infant seat.

"You bet," Cal said, backing toward the door. He waved at the kids and winked at her, which she was sure Dr. Logan not only caught, but was the primary reason for his scowl deepening.

Then Dr. Logan looked at her, his brow knotted in what she could only surmise was confusion, mumbled something about being right back, and disappeared after his brother, leaving Maddie to wonder if the moon was full or what.

Chapter 5

"Okay, Ry—you mind telling me what's got your drawers in such a knot?"

Ryan grabbed hold of his little brother's arm and yanked him down the driveway and away from the house, far enough to be out of earshot. "You, that's what."

Cal jerked his arm out of Ryan's grasp, then rammed his hands on his hips. "Meanin' what? All I did was bring over a damn cake—"

"You were flirting, numbskull. With a vulnerable woman who just lost her husband. Not to mention just gave birth. What *is* it with you, that you can't be around a woman for more'n five minutes without making a play for her?"

Cal stared him down for a moment, then stalked away toward his truck. "I'm not even gonna dignify that comment with a reply."

Ryan followed. "You were moving in on her faster'n lava from a volcano, for God's sake!"

"I was being *friendly,* you idiot!" Cal yanked open his truck door, but Ryan was right there, grabbing his brother's arm again.

"What you were doing is not what I call friendly."

"Well, then, that's where you and me have a difference of opinion, big brother. And let *go,* for the love of Pete. I'm not goin' anywhere. Although now I remember why I'm not inclined to seek out your company."

A pang of regret sliced through Ryan as he let go of Cal's arm, but not strongly enough to sidetrack him from the issue at hand. "I know your reputation, Cal. Hell, everybody east of Tulsa knows your reputation. Just figured I'd head you off at the pass, is all."

Anger flashed in his brother's eyes. "I don't mean anything by it, and you know that."

"Do I?"

"Well, you should, dammit. It's just my way. Which you would know if you'd tried a little harder to get to know me, instead of listening to every shred of gossip that manages to meander through town. I'm not goin' to apologize for liking women, for seeing if I can make them smile for me. Especially one as cute and sweet as that one is, who I gather has been through a lot this past little while. I can't help but want to make her feel a little nicer about herself. That she's worth being noticed. No law against it, last time I checked. But damned if I'm gonna stand here and listen to you going on about my *reputation.* I've never in my life taken advantage of a woman, or gone out with one who I didn't respect as much as I did our own mother." Cal's voice caught slightly on that last little bit, but he quickly recovered. "Liking women doesn't make me a womanizer, Ry."

Ryan let out a huff of air of his own, then stuffed his hands in his back pockets. After a moment, he said, "How could you possibly know how sweet Maddie is? You didn't talk but five minutes, if that."

"Shoot, Ry…" In the dim glow given off by the back porch light, Cal's green eyes had gone the color of a murky pond. "Every time I turned around today, somebody or other was telling me about the poor widow and her *darlin'* little kids who showed up on your doorstep in labor." He grinned. "You want my opinion, Maddie's in far more danger from the married womenfolk in this town than she'd ever be from me. If she sticks around, I guarantee every woman within a fifty-mile radius is gonna try her hand at fixin' her up with *somebody*. Which reminds me…'' Cal hauled himself up into the driver's seat, leaving the door hanging open. ''I hear Ned McAllister's her uncle or something?''

Despite himself, Ryan felt his anger begin to fade. Flirting really was just his brother's way. And even though Cal used to go through women like they were M&M's—maybe he did respect them, but let's just say there was a big turnover in the girlfriend department—Ryan guessed he hadn't really heard much dirt on his brother in the past few years. These days, Cal's business pretty much kept him out of trouble. And out of sight.

''Her husband's great-uncle, yeah,'' he now said. Damn, it was cold out here. And damp. Ryan folded his arms over his chest and glanced up, frowning at the clouds, then back at his brother. ''She's got this idea she's going to be able to stay with him out at his place.''

''You tell her that'd never work?''

''What do you think?''

''And judging from that just-ate-grapefruit look on your face, I'm guessing she wasn't dissuaded.''

''Well, in her position, I don't suppose I'd feel I could afford to be too picky, either. I reckon she'll change her mind soon enough, though, once she sets eyes on the place.''

''And then what?''

Ryan sighed, his breath coming out in a white puff. ''Yeah, well, that's the part I haven't figured out yet.''

Cal craned his neck, looked up at the house, then back at Ryan. ''No reason why she can't just stay here, is there? At least until she gets back on her feet?''

''Other than the fact that the last thing I need is a woman and her kids underfoot indefinitely? What's so blamed funny?''

''You are,'' Cal said, still chuckling. He grabbed his door, slammed it shut. ''You come roaring out here after me, clearly intent on defending Maddie Kincaid's honor, then turn around and give me this crock about her and the kids 'being under-foot.' The truth is, something about that gal's gotten to you. And you haven't got the slightest idea what to do about it, do you?''

Ryan ignored feeling that he'd just been suckerpunched and said, "And you're off your rocker."

"Oh, yeah?"

"Yeah. For one thing, I've known the woman exactly two and a half days. For another, she's more'n ten years younger than me. *And* she just buried her husband. Besides, you know full well why I can't get involved with anybody."

Cal didn't have anything to say to that for a moment. Then he twisted the key in the ignition, gunning the engine. "Yep. That's a nice crop of reasons you got there."

"I don't like the way you said that."

That got a chuckle. "You know, one of these days, you and Hank both are gonna realize I'm not your *kid* brother anymore. That maybe I know a thing or two. Especially about women," he added with a lopsided grin.

"Which brings me back to my earlier observation."

Cal let out a ragged sigh. "I'm not looking to start something with Maddie, okay? At least…not this week."

With that, he backed out of the driveway fast enough to get the neighbor's dog all riled up.

Another week passed before Ryan got around to taking Maddie into Claremore to see Ned. Maddie wasn't all that sold on the idea of leaving Amy Rose with anybody, not even Ivy—she'd gotten the boy enrolled in kindergarten and the girl seemed to take to the church day care right off—and not even for a couple hours, but she'd finally relented. She'd fed her right before they left, though, hoping the baby would sleep through until they got back. And even though Ryan reminded her they had his cell phone, just in case, he could tell she still worried. She was just one of those mothers who had a hard time being away from her babies, even for a little while.

"You can adjust that seatbelt if you need to," he said when they got into the truck.

"What? Oh, okay…"

Only he had to lean over her to help her when the old belt refused to cooperate. Which put him way too close to her, close enough to catch her sweet, natural scent, nothing more than shampoo and soap and freshly washed clothes. Lord above, the woman washed clothes more than anybody he'd ever seen, other than his mother. And yesterday, she'd taken it upon herself to wash his, too, when he was out on a call. There his shorts and things were, neatly folded on his bed, when he got back.

And she'd started…doing things to the house. Nothing major, and not cleaning, since he had Cherise to come in once a week to do that—not that he'd let Maddie clean, anyway, not this soon after giving birth. Just these little touches—flowers and stuff, you know?—that made the place look brighter.

Like a real home.

It irritated the life out of him. Not what she was doing: that he liked it as much as he did. Because soon Maddie would go away.

She *had* to go away.

"How long is it?" she asked as they pulled out of the driveway.

"Not far. Forty, forty-five minutes."

She nodded, pulled her bulky sweater more tightly together. "You cold?"

"No." Then she smiled. "Maybe a little."

"I can turn the heat on, if you like."

"Oh. Well…okay."

For crying out loud, what was the big deal with asking somebody to just turn up the heat? Ryan looked over, took in her denim jumper—a maternity one, the only skirtlike thing she owned, apparently—the old canvas slip-ons on her feet. Her stockings or panty hose or whatever they were had a small run in them. "So," he said, because the silence was beginning to drive him buggy, "you've never met Ned, you said?"

She shook her head. Her hair did that slithery thing that

caught the light. She'd begun to put on a little weight, Ryan noticed with a start. Enough to soften her features just a bit. Make her look even younger. More vulnerable.

"I talked to him once, right after we were married. Sent him Christmas cards with pictures of the kids, too, every year. Never got one back, though." She propped her elbow on the rest on the door, frowned down at her short nails, then looked at him. "You think I'm crazy, don't you? For thinking this could work?"

"I think you've got a lot of guts," he said, and meant it. When her brows lifted, vanishing underneath her bangs, he added, "But I guess it's the crazy people who have the courage to attempt all the stuff the sane ones don't."

She fiddled with her purse, lying on her lap, then laughed quietly. "That's not answering my question."

"No, I don't suppose it is. But…" He thought on how to put this, then said, "Ned's lived on his own ever since he retired from the Army, some thirty years ago. No wife, no kids. From time to time, he'll take up with some mangy mutt, but he doesn't even have one of those right now." He glanced over at her. "From what I know about Ned McAllister, it doesn't surprise me that he never sent you a Christmas card back. Even if you all could fit in that dump of his, he's too set in his ways to adjust to having family around, not at this point in his life."

She met his gaze, just for a second, a funny expression on her face. Then she resumed staring out the windshield.

Stayed quiet for the rest of the trip, too, only commenting now and again on something they'd pass along the way. Unfortunately for Ryan, this allowed him more time to think than was probably good for him, especially as the only thing he seemed to be able to think about was the woman sitting beside him with the determined look in her stormy eyes.

About how much of an idiot he'd made of himself with Cal. No wonder his brother had come to the conclusion he had. All he'd had to go on was what he saw, which, thinking back, could certainly have been easily enough mistaken for something it wasn't.

Now if Ryan could just figure why his brother's doing whatever it was his brother did around women—around Maddie—had provoked such a reaction on his part, he'd be a much happier man.

And here they were in the medical center's parking lot, where, strangely enough, Ryan felt as though his fate was about to be decided. Well, not in the parking lot, but later on. When Maddie met Ned. He'd been twisting his brain up into knots these past few days, trying to come up with a solution to the Maddie Kincaid Problem, only to come up blank every time. Although he wondered about that last set of foster parents, back in Fayetteville. Whenever he tried to bring them up, Maddie got all cagey, changing the subject. But what little she had said had given him to believe they'd been close at one time. He just wondered if they had any idea the mess she was in now.

He glanced over, saw she looked a little paler than normal. Which was pretty pale. "We're here," he said, unnecessarily.

She nodded. Took a deep breath. Closed her fingers around the door handle.

"You want me to come with you?"

"No," she said, practically before he'd gotten the whole sentence out of his mouth. When Ryan told Ned about Maddie, the old man hadn't let on as to whether her being here pleased him or not. Hard to tell with Ned.

"You sure?"

She gave him one of those steely eyed looks of hers. "I don't need you to hold my hand," she said, which stirred the strangest, most unexpected reaction in the pit of Ryan's stomach. So he nodded, quickly, before he started thinking too hard about that strange and unexpected reaction, then got out of the truck to help her out. Except, of course, she was already out and halfway through the parking lot, making tracks toward the entrance like nobody's business.

Ryan just stood there, one hand braced on the truck's roof, and shook his head. Then he shouted out Ned's room number after her, in case she'd forgotten, although he pretty well fig-

ured he'd wasted his breath because he somehow doubted
Maddie Kincaid ever forgot anything.

She'd had to get away, from…whatever it was that was
shaking her up so much about Dr. Logan. Before he could
take her by the elbow or something, lead her inside. Not that
he would have, but you never know. She didn't figure it was
worth taking the chance to find out.

Maddie marched up to the desk, asked how to get to Ned's
room and was on her way before she could think about that,
either. Dr. Logan had already told her that Ned would have
to be in rehab for his physical therapy for a good four weeks,
and that the old man had apparently made it his personal
mission to try everybody's patience in the hospital. Lord, but
her heart was pounding so loudly, her teeth were rattling. Not
because she was afraid of dealing with a crotchety old man—
most people, she'd discovered, just used ill temper as an excuse to cover up their fears, and once you knew that, they
weren't nearly so scary anymore—but because she knew this
meeting was likely to be some kind of turning point. Once in
the elevator, she practiced her deep breathing, like she was
supposed to have used when she gave birth but never seemed
to remember until it was too late. It did seem to help, some,
because although her heart was still beating pretty loudly, at
least her teeth had stopped clacking together.

The elevator dinged at Ned's floor; Maddie waited impa-
tiently the few seconds it took for the doors to *shoosh* open,
then stepped out into the quiet hallway.

This had to work. Had to. Because if she couldn't stay with
Ned, what she was going to do or where she was going
to go once she left Dr. Logan's?

She was so engrossed in her worrying that she passed right
by Ned's room. Muttering to herself, she backed up, only to
realize she'd worked herself up into such a state, her teeth
were rattling again. So she took a moment—okay, several
moments—to pray for strength, then opened the door to
Ned's room.

* * *

"Uncle Ned?"

Starting at the soft voice, he carefully twisted in the chair they made him sit up in. Had to sit up, they insisted, too much of a risk for pneumonia if he laid down all the time. Hogwash. Wasn't his lungs that was the problem, it was his hip. Which now had a pin in it, holding it together like he was some old patched up babydoll. Except dolls couldn't feel any pain.

"Uncle Ned?" the gal said again, taking another step into the room. "It's Maddie. Maddie Kincaid. Jimmy's wife?"

Lord, but she looked scared half to death, those big gray eyes of hers taking up half of her skinny little face. Pretty enough little thing, he supposed, if you liked 'em scrawny.

Figured she'd come right in the middle of his favorite program.

"Well, come on in, gal, and sit down," Ned barked at her. Only fun he got out of life these days was making people jump. Not that many of 'em did around here, but it never hurt to try. "But you can only talk when the commercials is on."

"Oh. All right." She crossed to the other chair in the room—they'd taken Ned's roommate away for his morning session in the torture chamber, as Ned liked to call it—and sat on its edge, her hands folded neatly in her lap. Ned kept one eye and both ears—nothing wrong with those, either—on his show, the other eye on her. Just had a baby, Doc Ryan had said. And Jimmy was gone, too. Doc hadn't gone into many details, out of deference to Ned's being kin to Jimmy, was his guess, but Ned got the feeling that Jimmy's death hadn't been quite as "accidental" as Doc was making out.

Doc had also warned him that the gal wasn't here just for a visit, that she'd come to Haven because Ned was her only living relative.

Imagine that.

Still, what could he possibly do for her? He barely had a pot to pee in himself. And he was a pain in the butt to be around. Just ask anybody.

When a commercial for some toilet bowl cleaner came on, Ned tore his attention away from the TV, saw the gal had brightened up some.

"How're you feeling?" she asked.

"Lousy," Ned answered. "Take my advice, gal—don't grow old. And for God's sake, don't break anything if you do. Now I know you didn't come all the way here to make chitchat, so just come to the point. Whaddya want from me?"

She looked a little taken aback, but only for a second. "Well, okay, the fact of the matter is...I need someplace to stay, me and the kids. And since we're kin, I was hoping maybe I could stay at your place. Just until I get on my feet," she added quickly. "Soon as I can work, I can probably rent a place of my own, but that won't be for another four weeks yet, and you'll be here for a while, anyway. And if you like, I could even stay around to help you after you come home. So this could work out really well for both of us, couldn't it?"

Heavens to Betsy. Now he remembered why he'd never had much use for women. They could talk a man to death.

The commercial over, he turned back to the TV. From a few feet away, he heard an exasperated huff. Women did that a lot, too, as he recalled.

But he'd no sooner had this thought when she reached over, big as you please, and grabbed the remote from his hand, shutting off the TV.

"Hey—!"

"I'm sorry," she said, and he saw tears glittering in her eyes. "I don't mean to be rude, but you obviously do, and I don't care if you have lived alone all your life, this is an emergency and it took a lot for me to come here ask this of you. Now, if you don't want me to stay with you, well, that's your choice, it's your house after all, but the least you could do is put me out of my misery now instead of making me wait another—" she glanced up at the clock "—twelve minutes."

The silence when she was finally through—though a blessed relief—rang in his ears just the same. Ned tried to lean forward, but his hip let him hear about it, boy, good and loud, so he stayed put. They'd come and make him move soon enough. "What I don't get is, why you'd *want* to live with me. I'm not a nice man, Maddie. Don't have much use for people. Even less for little kids. We don't even know each other, for pity's sake—''

''I know all that,'' she said. ''Well, not the part about you not having any use for people, but…'' She sucked in a breath, let it out in a rush. ''But I'm desperate. I don't have any other place to go—''

''You're already staying with Doc, though, right?''

''Because I had the baby in his house, he feels responsible. But I can't stay there forever. Please, Uncle Ned…''

''No.''

He saw what little color she had drain right out of her face. ''But—''

''I said no, gal. My place is mine. Got it arranged just the way I like it. Don't need no woman coming in, rearrangin' it to suit her, don't need kids gettin' into my things—''

''I wouldn't let them do that.''

He turned back to the TV, before the hurt in those big gray eyes got to him. ''This discussion is over. Now if you don't mind, would you please turn the TV back on before you leave?''

She stood, tossing the remote onto the bed where she knew he couldn't reach it. ''Get it yourself, you horrible old man.''

Then she stormed from the room, that little chin of hers stuck out clear to Texas. Only, once she was gone, Ned didn't feel all that satisfied about the way things had turned out.

After Ryan finished checking up on a couple of patients, he found Maddie sitting stiffly in the Rehab waiting room, her arms crossed so tightly over her midsection he wondered how she was breathing. Judging from the expression on her face, things had gone about the way he'd feared they would.

Which meant they were back at square one.

She glanced at him, said, ''Can we go now?'' and sprang up, taking off down the hall. Ryan had been about to check on Ned, but figured there wasn't much use, anyway, seeing as the old cuss was doing as well as could be expected. So he followed in the wake of Maddie's brittle silence, weighing his options.

Wasn't until they got all the way back to the truck that she finally let loose.

"I've never in my life met anybody as cold and mean as that old man! He wouldn't even discuss it! Just said 'no' without even thinking it over! Some dumb TV show was more important than what happened to his own kin!"

She whapped her palm but good on the truck's front bumper, hard enough that Ryan feared for the fragile bones in her small hand. Not to mention the bumper. Ryan grabbed her wrist before she could get in a second blow, jerking her away from the truck with enough force to spin her around so they were face to face. Her eyes got all big, for a split-second, before she launched herself against his chest, sobbing her heart out.

Well, what else could he do but wrap his arms around her and tuck her head underneath his chin, letting her know she was safe? For the moment, at least. Of course, she only sobbed harder, all that pride and stubbornness just melting away, right in his arms.

Unfortunately he melted right back. Oh, he tried not to, but it was a lost cause and he knew it. His heart just ached all to hell for this scrappy little thing who had so much on her narrow shoulders right now. And even though he'd known all along what Ned's reaction was likely to be, it still chapped his hide that the old man could be so deliberately cruel that he couldn't even try to help his niece—even if only by marriage—find a solution to her dilemma.

So he let her cling to him, if that's what she needed right now. And if his hand found its way to that soft, sweet-smelling hair, cradling her head against him where she could likely hear his heart thumping inside his chest, she'd understand he was just comforting her, right?

It had been a long time since he'd held a woman in his arms.

A long time without a little softness in his life.

After a minute or two, the storm passed, so he could finally peel her off of him without feeling bad about it, get some space between them before he started thinking about things he didn't need to be thinking about.

But once he had her at arm's length, it wasn't so bad. In fact, while he stood there, rubbing her frail shoulders while she blew her nose on a tissue and apologized for getting his jacket wet and hiccuped once or twice, he got his bearings again. She was his patient, after all. If his shoulder had been the only one to cry on in the immediate vicinity, that couldn't be helped.

Nothing more to it than that.

Then she let out this shaky, rattly sigh, and it hit him how much he'd grown to care about Maddie Kincaid, just in a few days. About her, and her kids. About what happened to them. Maybe he couldn't take them on as a permanent responsibility—nor would she want him to, he didn't imagine—but he'd do what he could for this gal and her babies, just because…well, because apparently that's the lot that had fallen to him.

He guessed he'd figure out the "whys" at some point down the road.

"Feel better?" he asked, unable to stop himself from brushing a piece of hair out of her eyes.

She nodded, sighed…and set her mouth in that way that Ryan had already learned meant trouble. Her eyes might have been all red and puffy, but he could practically hear all those cogs and gears whirring away in her head.

"You ready to go back?"

A breeze toyed with her hair. Like a little kid, she swiped at first one cheek, then the other, with the back of her hand. "Guess so. Don't want to keep you from whatever you have to do."

Ryan angled his head at her, one hand planted on the truck's roof. "What you don't seem to realize is that helping you figure all this out *is* part of what I have to do. So you're not keeping me from anything, okay?"

A second passed before she nodded. "Okay."

Then a thought struck him. "I've got some housecalls to

make. Wanna come along? Might take your mind off things for a bit.''

She appeared to think on this a minute, then said, "Long as we make it back within two hours, so I can feed Amy Rose."

"We probably could, but didn't you leave a bottle with Ivy?"

"Well, that would take care of Amy Rose's problem," she said with a smirk, "but it sure wouldn't do anything for me."

Naturally Ryan's gaze shot right to Maddie's chest.

Oh, Lord.

He opened the truck door on Maddie's side, gestured for her to get in. "We'll be back in plenty of time," he muttered.

They'd made two stops before this one, the first time to check up on a four-year-old named Howie who'd been through a bad bout of ear infections, the second to decide whether or not Todd Andrews, the boy whose mother had called Dr. Logan away that first night, was really ready to go back to school yet. Both kids had been given clean bills of health, much to their mothers' relief, and now Maddie and the doctor were pulling up next to a single-wide trailer nestled in a grove of evergreens and maples about a quarter mile off the main road.

"Who lives out here?" Maddie asked when Dr. Logan cut the engine. In the resulting silence, you could hear the wind teasing the reddening leaves.

"Mildred Rafferty. Seventy-four. Widowed nearly twenty-five years ago." The doctor linked his hands on top of the steering wheel, leaning forward a little to contemplate the dingy white trailer, the dusty blue trim a mite dustier than it probably should be. There'd been a fire going in one of the other houses; his jacket smelled like wood smoke.

She could still feel the sensation of the worn denim against her cheek when he'd wrapped his arms around her, back in the parking lot, the muted thumping of his heartbeat in her ear. The way he held her, not all awkward the way most men do when they find a hysterical woman in their arms and don't know what to do with them, but like he really cared.

Foolishness, she told herself. Plain, good-for-nothin' foolishness.

"Her arthritis acts up now and again," the doctor was saying, "making it hard for her to do much of anything. She's got one daughter, who's stuck in Phoenix because of her husband's job, and it drives poor Justine nuts that her mother won't either go into a retirement home, or at least move back into town where people could look after her more."

"Why won't she move?"

The doctor smiled just enough to crinkle the corners of his eyes. "Thirty years ago, Mildred and her husband, J.T., bought this land, intending to build on it. The mobile home was only supposed to have been temporary. Except J.T. had a heart attack and died while he was framing the house. He wasn't even fifty yet." He nodded straight ahead. "You can see what's left of the half-finished house through the trees. Would've been a nice one, too," he said, almost wistfully. "Mildred has refused to sell, or even leave, insisting this is the only way she has of still feeling close to her husband. In fact, I've come out here on more than one occasion to find her out by the unfinished house, talking to J.T. as if he was standing right there in front her."

Maddie thought on this a second, then said, "Maybe he was."

She felt the doctor's gaze on the side of her face for a long moment. Then he said, "Well, I suppose we best be getting a move on."

Her white hair cut almost as short as a man's, her tiny body nearly lost in layers of sweatshirts and sweaters over droopy, brown polyester pants, Mildred Rafferty answered her door with a big smile for the doctor, and almost as big a one for Maddie, who Dr. Logan introduced to her. Behind her, either dozing or milling about, were at least four cats. Which probably accounted for the pungent, room-freshener-trying-to-mask-the-cat-pan aroma. Wasn't too bad, though. Lord knows, Maddie had smelled worse in her life.

"C'n I get you somethin' to drink? A snack, maybe? I just opened a new bag of Pecan Sandies yesterday, so they're still fresh."

"Well, now that you mention it," the doctor said with a slow, almost lazy smile, "that sounds pretty good. Maddie?" He looked over at her, his wink so fast she barely caught it. "How about you?"

She gave him a puzzled look for a second or two, until his slightly raised eyebrows made her snap to.

"Oh…okay, that'd be real nice," she said to the old woman, unable to keep from smiling herself. "It's been a long time since I had a Pecan Sandie. Do you need any help?" she called after Mildred, who was already making slow, steady tracks back to the kitchen.

"Oh, no, you two just sit right down, make yourselves comfortable."

Maddie perched on the edge of an arm chair that'd seen better days, while the doctor sat on a woebegone couch the color of baby poop, his legs spread, his cowboy hat propped on one knee, neither of which prevented one of the cats from jumping up and trying to find a place to roost. Chuckling, he teased the cat with his hat until it finally got bored and left, then called back into the kitchen, "I see you're on the prowl today, Miss Mildred. You must be feeling pretty good."

"I am at that," the old woman said, shuffling back into the living area with a plate of cookies, which she set on the coffee table in front of them. "Praise the Lord, I truly am. Take a look at these, would you?"

She lifted her hands to the doctor for his inspection. The knuckles were swollen almost to the point of being deformed, but she slowly flexed them for him, beaming like a child at her accomplishment. "You know I'm not one for takin' lots of medicine just because I'm old, but I have to say, that new stuff you gave me sure seems to be doin' the trick. I haven't had a really bad spell in some time, not even when it rained a couple weeks ago."

Gently—so gently—the doctor took the small, knobby

hands in his big ones, then nodded in approval. "Swelling even seems to be down some."

"That's what I thought, too, but I thought maybe it was just wishful thinkin'."

"No, ma'am, from the looks of things, I'd definitely say we finally hit on the right thing." Ryan took a cookie, bit into it. "Any side effects?"

"Nary a one." She reached up and rapped on her own head. "Knock on wood."

He laughed, then got her to talking about, oh, ordinary stuff, like the weather and her cats and what she heard from Justine, her daughter. As she had on the other two calls, Maddie sat quietly and observed him in action. No wonder his patients adored him. Even though they hadn't spent more than ten or fifteen minutes at each house, Dr. Ryan—which Maddie noticed was what most folks called him—never made anybody feel rushed, or like there was anything more pressing on his agenda at that moment than tending to them. And the man knew how to *listen,* a quality that few men—in her admittedly limited experience—took the time or trouble to cultivate.

"What do you hear from J.T. lately?"

Thinking she hadn't heard right, Maddie looked over at Ryan, who was calmly munching another cookie.

Mildred had sat down beside him some time ago; now she laid a hand on his arm, her expression serious and just this side of worried. "Funny you should ask me that, since I was just thinking, right before you got here, that he hasn't come to me since the last time you were out here. I'm a little concerned, to tell you the truth. In more'n twenty-five years, he's never stayed away this long." Eyes the color of wilted celery lifted to Maddie. "What do you think it means, honey?"

"I—I'm afraid I don't know," she said, glancing over at the doctor, who wasn't giving her a clue. "You...talk to your husband a lot?"

The slightest glimmer of amusement appeared in Mildred's eyes. "Well, I don't know as 'talk' is quite the right word, since he's dead and all. But, well, just because I can't see him anymore, or touch him, doesn't mean I can't *feel* him."

She pressed a hand to the center of her chest. "In here. It's why I never left this place, even though I know most folks think I'm just tetched in the head. This is where J.T. is. So this is where I belong."

Maddie could feel Dr. Ryan watching her, waiting for her reaction.

"I don't think you're touched in the head at all, Miz Rafferty," she said softly, reaching over to grasp the old lady's frail hand. "You and your husband must have loved each other very much."

Moisture sheened Mildred's eyes, even though she was smiling. "Yes, honey, we sure did." Then her smile broadened. "But enough of that. Dr. Ryan told me, last time he was out, that you have three beautiful children, including a brand new baby girl."

Maddie sat back in her chair. Just the mention of Amy Rose had signaled her letdown reflex. As with the other two children, her puny little breasts produced more milk than they could hold. "Yes, ma'am, I sure do."

"Oh, I just love children. Don't get much of a chance to see any these days, but I remember taking care of my daughter when she was little as one of the happiest times of my life. Oh! Are you okay, honey?"

Maddie nodded, waiting for the stinging sensation to pass. "It's just…getting close to time to feed my daughter."

"Oh, for heaven's sake! Then you need to get going!" The old woman practically bounded off the sofa, as if there was something she could personally do to relieve Maddie's discomfort. "I remember only too well how uncomfortable I got, when I couldn't get to Justy fast enough."

Cats weaving around their feet, they all headed toward the door. But just as Maddie set foot outside, she turned to Mildred and asked, "Would you…would it be okay if I brought the kids out sometime for a short visit?"

The look on the old woman's face nearly brought tears to Maddie's eyes. "Oh…" she breathed. "Could you?"

"I'd love to. And I'm sure they'd love it out here, too. How about…next Tuesday, after lunch?"

"Oh, yes, honey, that'd be fine!"

It was some time after they were back in the truck before the doctor spoke, leading Maddie to worry that maybe she'd done something wrong. But then he finally said, his quiet, steady voice laced with something that sounded to Maddie almost like wonder, "What on earth made you decide to do that?"

She looked at him, something inside her clutching at the expression in his clear blue eyes. "Probably much the same reason you stop in to see her. Because you can't stand the thought of that sweet, lonely old woman out here all by herself with nobody to talk to. Well, except her husband," she added with a smile, which the doctor returned. As he started up the truck, she said, "I can't stand the thought of anybody being lonely. Never could. I know too much how it feels." She glanced over at him, but he was too busy reversing the truck to notice. "Who brings her her groceries and things?"

He reached up, adjusted his hat. "I do."

They jostled along the rutted dirt road for a minute or so before she said, "You like that will all your patients?"

"If you mean do I bring them all their groceries, no."

She laughed. "I don't mean that. I mean, the way you…I don't know how to put it exactly. The way you make each one feel like nobody's more important than they are, just at that moment." She looked over at him. "You really, really love what you do, don't you?"

They'd reached the main road which would take them back to town. Dr. Ryan stopped the truck, hesitating for a bit before finally meeting her gaze. Maybe it was just the light, but Maddie could have sworn his cheeks were pinker than usual. "Yeah. I really do." He flexed his hands on the wheel, like he was trying to make up his mind about something, then said, "Only one more stop. Think you can hold out?"

"Thought you said Mildred's was the last stop?"

"This one just came to mind," he said quietly, looking out the windshield. "Wouldn't take but another half hour at the most." Then he turned back to her. "There's something I think you should see."

Chapter 6

"Oh, dear," was all she said when they pulled up in front of Ned's shack.

Ryan's insides twisted at her obvious dismay. And no wonder. Besides the mangled, wheelless sedan listing south that as far as Ryan knew hadn't run since the early eighties, the yard boasted half a chicken coop, piles of...junk from any number of unfinished projects the old man had abandoned over the years, and an outhouse at the back that looked as if it'd fall over if the occupant sneezed too hard. Not that you could see any of it too well through the waist-high weeds.

"I figured you weren't going to let this go until you saw for yourself," he said, and Maddie hauled in a shuddering breath.

"It looks like one of the little pig's houses. *After* the wolf huffed and puffed. And I don't suppose the inside's any improvement?"

"'Fraid not."

Then Maddie's mouth screwed up to one side. "I really couldn't've brought my babies here to live, could I?" she said, only to swat away whatever reply he might have made, her whole body going limp with defeat. "Take me back. I won't bother you—or Uncle Ned—about this again."

"I'm sorry, Maddie—"

"No, it's okay." She turned to him, her smile sad. "I'm glad you showed me. But honestly…" Frowning, she looked back. "How on earth a human being could *want* to live like this is beyond me."

Ryan swung the truck around and headed back toward Haven, his thoughts bumping around inside his head. Where the impulse had come from to take her to see Ned's for herself, he had no idea. But after she'd so neatly…defined him, in a way that nobody—not his parents, not his brothers, not even Suzanne—had ever been able to do, he felt he owed her that much, at least.

Nobody had ever seen clear to his soul the way this woman apparently did.

And it scared the bejesus out of him.

A good ten minutes later, Maddie was frowning at the passing scenery, wincing every time they hit a bump, wondering what on earth she was going to do now, since Plan A had fallen apart. Which meant she needed to come up with Plan B real fast. Preferably before they got back home.

No, not *home,* she corrected herself. *Back.* Dr. Logan's house wasn't her home, and it scared her just how easily the word had come to roost in her thoughts.

"You're too quiet," he said, scattering her thoughts to kingdom come.

"Just thinking, is all. How'd you find out Ned had broken his hip, anyway?"

"Luckily, he was in town when it happened. Fell off the curb, right in front of the café. If he'd been out at his place, no telling when somebody might have found him."

Maddie shuddered. "Doesn't anybody go out and check on him?"

"Folks used to, from time to time. Until Ned took to firing his shotgun to warn people off."

She shook her head. "I still don't understand why anybody would want to be alone like that. I mean, *that* alone."

After a moment, Dr. Logan said, "Some people just do, Maddie. It's not worth worrying over."

Something in his voice made her glance over, but his attention was focused on the road, his thoughts all locked up inside him.

With a sigh, Maddie returned to watching trees zipping past and trying not to think about how full her breasts were getting. Maybe because her mama had abandoned her, she didn't know, but she'd always liked having people around her. Not that she didn't like a little alone time, now and again, but to go for days or months, or even years, without company would drive her nuts.

And by company, she thought, she didn't mean people you *had* to be around because taking care of them was your job.

But thinking about all of this wasn't addressing the problem at hand, which was what was going to happen now. Since it had been more than a week since she had the baby and they were both fine, she didn't need to be under the doctor's care anymore. Only, once she got that far in her thinking, she ran into a dead end.

And judging from the doctor's pensive expression, so had he. Except then he looked right at her, like he could read her mind, and said, "You know you and the children can stay in my house as long as you need to."

"Thank you," she said. "But I don't want your charity."

His mouth went all tight, like he was holding back from saying what he was thinking, which was just fine with her. Then his cell phone rang.

"Okay, Marybeth," she heard him say as they pulled into his driveway. "I'm on my way, but I'm sending the ambulance, too. See if you can get an aspirin in him, it might help until we can get there."

"Is everything all right?"

He was out of the truck and around to her side, opening her door for her before she had a chance to open it herself. "It's Sherman Mosely," he said distractedly as she got out, "the town's lawyer. His secretary thinks he's having a heart attack—"

"Then why're you still here?"

Five seconds later, he wasn't.

An hour later, her breasts no longer felt like they were about to pop. Unfortunately she couldn't say the same for her brain. Especially as now she was worrying about somebody she didn't even know. Or maybe it was more that she was worrying about the man that everybody was looking to to make sure this Mr. Mosely would be okay.

Sure seemed like a lot of people leaned on Dr. Ryan. Which would be okay if he had somebody to help bear the load from time to time. Far as she could tell, though, he didn't, not really. Not even his brothers. What a shame, to have family right here in town and not be close to them.

Not that this was any of her business.

Now wearing a ratty old pair of leggings and a loose shirt that buttoned up the front, she wandered around the too-quiet house for a little bit, patting her daughter on her back as she walked. She had a good half hour to kill before she had to pick up the other two kids: it occurred to her she hadn't seen the doctor's office yet, and since she didn't think it was any big deal if she peeked, she did.

The waiting room, painted ivory with dark wood trim, smelled comfortably of steam heat and old wood. Assorted chairs and benches lined the walls, as well as a shelf full of toys and books, the usual assortment of old magazines. Off of that was an exam room with lots of glass-doored cabinets and counters and drawers and such, that looked pretty spiffy and up-to-date, and past that, what she took to be a records room with wall-to-wall filing cabinets, some of the drawers half open. Finally she reached the doctor's office, a fair-size room all in browns and tans. In front of a bay window looking out over the backyard sat the biggest wooden desk she'd ever seen. An old-fashioned blotter, bare except for a prescription pad and a Bic pen, nestled in the middle of piles of charts, folders and assorted official-looking papers.

Still rubbing the baby's back, Maddie made her way over to the desk. She saw her own chart in the wreckage, saw dates written on others going back a good two months. There were what looked like insurance claim forms, too, a whole stack of them, sitting drunkenly in a bin on one corner.

She blew out a stream of air that tickled her bangs: judging from the state of this office, everything she'd heard about Oklahoma tornadoes was true.

Clearly Dr. Logan had fallen way behind in his paperwork. Frowning, Maddie shifted the baby to hold her in one arm, gently sifting through the nearest pile. Not that she meant to pry, but...

Lord, this man needed a keeper.

Not that this was any of her business.

The grandfather clock out in the front hall chimed, alerting her that she needed to get a move-on if she was going to get the children on time. It was faster to take the car, but both the church and the school were within walking distance, which sounded like a good idea right now. She needed to do something to work off all these jittery feelings. Besides, she hadn't really had a chance to explore the town. And maybe something would pop up in her face while she was out. A job. Someplace to stay. A million dollars.

Well, she thought, bundling Amy Rose into the stroller Didi Meyerhauser's daughter Faith had brought over, you never knew, did you?

''Mama! Please?'' Noah looked up at her, his eyes like a pair of chocolate drops. ''Can't we eat in there?''

If Maddie had realized their walk through town would take them by way of the town's only eating establishment (that she could tell, anyway), she would probably have chosen a different route.

''I'm sorry, baby, but I didn't bring my wallet with me.'' Not that it would have made any difference, even if Hank Logan had refused payment for her motel room, or so Dr. Logan had said. Although she had to admit, the smells coming out of the Haven Café were real tempting. She couldn't remember the last time she'd had a hamburger and french fries. Or a chocolate shake.

Maddie looked down into her son's eyes and just managed not to let out a weary sigh. She really shouldn't've thought about that chocolate shake. "There's tons of food at ho…at the house, sugar. We don't need to be buyin' anymore."

"Mama, I gots money."

Now Maddie turned her attention to Katie Grace, who was standing there holding a dollar bill in her hand. "Where on earth did you get that?"

"Ivy gived it to me yesterday. She gived one to Noah, too."

Maddie looked at Noah. "She did?"

Noah was busy searching the pockets of his coat, finally coming up with the dollar bill on the fifth or sixth try. He gave Maddie a big grin. "I forgot. So can we go eat lunch in there, Mama?"

Well, she didn't know whether to be ticked at Ivy or not, although she supposed the midwife was just acting like a granny, was all. But she did know that two dollars wasn't going to get them very far, even though the prices listed on the menu posted in one corner of the window were pretty reasonable. And the chalkboard sign said they were serving homemade split pea soup today. Lord, Maddie hadn't had split pea soup in a dog's age…

"Mama?"

She sighed. "Two dollars, huh? Well, I suppose we could swing some french fries and one Coke, but you'll have to share, okay? Then I'll give you your real lunch after."

The kids let out whoops of glee, then practically killed themselves seeing which one could get inside first. Noah won, then remembered he needed to hold the door open so Maddie could manuever the stroller inside.

Warmth and noise and delicious cooking smells swirled around her when she entered, the conversation level dipping slightly as many of the patrons—mostly male, she noticed—stopped chewing and talking long enough to give her and the kids a curious look. But that only lasted a second or two.

Behind the counter, a round, brown-faced woman in a gussied-up black sweatshirt and dangly earrings, her short gray hair cut close to her head, was holding forth about something with a young man who was pretty much all legs and cowboy hat. Every once in a while, she'd let loose with a belly laugh that made Maddie smile in return. There were two other waitresses in pink uniforms and sneakers, one young and blond, one middle-aged and suspiciously brunette, zipping from table to table, yakking away as well.

The woman behind the counter glanced over, caught Maddie's eye, said something to the young man and made tracks in Maddie's direction, wearing the brightest smile Maddie had ever seen.

She grasped Maddie's hand in both of hers, said her name was Ruby Kennedy, that she and her husband Jordy ran the diner, then added, "You must be the gal stayin' up at Doc Ryan's place."

"Yes, ma'am," Maddie said, but the woman had already turned that bright, loving smile on the children, asking them their names and cupping each of their heads in turn when they told her. "And who's this little angel?" she asked Maddie, squatting even lower to softly touch the baby's hand.

"Amy Rose."

Ruby grinned up at Maddie. "You sure picked some pretty names for your babies, Mama," she said, then turned back to the children. "Y'all hungry?"

"Oh!" Maddie touched the woman's arm, lowering her voice so nobody else would hear. "I'm sorry, but I've only got two dollars, uh, with me, I told them they could share some fries and a Coke—"

"Never you mind about that," the woman said, straightening up. "You just go on ahead and sit over there—" she nodded toward an empty booth by the window "—and we'll get these babies fixed up. You, too, Mama," she added, giving Maddie the once-over.

"But I can't—"

"Got us a tradition here, honey—all newcomers to town get their first meal free. Now get on over there before these poor little things fall over from hunger. You all like hamburgers?'' she asked the children.

And that, apparently, was the end to the discussion.

By the time they'd all finished, it was so late they pretty much had the place to themselves, since the waitresses were gone until five when the dinner rush would start up. Ruby's husband Jordan, who did most of the cooking, came out to say ''hey,'' and the kids' eyes just about bugged out of their skulls at the sight of the huge, bald-headed man with the single gold loop in his ear. But his smile was just as big and bright as his wife's, and his low, rumbly voice soon put them both at ease. When he left, Ruby joined them in the booth, clearly settling in for a good old-fashioned gossip session.

''Gotta get my baby fix,'' she said, swooping the now awake Amy Rose out of the stroller and settling her into the crook of her ample arm. Apparently Ruby knew all about Maddie's predicament, although Maddie had felt obliged to straighten out one or two minor alterations to her story that had transpired somewhere along the grapevine.

''So you planning on sticking around?''

''I don't see as I have much of a choice…what is it, Noah?'' she said when he tugged on her sleeve.

''C'n I go look at the candy and stuff?'' he asked, pointing at the goodies lined up by the cash register.

''I suppose, long as you take your sister with you.''

Then Ivy Gardner breezed in, skirts and poncho flapping. She waved at Ruby, grinned and yelled out ''Hey!'' to Maddie, then helped herself to a cup of coffee from the pot still steeping behind the counter.

''Clouding up again,'' she said, clomping over to the table. She'd looped her long braids up around her ears today, which made her cheeks look even rounder than ever. As Maddie was skootching over in the booth to make room for Ivy, another woman, this one sporting a hairdo that defied both gravity and time, hustled into the diner, her arms wrapped around herself over what was clearly a beauty shop smock in a shade of purple picked expressly, Maddie decided, to set off the orange hair. Even from here, Maddie could see the turquoise eye shadow. Clearly this was somebody unafraid of strong color.

She, too, waltzed on behind the counter and poured herself a cup of coffee, grabbed a creamer from a tub under the coffeemaker, and made her way over to the table. Noticing that it was already full up, however, she grabbed an empty chair and swung it around so she could sit at the end of the table.

"Lord, but it's nippy out there," she said, ripping off the top to the creamer with long, shocking pink fingernails that Maddie bet the farm weren't hers. "Nearly froze my butt off, just in that short walk." Then she smiled at Maddie and extended one many-ringed hand. Maddie half expected the woman's face to crack and fall off in pieces into her coffee. "I'm Luralene Hastings, I run the Hair We Are, two doors down. And don't take this the wrong way, sugar, but who the hell did that to your hair?"

Maddie blushed a little, reaching up to touch her hair as Ruby said, "Honestly, Luralene—that last dye job must've seeped into your brain!"

"For your information, Ruby Kennedy, I do not *dye* my hair. This is just a rinse, you know, to give it some highlights. And I'm sorry, honey," the redhead said to Maddie. "I honestly didn't mean to be rude—"

"No, it's okay," Maddie said, badly wanting to look away before her retinas melted. "It was a beauty school cut. And that was some months back. I keep meaning to get it trimmed but…"

The other two women immediately jumped in with how Maddie's hair looked just fine and all that, but Luralene must've felt her honor was at stake or something, because she ended up telling Maddie she could come in to her shop anytime and she'd have her new girl, Stacey, give her a trim for free because most of their clients liked a more formal style, you know, so Stacey didn't get much chance to practice cutting hair worn natural like Maddie's.

"Oh. Okay," she said, wondering why her children weren't pestering her to go home so she could gracefully extricate herself from all this.

But then the women got to talking about the Logan boys, as they called them, and Maddie's ears perked up. Since Amy Rose was making noises about eating again, anyway, she just unbuttoned her shirt and let her have at it, which in turn provoked no end of ooohs and ahhs from the women, while Noah and Katie Grace played tag around the tables.

Ivy got up to get another cup of coffee, returning moments later. "Never saw two people more in love than those boys' mama and daddy," she said, dumping three packs of sugar into her coffee. After a slurping sip, she added, "But it took close to ten years before she got pregnant with Hank...."

Well, that led to several minutes' worth of stories about the three brothers as boys, until Luralene leaned forward, talking out of the corner of her mouth. "But what nobody can figure out is why none of 'em are married."

"No problem figurin' out why Hank's not." Ruby's face got all pinched with concern. "That boy's still grievin', anybody can see that," she said, then filled Maddie in about Hank's loss.

"And what really tore Hank up," Ivy put in, "was that, even with him being a cop, he couldn't do anything to help find the killer. So I guess he's been using that motel of his like some kind of therapy. But it's still not healthy, the way he keeps to himself."

"Then there's Cal," Luralene said, "who just can't seem to make up his mind. Of course," she said with a pointed look at Ivy, "I suppose there's a reason for that."

Ivy huffed out a sigh. "Oh, Luralene...the boy hasn't even laid eyes on Dawn but a couple times since she went away to college. A high school crush, is all that was. Over and done with. Anyway, he's young yet. He'll settle down when he's ready."

After several minutes' worth of surmising about Cal and Ivy's daughter Dawn, the discussion finally snaked around to the only subject that interested Maddie.

"As for the good doctor," Ivy started out, but Luralene interrupted her with, "Which reminds me, I still haven't gotten a bill from him from when I had, you know—" she lowered her voice again "—my little problem," which of course prompted appropriate inquiries as to her health.

After Luralene assured them she was fine, Ruby said, "Come to think of it, we haven't gotten a bill yet for Jordy's sprained wrist. I've been so busy, I plumb forgot about it. You suppose they got lost in the mail?"

"Um…"

All three heads turned to Maddie.

"Well, I don't know for sure, but when I happened to see into his office this morning, I noticed his desk piled to kingdom come with papers and things. So maybe he never got around to sending his bills?"

"That could be," Ivy said, toying with one of her braids. "He had somebody handling that for him, but she got married and moved away, and he hadn't done a blessed thing about replacing her—"

"Talk about keeping to himself," Luralene put in, her tastefully arched brows drawn together. "At least Hank has an excuse. With Ryan, though, he's just been alone for so long, it's gotten to be a habit."

That got a chorus of "uh-huhs" and "that's rights", which Maddie—who had reached the limit of her patience, especially because her butt was getting numb from sitting so long—interrupted by asking flat out what they thought the problem was.

Ivy blew out a stream of air. "Not that I'm one for telling tales out of school, but he's got this notion in his head that no woman would ever be able to deal with his crazy schedule, what with him being a country doctor and all."

"Well," Ruby said, her mouth all twisted up, "I don't suppose it's that crazy a notion. After all, Doc Patterson was divorced twice."

"Oh, please, Ruby," Ivy said. "You know I thought the world of that man, but he didn't have a lick of sense when it came to picking women. In any case, Ryan didn't always feel that way. True, he didn't have the girls hanging off him in high school like his brothers did, but he dated Suzanne Potts for years—"

"Potts," Maddie said, her brow crinkled. "As in, don't-eat-that-tuna-casserole Potts?"

All three ladies burst out laughing. "Suzanne is Arliss's daughter," Ivy said. "Sweet girl, actually. But clueless, if you ask me. It's not like she didn't know what she was getting into long before she and Ryan got engaged, seeing as Doc Patterson had been the family doctor for years. And I guess things were okay as long as Ryan was just sharing the practice. Unfortunately, maybe three months or so before the wedding, Doc Patterson suddenly passed on, and the whole she-bang fell into Ryan's lap. Didn't seem to bother him any—he'd always expected to take over when Doc retired, anyway—but Suzanne was another story. Didn't help it was that spring we had that late outbreak of flu, you remember?" she said to Luralene and Ruby, who both nodded. "Ryan was kept hopping for two weeks. And to hear Suzanne's mama tell it, I guess Suzanne felt she'd always come second in Ryan's life." Ivy shrugged. "So she called off the wedding."

Maddie waited out the spurt of anger, then asked, "Is she still around?"

"Oh, no. She moved to Oklahoma City shortly after they broke up, got married to somebody else. I don't think she's been back to visit her folks but two or three times since she left."

"And the doctor doesn't date at all?"

"He did some, after Suzanne left. But not seriously. And then he just…gave up."

From the back, the phone rang, followed immediately by Jordy's bellow out to Ruby that it was for her. Then Luralene looked at her watch and let out a squawk, jumping up from the table. "I plumb forgot I had a three o'clock! Eunice'll never let me hear the end of it if I'm late! Nice meeting you, Maddie!" she said, yelling over her shoulder on her way out for Maddie to drop in anytime for that trim.

Thinking she really needed to get going as well, Maddie glanced over at the children, who were lying across the stools on their stomachs and spinning themselves silly, only to jump slightly when Ivy, who'd switched to the other side of the booth, touched her wrist.

"There's something else," the older woman said when Maddie looked over. "I didn't want to say anything in front of the others, because Ryan doesn't know I know…" She backed up a little, squinting at Maddie. "You promise not to breathe a word of this to anybody?"

Well, for pity's sake—who would she tell? "I promise."

Apparently satisfied, Ivy leaned closer. "See, I know there's a couple other doctors who're wanting to set up a centralized clinic for the area. You know, so they could spell each other sometimes, maybe split the salary of two nurses between them? They've approached Ryan I don't know how many times in the past year about going in with them, but he's not having any of it."

Maddie frowned. "Why?"

Ivy shrugged. "Damned if I know."

"But if anybody needs a partner, it's him!"

Ivy's brows lifted. Maddie flushed.

"In his practice, I mean," she said, even though, yes, she knew what Ivy was thinking, that Ryan needed a partner on a much more personal level as well.

But what did this have to do with her?

Lucky for her, the kids started up with the afternoon crankies right about then, so she had her excuse to leave before the conversation got any more complicated. Although, by the time she got home and got the youngest two down for their naps, her thoughts, which had been swirling around inside her head like the fake snow inside a glass globe, suddenly settled into place.

Whatever leftover feelings Dr. Logan had for his fiancée, or how he chose to handle his private life, were none of her business. She was more than done with the foolishness of trying to change a man—even if it weren't way too soon after Jimmy to even be entertaining the *idea* of becoming interested in somebody else. But the fact of the matter was, Dr. Logan needed someone to help him straighten out his paperwork— and maybe make sure he got a decent meal every now and again—and she needed to not only work off her medical bills, but to keep a roof over her babies' heads until such time as she could make her own way....

Well, the solution was obvious, wasn't it?

It was nearly seven o'clock by the time Ryan finally got back to the house. No sooner had he left Sherman at the hospital—as Ryan had hoped, the middle-aged, potbellied lawyer had had more of a fright than an attack, although now maybe he'd actually start doing something about losing that extra forty pounds he was hauling around—than he'd gotten a call from the high school to check out three football players who'd gotten a little overenthusiastic in their tackling. The boys were banged up some, but otherwise fine…and God willing, nobody would need Ryan until tomorrow morning. A full night's sleep would be a godsend. Not that he was holding his breath.

Speaking of holding his breath—the instant he walked through the door, his stomach sat up and begged. Fried chicken, if he wasn't mistaken. Some kind of baking, too. Then he heard the laughter. Maddie's, primarily, but the kids' were giggling their heads off about something as well.

Ryan shut his eyes, as if he could shut out the sound any more than he could the enticing scent, tempted to think *Not fair.* Still, he yanked off his muddy boots—years of his mother's fussing about tracking up the house had, in Ryan's case, taken hold, although the same couldn't be said for his brothers—and set them on the mat by the front door, then padded in his stockinged feet to the kitchen.

Somehow, at this moment, having his solitude invaded didn't seem so bad.

A pair of small heads, one blond, one dark, were bent over his kitchen table, intent on coloring what looked like those placemats with the maps of Oklahoma on them that Ruby gave out to her younger customers. The baby was in her swing, no-color eyes big as all get out, calmly taking it all in. And Maddie was flitting from place to place in the kitchen, doing…cooking things.

Katie looked up and saw him, breaking into an instant,

dimpled smile that came damn close to knocking him for a loop. "Look, Dokker Rine!" she said in a scratchy voice reminiscent of her mother's. The child held up her map, which was covered top to bottom with bright, enthusiastic scribbles. "I drawed!"

"You sure did, honey." Ryan took the map from her to get a better look, tucking down the corners of his mouth in mock seriousness as he studied it, then returned it to her with an approving nod, palming her silky head. "Wish I could draw like that."

Ryan glanced over at Noah, who was painstakingly coloring within the lines, his tongue stuck out in concentration. The boy's slender fingers clutched an orange crayon so tightly, Ryan half expected it to snap.

"Hey, grasshopper—whatcha got there?"

"Nothin'." The boy angled his body over the paper, his brow tightly knit. "You can't see."

Brows lifted in question, Ryan looked over at Maddie, who'd stopped her fluttering about to watch; she met his gaze for a second, if that, only to sigh and lift one shoulder in response. Close enough to Noah to touch him, she reached out, stroked his hair.

"Go on, now," she said, her voice barely audible over the sound of the chicken sputtering and sizzling on the stove behind her. "Show the doctor what a good job you're doing."

The boy's shoulders tensed; clamping down on the crayon even harder, he shook his head.

There were shadows in Maddie's eyes when she returned her gaze to Ryan's, shadows which didn't quite vanish when she smiled.

"Well. Good. You're back. I timed it just right, then," she said, swiping her hair out of her eyes with her wrist. "The kids already ate, but I figured you wouldn't mind something that didn't come out of a casserole dish for a change. So why don't you go on ahead and get washed up, dinner'll be in about ten minutes. And afterward, we can discuss my idea."

Uh-oh. "Idea?"

Her smile was just the slightest bit unsteady. "Uh-huh. And this one makes a lot more sense than the first one did."

He could only hope.

He'd eaten four pieces of chicken. No, make that five. And mashed potatoes with gravy and fresh steamed broccoli—which actually wasn't all that bad, the way Maddie cooked it—and biscuits. Oh, sweet merciful heaven, the woman could make biscuits. Then she put the older two to bed, saying he'd need the time to let his dinner settle before the cherry pie.

Cherry pie?

They'd managed to redistribute a lot of the offerings from the week before, including most of the desserts, but there hadn't been a cherry pie among them. And Ryan was quite partial to cherry pie.

Quite partial.

Maddie came back to the kitchen, met his gaze, then let out a sigh. "I'm real sorry about the way Noah acted before dinner. When you tried to see what he was coloring? That last year or so, Jimmy…well, he seemed to forget a lot that Noah was just a little boy. He got on his case about a lot of things he shouldn't've. It's made Noah real sensitive, afraid of being criticized, you know? He didn't mean to be rude—"

"Maddie," Ryan said quietly, "it's okay. Little guy's been through a lot." He felt his mouth twitch. "And I don't offend easily, believe me."

She smiled a little at that, then stood there fiddling with her hands, as if she wasn't sure what came next.

Ryan sat back in his chair, his hands braced on the edge of the table. "Been a long time since I had a meal like that in my own kitchen. In fact, I don't think I've *ever* had a meal like that in my own kitchen."

Her smile loosened up some. "So it was okay?"

"A lot more than okay, Maddie. I may not be able to move for a week. Where'd you learn to cook like that?"

A cloud flitted across her eyes before she went to clear the plates. "From my last foster mother. Grace Idlewild…no, no—it's okay, I've got it," she said when Ryan tried to help her. "Anyway, Grace figured learning how to cook would give me something to do other than sit around and mope all day."

"Did it work?"

"Not at first. Until she told me if I wanted to eat, I'd have to cook. So I learned. It's all just plain home-cooking, though."

"Nothing wrong with that."

Her gaze flicked to his. "I was afraid you'd maybe compare me to your mother or something."

"My mother?" He shook his head. "Not a chance. Mama was a musician—she taught piano and violin—not a domestic. In fact, if it hadn't been for Ethel, our housekeeper, no telling what we would have eaten."

"Ethel? The same Ethel Cal was talking about?"

"The very same. She's in her seventies now, but tough as they come." Then something occurred to him. "Where'd you get the food? Don't tell me you spent your own money on this."

She'd been gathering up the pie and what-all at the counter; he saw her hesitate a moment before carting it all over to the table. "It was all on special," she said. "But even so, I considered it…an investment. Look," she went on before he could question her, "why don't you serve up the pie while I get Amy Rose settled in for her feed? I can eat one-handed, but I can't cut a pie that way."

So he did, just as glad for something to do while Maddie unbuttoned her blouse and put the baby to breast. But… "What do you mean, this was an 'investment'?"

He saw the flush sweep up her cheeks, had a devil of a time tamping down his protective response to it.

"Okay." She cleared her throat, then started in about her bill and needing a place to stay and how he probably wouldn't mind coming home to a real meal now and again, adding, "And then I saw all that paperwork piled up on your desk and I thought—"

"You were in my office?"

She'd been busy poking her fork over and over again into her pie crust while she'd been prattling on, but now she lifted her chin and she looked right at him, which he'd already learned was a clear sign that she was both nervous and determined not to let it stop her. "Since the door wasn't closed, I didn't figure I was exactly breaking any rules. And if I was, I'm sorry."

"You don't look sorry."

A tiny smile flickered around her mouth. "Well, I don't suppose I saw anything your other patients don't. Anyway, my point is…before I got married, I used to work summers for a construction company, doing filing and billing and what-all, so I thought maybe I could help you out, too."

He frowned. "Maddie, this is a doctor's office. Not a construction company."

Now she lowered her chin. The better to stare him down, he thought. "It's all just record keeping, isn't it? And I'm a real fast learner. You only have to show me once what to do, and I've got it. Or tell me where to call for the insurance stuff and let them help me figure it out, whatever. But from the looks of things, Dr. Logan, I'd say you need me. You need me real bad."

He'd never seen a pair of eyes that could manage to look so innocent and so…not at the same time.

Or that held the potential to make him feel foolish things.

Want to do foolish things.

Now it was Ryan's turn to poke at his piecrust. Well, he would have if he'd left anything on his plate to poke at. The problem was, on the surface, he couldn't find a single thing to object to about her plan. Swapping services was just a way of life around here, after all. Hell, he hadn't had to pay to have his truck fixed in years, especially not since Darryl Andrews, the town mechanic, and his wife Faith starting having all those kids.

But…

But.

He'd lowered his head, mulling things over; Maddie dipped hers to peer up at him.

"I know what you're thinkin'."

He jerked. "You do?"

"Uh-huh. You're worried about us being together in the house for too long. That I might start getting ideas."

"No, it's not that—"

She half-laughed, half-sighed. He told himself she was sitting too far away for him to feel her breath on his face.

That the last thing he wanted was to feel her breath on his face.

She adjusted the baby in her arms, then cocked her head at him, which made her hair do that shifting, sifting thing it did. "Well, shoot, if I were in your shoes, I'd sure be nervous about the idea of having a young widow with three kids living in my house. What if they get too attached? I'd be thinking. What if she starts looking at me and seeing her next husband, a father for her kids? Well, that's not gonna happen. Trust me, after what I've been through? Marriage is the last thing on my mind. So you can rest easy on that score. Far as I'm concerned, this is as a strictly temporary solution."

Their eyes locked for several seconds, Maddie's slender hand stroking her baby's head, over and over. It was everything Ryan could do to tell her to let out the breath she was holding.

He looked away, so he could think.

Then she said, probably because she felt she needed to get in one final argument, "All I want is a place to stay and a way to work off what I owe you, until I can save up to get a place of our own. I'm not looking for anything beyond that. Any more than you are."

Ryan's gaze jerked up from the pie, which he'd been eyeing, considering a second piece. "How do you know what I am or am not looking for?"

The baby had fallen asleep. Maddie pulled herself together, then got up, not looking at him. "A woman just senses these things, Dr. Logan," she said quietly, gently bouncing the baby as she stood there, the way mothers did. "So. Is it a deal or not?"

Some *deal*, Ryan thought, feeling a rueful grin tug at his

mouth. Wasn't as if he was going to throw the woman out, whether there was any way of her paying off her debt or not. That there was only made things worse. No, worse than worse. Impossible.

Yep. What he had here was one of those impossible situations, all right. The kind of impossible situation that made a man's stomach roil with apprehension. Never mind the line they'd both duly noted and sworn would never be crossed. Lines were all well and good, but that didn't mean a body wouldn't be tempted to cross that line. Especially a body as deprived as Ryan's. Having Maddie and her kids around...

Oh, hell—it wasn't his *privacy* he feared for.

Ryan leaned back in his chair, crossed his arms over that roiling stomach, and said, "You feel up to going over some of that mess in the office tonight, or would you rather wait until tomorrow?"

In short order, she gasped, squealed, and leaned over and gave him a peck on his cheek.

His skin fairly burned where her lips had touched.

Chapter 7

"**Y**ou here *again?* Dammit, woman—I do not understand why you can't just leave me the hell alone!"

Since, word for word, this was how Jimmy's uncle had greeted her every time she'd come to visit him during the past two weeks, Maddie didn't even blink.

And each time, her reply was the same.

"Because," she said over the drone of the TV as she walked right past where her uncle was sitting and over to his roommate, Charlie, "you are my only living relative and I care about you whether you want me to or not." She smiled brightly for the old black man, his cast leg extended in front of him. "How are you today, Charlie?"

"Well, I reckon I'm doin' okay, Miz Maddie." At the sight of the cookie tin in her hands, a pair of bushy gray brows lifted over yellowing eyes. "What's that you got there?"

"Since it's nearly Halloween, I thought you all might like some pumpkin cookies." She opened the tin; Charlie wasted no time in reaching for one with a gnarled brown hand. Behind her, her uncle continued muttering rude things she'd just as soon not hear, but whether they were aimed at her or Jenny Jones, she couldn't quite tell.

"Mmm-*mmm*," Charlie said, "these are sure good. Got cinnamon in 'em, right? And some nutmeg, too."

Maddie grinned. "They sure do."

Charlie took another bite of cookie, careful to keep crumbs from dripping all over his bright yellow sweatshirt, then waved the remnant in Ned's direction. "Mr. Hard Head over there don't know what he's missin'. You know, I'm not sure but that these are even better than those lemon squares you brought last week."

"Oh, for the love of—" Ned reached over, poked Maddie in the arm. "Just give me one of the damn things before the two of you drive me out of my skull."

She turned, deliberately keeping the tin out of Ned's reach. Santa Claus's evil twin, is what he looked like, with his thick, white hair pulled back into a ponytail, his bushy beard. "Don't do me any favors, Uncle Ned. No skin off my nose whether you eat 'em or not."

"I *said,* give me one!"

Maddie held out the tin, smothering a smile as Ned snatched a cookie like he was afraid she'd yank them away from him. Then, chewing, he squinted up at her. "What's different about you?"

"Got my hair cut. That new girl at Luralene's did it for me. You like it?"

Ned shrugged. "I s'pose it's okay. Lemme have another one of those pumpkin things." He waved his hand at her. "That sweater new, too?"

Maddie's brows lifted. It would appear they were having an actual conversation. Of course, a commercial was on, so she didn't suppose she should get too excited. Still, it was more than she'd had in the beginning. A lot more. In fact, it wasn't until the third visit that he'd relaxed enough to talk to her at all. Most folks would probably call her nuts, trying her hand at taming the old pook after the way he'd treated her. But that's just the way she was. And all in all, she wasn't doing too badly, considering. Now, moving slowly so she wouldn't spook him, she sat on the edge of the remaining free chair in the room.

"Got my first paycheck yesterday," she said, grinning.

That got a frown. "Thought you were working for Doc Ryan for swaps?"

Her skin heated a little. "I was. But he said he figured two weeks was long enough to pay off my debt. It's not much, though, since the kids and I are getting free room and board. But it's somethin'." *And I earned it,* she thought, satisfaction lapping through her.

Ned grunted. "And naturally, you went and spent it on new clothes."

"Honestly, Uncle Ned—" She put the tin down on Ned's bed, then reached over to straighten out his collar. Only took five visits to get to this point, but by now it was clear he was not averse to her fussing over him. "It's just one sweater, and I got it at Wal-Mart at that. I'm saving at least half of every paycheck, so I can eventually get the kids and me a place of our own."

She decided not to let on that she fully intended for Ned to come live with her, too, soon as that was possible. Anything to keep him from going back to that hovel of his, which she was sorely tempted to set fire to. Seemed a shame to spend all this time and energy recivilizing him, just to have it go down the tubes.

Yet another reason why she couldn't stay at the doctor's any longer than she absolutely had to.

Ned took a third cookie, then squinted at her. "You're one determined little gal, ain'tcha?"

"Yes, I am."

She managed to keep the conversation going for another twenty minutes or so, but when she stood to leave, putting the cookies where both men could reach them without killing themselves, Ned looked almost…stricken.

"You goin' already?"

Maddie tried to school her expression, but this was the first time he'd seemed to care whether she came or went. "I've got a lot to do before I have to pick up the kids. I'll be back in a day or two."

He folded his hands together in his lap, the corners of his mouth turned down. "Don't hurry back on my account."

"Don't worry, I won't," she said back when all she really wanted to do was lean over and kiss him on the cheek. But that would be a mistake.

Too bad her early warning signals hadn't been working two weeks ago, she thought a few minutes later as she got into her car.

Maddie had told herself a million times it had just been a quick peck on the cheek, for pity's sake. Nothing for anybody to get riled up about, even if her impetuousness had come as much of a shock to Dr. Logan as it had to her. But the look on his face...well. She would just have to control her natural inclination for touching people, that's all.

She supposed learning to control one's impulses was part of what growing up was all about.

She also supposed she shouldn't be surprised that all she'd done was to trade one set of worries for another.

Oh, on the surface, things were going pretty well. Noah seemed to be doing okay in kindergarten, Katie Grace was getting on fine with the other kids in the church day care—and Maddie enjoyed her one morning a week shift there, as well—and Amy Rose was not only growing like a little weed, but almost sleeping through the night already. Maddie was getting caught up on all the doctor's paperwork and had just filed the last old insurance claim yesterday. And the best part of it was, on those mornings when the older two were out of the house and Amy Rose was down for her nap, she'd taken to helping out a little when the patients were in for their appointments, which helped her to get to know her new neighbors more quickly than she might have otherwise done. In other words, Haven was becoming just that for Maddie and her kids. Every day, the town felt a little more like home.

Even if Dr. Logan's house didn't.

Not that it should, after all. Since this was just temporary and all. And it wasn't like the doctor wasn't as good to her as ever. In fact, those nights he made it home for supper, or got all the way through it without being called away, he always made sure to let her know how much he appreciated the meal. Which was a darn sight more than Jimmy did, especially at the end. Still, despite their agreement—and how well the arrangement seemed to be working out otherwise—she just couldn't shake the feeling that her being there still made him uncomfortable.

Hence, her worries.

When she got back to Haven, her spirits lifted at finding a parking place practically right in front of the Homeland. She'd truly gotten spoiled, being able to go to the supermarket without having to take everybody with her, although she practically had to referee between Ivy, Ruby and Luralene, who all wanted their turns watching Amy Rose whenever Maddie went over to Claremore to see Ned. Next time, though, she thought she might take Amy Rose with her. The nurses had all said it was okay with them, and Maddie figured it was about time to move into the next phase of Ned's taming, which was introducing him to her kids, one at a time. And not even grumpy old Ned McAllister would be able to resist a month-old, toothless baby with dark hair that stuck up every-which-way all over her head.

At least, that's what she was hoping.

Maddie grabbed a buggy and headed toward the produce section, still having a hard time believing she could basically buy anything she wanted. Dr. Logan gave her a healthy food allowance every week, although she was still careful to take advantage of all the sales, since she was not a person inclined to extravagance in any case.

The string beans being too scraggly to warrant more than a passing glance, she moved on.

"Hey…Maddie, isn't it?"

Startled, she looked around, a plastic bag filled with cucumbers dangling from her hand, only to jump a foot when a tall, beanpolelike man she only vaguely recognized suddenly appeared right in front of her buggy.

"I'm sorry, I don't—"

"Hootch Atkins. I was in to see Doc Logan t'other day." She frowned, shaking her head. He held up a bandaged arm. "Fish hook."

"Oh, right. Well." Clearing her throat, she returned to her task, which was picking out the biggest head of lettuce she could find. Lord, the price'd gone up so much, she was tempted to go without. She spared Hootch a quick glance and an even quicker smile. "Arm healin' okay?"

"Yes, ma'am, just fine. Doc really knows what he's doing. 'Course, he's had lot of practice on me."

The chosen head got dumped into the buggy. On to the tomatoes. "Oh?"

"Uh-huh. This makes the tenth hook he's taken out for me. Maybe the eleventh."

Oh, Lordy.

"You're looking real pretty today, Miss Maddie."

Oh, *Lordy*.

For some reason, there seemed to be a lot of single men in this town. As there were a lot of single women. Unfortunately the average age of the women exceeded that of the men by a good thirty years. Which she supposed accounted for why a single mother with three young children looked downright good by comparison. Hootch Atkins, bless his heart—he was a sweet soul, but not exactly the type to stir wild, passionate longings in a girl—was the third man this week to try cozying up to her. While such attentions were flattering, to a degree, they were also getting tiresome.

"Um, thank you, Hootch—"

"Maddie! Hey!"

She caught a glimpse of Hootch's crestfallen—and more than slightly annoyed—expression as she turned around. Wearing an up-to-no-good grin, Cal Logan was about fifteen feet away and closing in fast. Once there, Dr. Logan's brother slipped the hand that wasn't hanging on to his grocery basket—which Maddie noted was filled with frozen dinners and packaged cold cuts—into his jeans' back pocket, allowed a tight smile for the other man.

"Hootch."

The taller man nodded. "Cal. What're you doin' here?"

"Same as everybody else. Shoppin'."

"Thought Ethel did that for you?"

"Went to visit her daughter in Kansas City for the week. So I'm on my own."

The two men stood there, staring at each other, while Maddie wished they'd just both go away so she could get on with what she had to do.

"Well." Deliberately she wheeled the buggy between them, headed for the milk section. "Nice seeing both of you."

Hootch took the hint, apparently, said his goodbyes, and left. Cal didn't.

"You gotta watch out for that guy," Cal said, trotting a little to keep up with her. "He tries to hit on everything in a skirt."

"I'm wearing pants today."

"I noticed. Nice sweater, by the way. And I like the hair, too."

Maddie stopped the buggy dead, then looked up into Cal's grinning face. Now here *was* a man to stir wild, passionate longings in a girl. Just not this one. "But *you* wouldn't be comin' on to me, would you?"

"Me? Hell, no." But he was wearing that goofy smile.

On a sigh that was equal parts amusement and exasperation, she continued on to the milk, heaving the first gallon of four up into the buggy. Naturally Cal took over—men just did that around here, she'd finally gotten used to it—still grinning like a fool. She'd run into Ryan's baby brother a couple of times in the past two weeks, and he was always like this. Just an overgrown puppy, is what she'd decided. A little overenthusiastic, but basically harmless.

"How're the kids doing?" Cal asked.

"What? Oh, fine." Maddie made a big show out of dragging out her list, then heading for the rice and beans aisle. She'd done a ham the other night; the leftovers would make a real good ham-and-bean crockpot. Then she had to pick up a few things for Mildred Rafferty—she'd taken over doing the grocery delivery for the old woman, who now looked forward to seeing Maddie and the kids every Tuesday afternoon. She glanced over, decided Cal really was like a great big dog. One you wished would just go on back home. "Is there something you want, Cal?"

"Now, Maddie, if I didn't know better, I'd say you were trying to give me the brush off."

"And you would be right." She tossed a bag of navy beans into the cart. "Your brother warned me about you, you know."

"Oh, yeah?"

"Uh-huh. And from what he'd said, Hootch Atkins is an amateur compared to you."

Cal's grin grew even more smug. "Hey, you'll get no arguments from me on that score. But actually, I was thinking…what about bringing the kids out to the farm on Saturday? Think they might like that?"

"They probably would. I wouldn't."

"Oh, come on. I had a mare foal a couple weeks ago. And maybe the kids'd like to pick out a few pumpkins from our patch."

"Uh-huh. And what're you trying to pick out?"

He laughed. "My intentions are completely honorable, Maddie," he said gently. "I swear."

For some reason, she believed him. "Well…you sure the kids wouldn't get in the way?"

His brows lifted. "Of what? The pumpkins? I'm crazy about kids, Maddie. And I'm boarding a pony right now that'd be just right for them to take a ride on, if they want."

She picked up a can of creamed corn and pretended to study the label. But instead of ingredients and nutritional values, all she saw was Dr. Logan's scowl.

With a bright smile, she looked up at Cal. "Sure, that sounds like fun. What time?"

"I'll call you," he said. Then he swung one arm around her shoulders and gave her a quick hug. "All I can say is, I'm just sorry I didn't see you first."

Then he left, swaggering down the aisle, his basket banging into his thigh.

Oh, Lord.

After she finished up her shopping, she picked up the kids, then Amy Rose from Ruby's, took everybody home and fed them, then put them all down for a nap before they went out to Mildred's. When she was sure they were all asleep, she went on into the office so she could get in a couple hours' work.

Dr. Ryan was at his desk, frowning so hard through his glasses at the journal he was reading he didn't notice her standing there in the doorway. He still had on his white coat, which made his shoulders look broader than usual; his hair was sticking up funny, like he'd been plowing his hand through it. As usual, classical music was playing on the small clock radio set in front of him.

Something heated and scary and familiar trickled through Maddie as she stood there, watching him. All those men, some of whom really were very sweet—including the doctor's no-account brother, she thought with a half smile—and not a single one of them made her pulse kick up like this. This man, however…

She'd gotten her hair cut almost a week ago. He hadn't mentioned it once.

The doctor looked up. Maddie's thoughts scattered.

"Oh." He squinted at the clock. "It's later than I thought."

"I can always come back—"

"No, no, that's okay." He got up, tucking the journal underneath his arm. If the man wasn't tending to patients, he was reading up on how to tend to them. He'd said once that the older he got, the more often he ran across some study or other that totally disproved a theory previously taken as gospel. "Educated guesswork," he'd said one evening. "That's all this is."

Well, that's all life was, wasn't it?

"You can change the station if you like," he said.

"No, no…it's fine. What is this, do you know?"

He stopped in the middle of slipping off his lab coat to listen. "Tchaikovsky. His sixth symphony. Do you…like it?"

"I've heard worse."

He chuckled.

As the doctor hung the coat up on a hook on the back of the office door, Maddie sat behind his desk to begin sorting out the morning's work. The wooden seat still held his body heat; the air, his scent. Nothing she could define, certainly— well, other than a hint of Old Spice—but an aroma that was uniquely his, just the same. She breathed deeply, shivering a little.

"How'd your visit go with Ned?" he asked, leaning one hip on the front of the desk. On office hour days, they'd spend twenty minutes or so together sorting through the files and what-all, so he wouldn't get behind again.

"Better." She opened the first file. "I figure in twenty, maybe thirty years, he might not even growl at me anymore. Honestly, you have the world's worst handwriting." She flipped the file around. "What's this say?"

The doctor squinted a little—he'd taken his glasses off and apparently didn't want to bother putting them back on—then tapped the page. "Remove stitches. No charge." Then he said, "You know what they say about old dogs."

Maddie entered the notation in the journal she'd started keeping. "I'm not much for old wives' tales, Dr. Ryan. And as far as I can tell, most grouches are that way because they're unhappy."

"And you've decided you're the one to change that."

What was that she'd told herself about the foolishness of trying to change a man who doesn't want to be changed? Now she shrugged, picking up the next file. "I didn't say it would be easy. But I can't help it. I took this personality test once in a magazine, and it said I was a 'fixer'. You know, one of those people—"

"I know what a fixer is," he said. "My mother was one. Wait—is that Luke Hawkins's file?"

"What? Oh, yeah."

"That's a credit, not a bill. I'm still working off the new roof he put on the house two years ago."

Maddie made a note and set the folder aside to put away later. But her heart was just a rat-tat-tatting inside her, mainly because Dr. Ryan didn't usually talk much about his personal life. He didn't usually talk to her this much, period. She didn't know what it meant that he was now—if it meant anything at all—but she sure as heck wasn't going to do anything to break the spell.

"So…what do you mean? Your mother was a fixer, too?"

A smile turned up the corners of his mouth as he picked up one of the folders, scribbled something inside it. "Just that she couldn't stand to see folks at odds with each other, whether it was the neighbors squabbling over whose property a fence was on or the church membership about to come to blows over what color the new carpet should be." He glanced at her, then back at the folder. "What you're trying to do with Ned reminds me a lot of her. Not that she was always successful. Especially when it came to my brothers and me."

She tapped her pen on the blotter for a moment, then said, "Speaking of your brothers…I ran into Cal at the Homeland."

"Oh?"

So much weight for such a small word. "Yeah. He really does think he's God's gift, doesn't he?"

Dr. Logan returned his attention to the chart in his hand. "Just…be careful, Maddie. That charm of his can be lethal."

"And underneath that charm," she said, not looking at him, "is a really nice guy. Which you'd know if you two spent a little more time together."

"Forget it, Maddie. If my mother couldn't get us to see eye to eye, I seriously doubt you can."

She'd just picked up a stack of insurance claim forms, which she now laid flat on the desk. "Why not?"

"Oh, Lord…" He gave her a long-suffering look. "I let myself in for that one, didn't I?"

"Yes, you did. Well?"

"Look, it's not as if we hate each other or anything. It's just…we're just all real different. There's that big age difference between Cal and Hank and me, for one thing. Hank and I were closer when we were young, I guess. But then we hit junior high and he discovered sports." He grimaced. "And girls."

Maddie cocked her head. "You didn't like girls?"

"Oh, I liked 'em all right. They just didn't like me."

"I find that hard to believe."

He shrugged. "You wouldn't if you saw a picture of me at sixteen."

She shuffled things around for a good five seconds, then said softly, "You're not sixteen now."

Even more time passed while the very air molecules seemed to hum between them, as Maddie sat there listening to her heartbeat twang against her sternum. Then, finally, Dr. Logan said, "No, I'm not," then stood, brushing the palms of his hands together. "Any other questions before I go?"

She quickly sifted through the remaining folders. "None that I can see."

"Good. Then…I guess I'll see you later."

After he'd left, Maddie blew a stream of air through her lips. It was just as well she'd be leaving soon. Otherwise, she thought as she switched the radio station, the man would drive her completely nuts.

"Hey, Logan! Wait up!"

Just at the hospital's front door, Ryan turned at the sound of Nelson Burrell's voice booming behind him. He forced a smile for the large-boned, dark-haired man, one of the doctors who'd been pestering him for some time about joining forces in a clinic to serve the area.

"Hey, yourself," he said, shaking hands. He had nothing against Nelson, whom he'd known for years. Or Trudy Mason, either, the third doctor in the conspiracy. They were both fine physicians and good people. He just didn't agree with some of their philosophies, was all. Ryan also knew if he stayed in Nelson's company for more than thirty seconds—the time it took to exchange observations about the weather and inquire after Nelson's new wife as they both headed out to the parking lot—the other doctor would start in on him again. This, on top of his hair still standing on end from the crackling going on between him and Maddie earlier this afternoon, he did not need.

Apparently Nelson sensed Ryan's apprehension. Dark eyes twinkling, he said, "You can breathe now. I'm not going to get on your case about the clinic."

"Oh?" Ryan crossed his arms. "And when did the sun start coming up in the west?"

Nelson's stomach jumped when he laughed. "Oh, Trudy and I haven't given up on wanting you to join us. Just on bugging you about it."

"Nels, you know I think it's a fine idea. For you and Trudy. Not for me."

Nelson's hands lifted, his shiny new wedding band glinting in the fall sunlight. "You don't have to justify your reasons. Hey, I felt exactly the same way, before I finally stopped fighting the inevitable—how would I be able to give my patients the same kind of personal care they expect? And deserve? So far, so good, I have to say. And it's amazing how quickly a body gets used to actually having a night off now and again." He chuckled. "Might even find the time now to make that baby Ellie and I've been thinking about. It's pretty nice, feeling like you're part of the rest of the human race."

"Who says I'm not part of the human race?"

"Yeah, well…" Nelson shrugged. "Don't know about you, but I got damned tired of being lonely. Busy as hell, but lonely."

Ignoring the twist in his gut, Ryan said quietly, "I'm happy for you, Nelson. I really am. But I happen to like things the way they are."

"Fine, fine, suit yourself." The other man clapped Ryan's shoulder before turning to walk to where his own vehicle was parked. "You change your mind, though," he shouted over his shoulder, "you let us know, okay?"

Ryan waved, then hunched down against a sudden cold wind as he trudged over to his truck. After he got in, however, he just sat there, thinking. Or ruminatin', as his mother used to call it. *I swear,* Mary Logan used to say—often—*I never did see a boy* think *things to death the way you do.*

Damn, his mind was one scary place these days. Should be a sign stamped on his forehead: Enter At Your Own Risk.

Well, he did like things the way they were. Had been, anyway, before Maddie Logan and her kids had wriggled into his house, his life. So he was a creature of habit. Was that such a bad thing? He'd just never seen much reason to change how he did things simply for the sake of change. Not that he was so set in his ways that he'd hang on to an outdated treatment method if a better one came along. He just had to be convinced the new way *was* better, since nine times out of ten, it wasn't. *Different* didn't always mean *improved*.

So yes, he balked at most things that threatened the comfortable rut he'd carved for himself over the past few years. He was happy, his patients were happy—so why monkey around with something that didn't need fixing?

Like Maddie and her hair. He'd liked it just fine, the way she'd had it before. Now it was so short, it hardly moved at all. Of course, it did set off her eyes better this way, he had to admit....

Oh, yeah, like he needed to see her eyes better. Especially that...pitying look she got in them from time to time. What in tarnation was it about him that made women look at him like he needed saving? Especially *that* woman? Didn't she have enough on her plate, trying to straighten out her own life?

And why was it no matter what path his thoughts took, they always managed to end up in front of Maddie Kincaid?

He finally got around to starting up the truck. It'd be close to six by the time he got back. Supper time. They'd had pot roast last night, although he'd barely been able to get it down before Darryl Andrews had shown up with Darryl, Jr., who fallen off his skateboard and broken his wrist. Ryan silently thanked Doc Patterson for his foresight in getting an X-ray machine for the office, which had saved many a wounded soldier from an unnecessary trip to the Claremore E.R. And Darryl, Jr., was damn lucky that his break was simple enough for Ryan to set.

He frowned, thinking about some of the high-tech equipment Nelson had said they were planning to get for the clinic, thanks to some wealthy local benefactors. Still wouldn't be a full-service facility by any means, but it sure would be an improvement over what Ryan had on hand.

He rubbed the base of his neck, trying to massage out a budding headache. Too much to think about, too much. And his stomach was growling. He'd seen a package of pork chops in the refrigerator, defrosting.

He bet Maddie did a real good job with pork chops.

Then he frowned, wondering why thinking about pork chops should be making his headache worse?

About ten minutes from town, however, his cell phone rang. "Got two mamas ready to pop at the same time," Ivy said. "Which one you want?"

Ryan sighed. So much for those pork chops.

When he finally got home around nine-thirty, he heard Maddie talking to the baby, out in the living room. Too bushed to even take off his boots, he went up to the doorway leading from the hall, propping one forearm on the jamb. She was facing away from him, sitting with her back against the sofa arm, talking a mile a minute to Amy Rose who was bolstered against her thighs. The baby had on a little white sleeper with flowers or something all over it, her tiny brow furrowed in concentration as she clearly tried to make sense of those sounds coming out of her mama's mouth.

"Who's my pretty girl?" Maddie kept saying. "Who's my smart little girl?"

Ryan felt his lips curve as Amy Rose frowned even harder. She'd gotten through the red and wrinkled phase all right, but now her thick, black hair stuck up in tufts all over her tiny head, her thin features and oddly pointed nose making her look more like a little old lady in a bad wig than a month-old baby.

And every time Ryan saw her, or touched her, or smelled her, he thought his chest would explode.

Maddie suddenly twisted around, then sat up cross-legged on the sofa, lifting the baby to her shoulder. "Hey," she said softly, only to assume an expression much like her daughter's. "You look ready to drop."

Ryan skimmed a hand over his hair. "Good call."

"What was it?"

He'd called her, let her know he'd be late. And why. "A boy," he said with a smile. "Eight and a half pounds." He paused. "Sorry I missed supper. Again."

She gave him one of her would-you-please-get-over-yourself? looks. "There's a plate for you in the fridge. Just stick it in the microwave for a couple minutes."

"Thanks." He got as far as the armchair next to the sofa. Dropping into it, his eyes locked on the baby. Maddie laughed.

Ryan smirked. "Anybody ever tell you it's mean to laugh at a man who can't feel his feet anymore?"

She got to hers, lowering the baby into his lap. "Tell you what—why don't you hang on to Miss Stuff here, and I'll go warm up your supper?"

"No, it's okay—"

But she was gone before he found the energy to finish his damn sentence.

To better hold the baby, Ryan skootched down in the chair, hooking the sole of his boot up on the coffee table. "So, Miss Amy—learn any new tricks today?"

As if on cue, the baby's lips quivered, then spread into a crooked, toothless smile. Without warning, tears burned Ryan's eyes. Because a baby's smile was always a miracle, he told himself. Because he was so blamed tired, he could hardly think straight. Because there was a crazy, generous woman in his kitchen, warming up his supper, who didn't even seem to mind that he'd missed it.

Because…

Pain sliced through his heart, no duller now than it had been five years ago. Ryan tucked the tiny, scrappy baby against his chest, under his chin, shutting his eyes against memories of things he'd had no power to prevent.

Chapter 8

They were both out like lights when Maddie found them, their mouths hanging open in similar fashion, big man cradling itty-bitty baby. Feeling an actual tickle in her chest, she tiptoed over to take Amy Rose from the doctor. Only he jerked awake the instant she touched her, one large hand clasping the infant to his chest, the other seizing Maddie's wrist. A fierce protectiveness crackled in his half-asleep gaze, making her heart skip a beat.

"It's okay," she whispered, practically tingling from the urge to smooth the frown from his brow. His fingers were clamped around her wrist hard enough to almost hurt, but she didn't care. "You fell asleep. I just want to get her into bed."

It took another second or so before, with a shaky sigh, he relinquished both her wrist and the baby, slumping back against the chair and scrubbing his hand over his mouth. "Sorry. I'm..."

"Don't worry about it." Maddie allowed herself the indulgence of inhaling the sweet scent of her baby girl, now blended with the doctor's stronger masculine one. "Nice to know nobody could've come in and snatched her from you while I was gone. Your dinner's on the table, if you can make it into the kitchen.''

She came back downstairs a few minutes later to find the doctor scarfing down his food like he hadn't eaten in a week. Even so, she'd noticed that no matter how hungry he was, his table manners were always perfect. Unlike Jimmy, who she never could get to hold a fork like a civilized adult.

''It's okay, I take it?'' she asked, standing in the doorway, her hands stuffed into her back pockets.

''Oh, yeah.'' He forked a potato wedge, sighing as he looked at it. ''I'm really gonna miss this.'' He glanced at her, then back to his plate. ''When you go.''

Maddie told herself there was no reason why his words should sting.

''Which reminds me…'' She slid into the chair across from him. ''I think I might've found a house.''

Now she had his attention. And the frown again. ''Really? Where?''

''Over on Emerson. Closer to the school. It won't be available until New Year's, though, since they're fixing it up. Which is fine, since I won't have enough saved up for the deposit before then.'' She felt her cheeks warm. ''Listen to me, assuming it's okay for us to stay here that long.''

''Listen to you, is right,'' Dr. Logan said, his mouth rigid. ''How many times I have to tell you—you and the kids can stay as long as you need to. And I don't want to hear anything more about it.'' He cut another piece of pork, stuck it in his mouth. ''When can we go look at this house?''

''What are you talking about?''

He took a sip of water, gave her one of those looks. ''How many houses have you rented?''

''Well…none, actually. But heaven knows I've looked for enough apartments—''

''Not the same thing,'' he said, concentrating more on his food than her. ''Some of these old places are downright unsafe. I wouldn't be able to sleep nights knowing you and the kids are someplace I hadn't checked out.''

Her arms crossed, she stared at him until he looked up.

"What?"

"This may come as a shock, Dr. Logan, but you don't have to take care of the entire world."

A half-smile tilted his lips. "I'm not trying to. But I do feel a sense of responsibility for my patients. So deal with it."

It was dumb, and she knew it, but his words provoked a little spasm of disappointment, right underneath her heart. Not that she expected him to think of her and the kids in any other way. Or even that she wanted him to, because she didn't....

She got up from the table and started putting away the dishes she'd left to air-dry in the drainer, wondering when her feelings about...any of this were going to start making some sense.

"But I'm not exactly paying you the big bucks," the doctor said behind her. "How're you gonna pay rent on a new place?"

She swallowed and said, "By that time, Amy Rose'll be old enough to leave in day care, so I can get a full-time job."

"You comfortable with that idea? Of leaving her in day care?"

After setting the last plate in the cupboard, she turned back, leaning against the counter. "I don't see as I have a whole lotta choice in the matter. But at least I already got a job offer. Hootch Atkins said I could come work out at his bait and tackle shop."

The bite of potato headed for Dr. Logan's mouth stopped halfway up. "You're not serious."

"What's wrong with that? You got something against worms?"

"Worms, no. Hootch, yes."

"Well, he certainly seems nice enough to me."

"I just bet he is," the doctor mumbled under his breath.

"What's that?"

"Nothing." He fiddled with his fork for a second or two, then finally put that piece of potato into his mouth. "You could still keep working for me, you know," he said around it, then swallowed. "I mean, after you...leave. And now that money's coming in again—thanks to you—I can maybe raise your salary.''

"Thanks, but it's still only part-time. Like you said, it wouldn't be enough. Not unless I can find another part-time job or something to supplement.'' She nodded toward his empty plate. "You want seconds?''

"What? Oh…no, thanks…what are you doing?''

"Taking your plate so I can wash it. Got a problem with that?''

"What I have a problem with is your waiting on me.''

She stopped dead. "Is that what you think I'm doing?''

"Aren't you?''

"No.'' She carried his plate and glass over to the sink. "Being the most convenient person to do what needs doing isn't the same as waiting on somebody.'' With a glance over her shoulder, she added, "So next time I'm sitting down and you're up, you can do something for *me*.''

He chuckled, then said, "Can I ask you a personal question?''

"You know,'' she said over the running water as she sponged off the plate, "you're sure chatty for somebody who was next door to comatose a half hour ago.''

"Old med school trick. Ten minutes snooze, you're good for another four hours.''

Except, as she was setting the plate in the drainer, she noticed he was digging his fingers into the back of his neck. "Here,'' she said as she wiped her hands, "let me work out that kink for you—''

"No, no, it's okay…''

"Oh, for pity's sake! Why is it so blamed hard for you to let somebody do something for *you* for a change?''

Okay, so maybe Ryan didn't know all that much about women, other than from a physiological standpoint. But he sure as hell knew he was too tired to argue with one standing there with her hands fisted into her hips and her eyes blazing like that. Still, about a hundred troubled thoughts rose up in Ryan's mind like spooks on Halloween night, the chief spook being that the idea of Maddie's hands on his person was at once tempting and terrifying.

"You any good at working out kinks?"

But she was already standing behind him, her surprisingly strong thumbs intent on annihilating the knot at the base of his neck. "Drop your head forward and I'll show you."

It took everything Ryan had in him not to groan. Oh, yeah…she was good, all right.

"So what'd you want to ask me?" she said about a century later.

"Hmm…oh…um…oh, right—how were your grades in school?"

"Pretty good. A's and B's, mostly. Why?"

Now she was doing these little circling things up the sides of his neck. His whole body was going blissfully numb. Well, almost his whole body.

"How…how about in math and s-science?"

"I'm sorry—am I hurting you?"

Not exactly. "No, I'm good."

Actually, he wasn't good at all. Actually, he was on the verge of losing his mind. Not to mention his control. He told himself it was just because it had been a long time since a woman had touched him.

Then he told himself he was lying through his teeth.

"They were my best subjects," she said.

What? Oh. Right. Math and science.

"Where're you goin' with this?"

Nowhere, unfortunately, he thought as she started in on the area between his shoulder blades. How could such tiny hands be so strong?

How could he have forgotten how good this felt?

Focus, Logan.

"I was just wondering if you've ever thought about going back to school?"

"Well, sure, I used to think about it all the time."

"But not now?"

Her laugh was breathy. "I have three children under the age of six, remember? Right now, being their mama's my number one priority. I figure I've got plenty of time once they're older. And maybe by then I'll know what I want to be when I grow up. Hey—'' She gently cuffed him on the shoulder. ''This is supposed to be relaxing you. You seem to be getting more knotted up the longer I do this.''

After a long moment, he said, very softly and very deliberately, ''There's a reason for that, Maddie.''

Her hands stilled on his shoulders. Then there was nothing left but the void where her touch had been. ''Oh. Oh, Lord, I'm so sorry…''

Ryan twisted around in his chair. ''Not nearly as sorry as I am.''

She backed away, then, her cheeks so red she looked feverish. ''I'm sorry,'' she repeated, then started to turn away. Ryan lunged forward, snagged her hand.

''Don't go,'' he said quietly. And meant it, God help him.

''It's just I didn't mean anything by—''

''I know you didn't, Maddie. It's okay.''

''Is it?''

''Oh, hell,'' he said on an exhaled breath, then dropped her hand, leaning forward to clasp his own between his knees. Half smiling, he peered up at her, still standing there looking as if she didn't know what hit her. ''Did you think just because I live alone everything had shut down?''

Her color deepened even more.

''I…wasn't thinking about that at all, if you want to know the truth. I mean, I *should* have, I was married, and it never took much for Jimmy—'' She folded her arms over her stomach, shutting her eyes. ''You must think I'm the stupidest woman on God's green earth.''

Tenderness rushed through him. And something more. ''Not hardly. In fact, before my body went haywire on me, I was going to say…'' He cocked his head at her. ''You can sit down. The danger's passed.''

After a moment, she sat. As far away as she could, stiffly, her hands clutching the seat on either side of her legs.

He looked at her, hard, then said, ''For what it's worth, you might want to think about getting your degree in something in the medical field. Since you like taking care of people so much," he added with a smile.

"Oh." She frowned down at her lap, then looked back at him. "Grace—my last foster mother—was always at me about becoming a nurse, too."

"You'd make a good one, Maddie."

"Maybe." Her chin lifted. "But right now, I can't imagine anything more fulfilling than taking care of my family. Can you?"

Another strange, uncomfortable mix of emotions spiked through him as he sat there, watching this sweet, tough, vulnerable woman watching him. He shook his head. "No. I can't." Maybe it hadn't been the smartest thing he'd ever done, letting on the power she had over him. But it was either her or him, and a few minutes ago, self-preservation had clambered to the top of the pile. Still, maybe because he was tired, maybe because he really was as much of a fool as he was beginning to suspect he was, he found he was almost desperate to know more about her. "Can I ask another question?"

She shrugged, but wariness weighted her gaze.

"I get the feeling you were close to your last set of foster parents."

The wariness sharpened. "I was. Most of the time, at least."

"Then what happened?"

"We…lost touch, is all." She shrugged again. "It happens."

"So…they're still alive?"

"Far as I know…oh." Her mouth quirked to one side. "What you're really asking is, why didn't I contact *them* after Jimmy's death?"

"Okay. Let's go with that."

"Because…because I burned that bridge when I got married."

"You didn't think they'd help you?"

"It was more like I had no right to ask them for help. Now if you don't mind…" She got up, her expression shuttered.

"Amy Rose'll be wanting her breakfast by 6:00 a.m., so I'd best be getting to bed."

Ryan stood as well, only to call her back before she reached the kitchen door. "We can go look at the Emerson house tomorrow, if you like."

"I really don't think—"

"Sometimes, a person can think too much," he said, crossing his arms. Then he smiled. "If you can be friends with my brother, I'd like to think you could be friends with me, too. And friends help each other out."

After a second or two, she said, "Just remember *you* said that, not me."

Then she was gone, leaving Ryan wondering if there was any way he could examine his own brain.

The next day, Maddie got the key from the real estate agent handling the Emerson house, and they all trooped over to take a look-see. The houses were smaller on this side of town, but the neighborhood was neat enough. Maddie had high hopes that once the house was fixed up, it would look as good as its neighbors.

Dr. Logan, however, didn't look entirely convinced. But then, he'd started out in a grumpy mood. Which was fine with her, since she wasn't exactly feeling like sweetness and light today, either.

Talk about making a fool of herself. Honestly, offering to give the man a massage, of all things. And then to not catch on right away that he was...was...

Exactly what she'd been for the rest of the night.

Her cheeks burned. What in blue blazes was wrong with her, thinking along these lines? Except...

Except, was it such a bad thing, knowing her touch had done that to him?

She wasn't exactly what you'd call a sex goddess, after all. Well, she supposed she did okay with Jimmy, but then, they'd still been teenagers when they got married. There wasn't exactly much of a challenge turning on somebody who didn't have an off switch.

"There's a stain on the ceiling," the doctor was saying, his voice echoing in the empty, half-painted room cluttered with ladders, paint cans and drop cloths. Although considering how much paint there seemed to be on the bare wooden floor, Maddie wasn't sure how much good the drop cloths had done.

"Hmm?" She looked over, telling herself it couldn't affect her one way or the other, how he looked holding onto the stroller handles like that. After all, the doctor had insisted on pushing it. After the sleepless night she'd had, Maddie wasn't up to arguing.

"Stain. On the ceiling."

She looked where he was pointing. "Apparently the toilet backed up a time or two," she said, almost defensively. "The agent said it's been fixed, now all they have to do is repair the damage."

He nodded, then glanced around. "Seems small."

"Well, I suppose next to your house, it is. But it's big enough for us. There's the two rooms and a screened-in back porch plus an eat-in kitchen down here, then three bedrooms and a bath upstairs."

Ryan looked pointedly around the very empty room. "I suppose all the furniture's in storage?"

Maddie felt her cheeks heat up. "There's a kitchen table and chairs, and some beds upstairs. We can live without living room furniture for a while—"

Something crashed overhead, shaking the ceiling. Katie Grace screamed. The doctor took off, bounding up the stairs two at a time. Her heart racing, Maddie unhooked the baby from her stroller and quickly followed, almost afraid of what she'd see when she got up there.

"It's okay," Dr. Logan said when she arrived. "It was just a ladder going over." But he frowned hard at the kids. "Which I don't imagine happened on its own, did it?" There was a sternness in his voice she'd never heard before, one that sent Noah backing up against her.

Katie, ever helpful, pointed to her brother. "He tried to climb it an' it falled over."

"Yeah, that's what I figured." He took a step toward Noah,

who crammed himself against Maddie's thighs so hard she nearly lost her balance.

"S'was an accident," he said, his voice trembling. "I didn't mean to. P-please don't get mad at me."

The doctor's gaze shot to Maddie's for a moment before he crouched in front of Noah. "I'm not mad at you, grass-hopper," he said, more gently. "I just don't want you messing with something that could get you hurt, that's all."

"But you're a doctor. You can always fix it when some-body gets hurt."

His expression clouded over as he shook his head. "Not always, Noah. I'm a doctor. Not a magician. Which is why it's always better to avoid getting hurt in the first place." He stood, hesitating a moment before palming Noah's haywire hair. "Hey—no matter what I say to you, or how I say it, you don't ever, ever have to be afraid of me. Okay?"

After a second or two, Noah nodded, then twisted around to look up at Maddie. "C'n me and Katie go play now?"

Her chest tight with emotion, Maddie said, "Sure," hitch-ing the baby higher in her arms as she watched the two of them scamper off. Then she looked over at the doctor. "Thank you. He needs…more of that in his life. To see there's a difference between being strong and being mean."

Their gazes linked, for just a moment. Dr. Logan swal-lowed, then nodded, before wandering off into the next room, where he started knocking on walls and things with a serious expression on his face. Old, faded wallpaper molted off the walls in ragged strips; the closet door was off its hinges and propped next to the window. Still, sunlight danced across the uneven floor, chasing the gloom from otherwise dark corners. The doctor tapped something again.

Maddie chuckled. He turned to her, looking bemused.

"What's so blamed funny?"

"I keep expecting you to go, 'Say ah.'"

"Well. You never know," he said.

"You have any idea what you're looking for?"

He just frowned at her.

Just then, the kids came barrelling past them in the short

hall and on down the uncarpeted stairs, sounding like those crazy people who run from the bull every year in Spain or wherever that was.

"Those could be dangerous," the doctor said, nodding toward the stairs. "Especially when the baby starts walking."

"That's why there's baby gates."

"They don't always work. Some babies learn to climb over them."

"Honestly, Dr. Logan…" Exasperated, she headed down the stairs. "Anybody ever tell you you're a worry wort?"

Grumbling and mumbling, he followed her. Halfway down, he said, "How much did you say they're asking?"

She told him. He grunted.

"And they're sure it's going to be ready by New Year's?"

"I only know what the agent told me. And speaking of holidays…" She carted Amy Rose back over to the stroller to strap her in, wondering why she was about to suggest this. But the idea had been building up in her mind for the past week until there was no ignoring it. After scooping off a trickle of slobber from the baby's chin with her finger and wiping it on her jeans, she took a deep breath, said a mental prayer for her sanity, then said, "I've been meaning to ask you if it'd be okay with you if I cooked Thanksgiving dinner for you. As a way to say 'thank you' for everything you've done for me and the kids."

As expected, he gave her an odd look. But then, he was always giving her odd looks. She was beginning to get used to it.

"You got something against Thanksgiving?" she asked.

"No, no, it's just…it's been so long since…" He rubbed the back of his neck for a second, then seemed to catch himself, quickly lowering his hand to his side. "And I wouldn't want you to go to a lot of trouble for nothing. Holidays are usually my busiest days. Kitchen accidents, food poisoning, heart attacks from overeating." He smirked, crossing his arms. "Patching up the wounded after a family 'discussion.'"

Maddie laughed, then said, "Okay, I see your point. But I also want to do this for the kids." She looked back at the baby, who was trying to stuff her fist in her mouth. "It's been a while since we've had a real holiday celebration, too."

"Lord, woman," Ryan said softly behind her, "you sure do know which buttons to push, don't you?"

Her gaze whipped to his. "I'm not trying to—"

To her shock, he reached up, tenderly brushing her hair away from her face. "It's okay, honey," he said with a smile that was more sad than anything. "Knock yourself out. Just don't..." He lowered his hand, stuffing it in his pocket. "You just can't count on my being there, okay?"

"I won't, I promise." Her cheek still tingling from his touch, she crouched by the stroller, afraid to look at him, afraid he'd see something in her eyes that had no right to be there. "There's one more thing."

"And what's that?"

She straightened up, finding the wherewithal to face him again. "Long as I'm doing the cooking, is it okay if I invite one or two other people? Like maybe, Mildred and Ivy?"

"Sure, you can invite anybody you like—"

"Even your brothers?"

He frowned at that, just like she figured he would.

"My brothers and I haven't shared a holiday meal in nearly ten years."

"Then it's high time you did," she said, calling to the kids as she wheeled the stroller to the front door. "You can invite Hank," she added, "and I'll invite Cal when the kids and I are go out there on Saturday."

The doctor hardly said three words to her the rest of the way back to his house.

"This is really beautiful." Maddie fingered the folded lace tablecloth draped across her arm, then looked up at the doctor's younger brother. "You sure you don't mind me borrowing it?"

Accompanied by a small herd of grinning dogs—a pair of Australian shepherds, a Border collie, and one multicolored thing made out of scraps—they'd toured the Logan family home, a sturdy, rambling cinnamon-brown clapboard house that Maddie liked nearly as much as she liked the doctor's, as well as the grounds and stables. Then the kids had their pony rides, complete with one horror-stricken moment when the kids caught sight of pony poop for the first time and Maddie had thought she'd just about die laughing. Now they were standing out back, at one end of the large vegetable garden Cal's housekeeper, Ethel, maintained. Most of it was spent now, this late in the season, but there were still winter lettuces going and some Brussels sprouts…and pumpkins. Dozens and dozens of pumpkins, which the kids were now inspecting one by one, with the dogs' help.

"Nobody's used that tablecloth since Mama passed," Cal said, leaning his weight on top of the chain link fence surrounding the garden to keep the varmints out. "It's just been sitting in the buffet, gathering dust." He squinted up at her. "Thanks for inviting me, by the way."

"You're welcome."

"So what'd Ry think of the idea?"

"Hard to tell. Although I think he thinks I'm nuts."

Cal just laughed.

Visoring her eyes with her hand against the strong late-afternoon sun, Maddie watched the children for a moment, hopping from pumpkin to pumpkin like a pair of giggling fleas. Every day, they seemed to relax into their new lives a little more. Especially Noah, she thought with a wry smile, whose troublemaking skills had nearly returned to normal levels. Her smile flattened out some, though, when she thought about how attached they were both getting to Dr. Logan. What was it going to be like two months from now, when they had to move out?

"Hey. A man could go deaf from the sound of all those gears grinding in your head."

Maddie shook off her errant thoughts and looked over at Cal, standing there with that up-to-no-good grin on his face. "Sorry. Got a lot on my mind."

He shifted to face her, the grin dimming by a few hundred watts or so. "You know, I wasn't all that sure you'd come out today."

She squinted out at the kids. "Neither was I."

"Then why did you?"

"Because I thought it *would* be good for the kids. And because…" Her cheeks warmed.

"Because Ry told you not to?"

Her gaze flew to his. "He didn't tell me *not* to." She smoothed her hand over the tablecloth. "Not in so many words, at least."

Cal let out a bark of laughter, shaking his head. "You are something else, Maddie."

An indignant squeal caught their attention; they looked out to see both kids trying to sit on the same pumpkin. Katie Grace butt-bumped Noah in the hip, knocking him onto the ground. Unfazed, he simply got up and moved on to the next throne, the pumpkin nearly as big as he was.

"C'n we have this one?"

"You sure can, buddy. Now help your sister pick one out, then we'll load 'em up in your mama's car."

The kids scampered back further into the patch as Cal said, "So what you're saying is, you came out here to get a rise out of my brother."

"I did not!" Except then he angled his head at her, his grin all crooked and knowing, and she let out a sigh. "Well, maybe a little. And what's so funny?"

"Nothin'," he said, chuckling. "Just that I was thinking what a fine sister-in-law you'd make someday."

"*Sister-in—*" Maddie clamped shut her mouth and just gaped at him. When she found her voice again, she said, "You have definitely been out in the sun too long. And would you please wipe that exasperatin' grin off your face? Honestly, Cal—what on earth would even make you say such a thing?"

"My brother's attitude about you, for one thing." Katie Grace pointed out her pumpkin; with a wave of acknowledgement, Cal headed for a shed near the house. Maddie followed. So did Mooner, the scrap-dog.

"He's just being protective, is all. Because—"

"You work for him? You live with him? He delivered your

baby?'' Cal pushed open the door to the shed, stepped inside long enough to get a wheelbarrow. When he reappeared, he said, ''Hell, Maddie—he doesn't go around warning any *other* woman about me. And then—'' he steered the wheelbarrow through the garden toward Noah's pumpkin ''—you go and deliberately antagonize him by comin' out here. So what does that tell us?''

Stumbling along behind him, praying she didn't trip over a vine and break her neck, Maddie said, ''That I'm free to choose who I see and where I go?''

''Nope. Wrong answer. What that says to me is, you knew your coming out here would tick him off.'' He stopped, stared at her hard. Mooner sat down and stared, too, until an itch over his stubby tail distracted him. ''Might even make him jealous.''

''That's crazy!''

The late-afternoon sun made Cal's green eyes twinkle like emeralds. ''You're forgetting who's the experienced one here. There's not a man-woman game on earth I haven't played at one time or another.'' He leaned toward her. ''I know all the moves, Miss Maddie.'' Then he sobered. ''I also know my brother doesn't generally look at a woman the way I saw him look at you that night I was up to his house. Not since—'' He stopped.

''Suzanne?''

''So you know about her?''

''Only what Ivy's told me. Your brother never talks about her.''

''Yeah, that sounds about right.'' He took out a pocketknife to whack the pumpkin's stem. ''I'm sorry, but the man's not leading a normal life. Him and Hank both. I figure if you can get his heart started again…'' With a grunt and a thud, he loaded the pumpkin into the barrow.

''You're forgetting one important thing,'' Maddie said, as he jerked the loaded barrow around to push it to where Katie was squatting by her pumpkin, petting it like it was a dog.

''And what's that?''

''That you're deluded,'' she shouted toward his back.

Cal just laughed. Maddie felt like somebody'd screwed her brain in too tight. "Okay, so...so maybe it is time your brother came out of that stupid shell he's in. I don't disagree that what he's let happen to himself isn't good. But whatever he might need in a girlfriend—in a wife—I'm sure not it."

Cal thunked the second pumpkin into the barrow, then straightened up, dusting off his hands. "What makes you say that?"

"Where would you like me to start? For one thing, I'm not looking to get involved with anybody for a good long while. And for another, what do we have in common? Not to mention the fact that I'm so much younger than he is. I mean, he's got all that college education, and...and...shoot, Cal—there's only so much classical music I can take before I'm ready to scream."

A half smile curved Cal's mouth. "Yep. Nice set of objections you got there."

Maddie hugged the tablecloth to her chest and stared out toward the stables. An occasional soft whinny pricked the air as she stood there, thinking about the doctor's reaction to her touch the other night. About her reaction to his, when they were at the house on Emerson. The way her stomach flipped over at the sound of his voice when he talked to Amy Rose, when she heard him joshing with his patients.

If she was being honest with herself, she'd admit she was in serious trouble.

And Maddie always made it a point to be honest with herself.

She turned to Cal, frowning. "I won't deny that I care about him. Maybe even care *for* him. I mean, it would be kinda hard not to, considering how good he's been to me and all. But that doesn't change anything," she quickly added. "If anything, it just makes me more determined than ever to get out of there as soon as I can, before—" She caught her lip between her teeth.

"Before what?"

Shaking her head, she looked back over toward where the sun was thinking about bedding down for the night. "There was a time I believed in dreams, so much so that I turned my back on the only two people who'd ever cared two hoots about me. Well, five years of being married to a dreamer sure cured me of that.'' Poking at a clump of dirt with the toe of her canvas shoe, she said, ''If it's one thing I've learned, it's that there's no point in wishing for things that aren't going to happen. People can't help being who they are, feeling what they feel. And dreaming won't change that.''

''Then what was all that baloney you gave me about Ned?''

She'd told Cal about her mission to turn the old man's attitude around. Now she was sorry she had. ''Not the same thing. Ned was just waiting for somebody to come along who cared enough to save him from himself. Even if he didn't know it. Ryan...''

She stopped, realizing that was the first time she'd ever called the doctor by his first name.

''I don't know the particulars about him and Suzanne,'' she said, ''but my guess is that he's still hurting over her leaving him. And frankly, trying to heal something like that takes more energy than I've got.''

Cal was quiet for a moment, then turned the wheelbarrow around to leave the garden. ''I just have one thing to say about dreams, Maddie.'' He nodded over his shoulder, indicating the farm. ''Buying this farm was my father's dream, even when he didn't have two nickels to rub together. Turning it into a successful horse farm was mine, even though nobody thought I'd ever be able to knuckle down long enough to stick with it. No, dreams don't come true just by wishing, but they can be the spark that start things happening. Even if they don't make a lick of sense to anybody but ourselves. That doesn't make 'em any less worthwhile. And without 'em, you may as well just lay down and die.''

They'd reached her car; Cal popped open the trunk to put the pumpkins inside. Crossing her arms against the descending chill, Maddie stared out over the pastures. ''You love your brothers, don't you?''

He slammed shut the trunk. ''They don't make it easy, but yes. I do. Shoot, they were my idols when I was a kid. Watching what's happened to them in the past couple of years…it makes me sick, Maddie. They were always driven, both of 'em, but they used to be human, at least. I just want to see them happy.''

She looked over at him. ''What's your dream these days, Cal Logan?''

That funny smile stretched across his mouth. ''Ah, my mama told me that the thing about dreams is, sometimes you've gotta keep 'em close to your heart. Cherish 'em. Know they'll come to fruition in their own good time.'' He winked at her. ''Just as long as you don't give up on 'em.''

Chapter 9

More than once that afternoon, Ryan had thought about driving on out to Cal's farm to see for himself what was going on. Except that would be childish, for one thing. And give people the wrong impression, for another.

But, damn, he was in a rotten mood.

For the first time in what seemed like months, if not years, he'd had an entire afternoon without a single call. Which meant he'd been alone in the house the whole time. Savoring the quiet. The peace. Just the way it used to be, before Maddie came along. Just the way he liked it.

He rattled the journal he was trying to read.

The grandfather clock bonged.

Outside, a dog barked.

Somebody drove by.

The house made a creaky, settling noise.

Ryan got up, walked over to the window. Watched the street for a while. Went back to his desk. Sat down. Glowered at the journal.

A minute later, the house shuddered from the front door

opening, followed by a blast of children's voices, the baby crying, Maddie laughing over it all.

He resisted the urge to get up, go meet them.

In his mind's eye, he could see Maddie's smile. Knew all he had to do, to see that smile in person, was get up off his lazy duff and go out there—

"Dokker Rine, Dokker Rine!" Katie Grace burst into the office, her cheeks as pink as his mother's roses used to be, her blond hair a tangled mess. Before Ryan knew it, the child was on his lap, smelling of cold air and baby shampoo and her mama. "We gots two *huge* punkins, an' we gots to ride a pony at Uncle Cal's—"

Uncle Cal's?

"—an' there were kittens in the barn an' Uncle Cal said maybe we could have one, when Mama gets her own house—"

"Land, Katie Grace!" Out of breath and as flushed as her daughter, Maddie appeared in the doorway, juggling a squalling Amy Rose in her arms. All three females were wearing denim overalls. "Leave the man in peace!"

But what if the man doesn't want to be left in peace?

With that thought, the discombobulation that had been plaguing Ryan all afternoon suddenly undiscombobbled. Because the man very much *did* want to be left in peace. The man very much did not want to spend another afternoon like this one, wondering about Maddie Kincaid and her children.

Missing them.

Missing her.

Her eyes were bright, almost silver, almost as brilliant as her smile. She shoved a hank of hair behind her ear, the gesture relaxed.

She'd had a good time, this afternoon. With Cal.

Why should he begrudge her a few hours' innocent pleasure?

"Just let me get this little girl fed," she said, "then I'll start dinner. I've got some hamburger defrosting—would you rather have spaghetti or tacos?"

Oh, no…the man did not want to get used to having somebody coming home and asking him if he wanted spaghetti or tacos.

And most of all, the man did not want to have to avert his gaze from the woman asking him that question because every single one of his trillion cells was crying out with want for her.

"Ryan?"

His head snapped up at the sound of his Christian name on her lips.

"Ryan?" she said again, more softly. She'd stuck her pinkie finger in the baby's mouth to fake her out for a minute. "Is something wrong?"

"Whatever you want to make is fine with me," he said, hearing the curtness in his voice. At her puzzled look, he forced himself to ask, "Have a good time?"

"Land, yes," she said, then said, "Oh! Cal loaned me the lace tablecloth for Thanksgiving y'all used to use on holidays."

"Oh. Good."

"Don't bowl me over with your enthusiasm," she said, her lips curved in a teasing smile. "Have you asked Hank yet?"

"No. Haven't had a chance."

"Well, it's early yet, I guess. Okay, guys," she said to the kids, "why don't you go see what's on TV while I feed Amy Rose, then it's tacos for dinner!"

Amid shouts of glee, they all left.

And it was quiet again, although not as quiet as before. Ryan could still hear them, in the other part of the house. Could still feel their presence, shimmering around him. Inside him.

He got up again, went back over to the window. Stared out of it some more until his brain stopped acting all stupid and finally decided to cooperate.

Maddie Kincaid was the kind of woman who was meant to be married, he decided. Not to him, though. To somebody who'd truly appreciate her, who wouldn't feel invaded when she was around. Maybe to Cal—maybe Maddie was to be the one who'd finally rein his baby brother in?—maybe to somebody else. Maybe not right away—well, no, definitely not right away, she just lost her husband not too long ago, after all—but…but surely there were one or two single men around he'd consider worthy of her. Not that he could think of any at the moment, but still. Because, see, this wanting Maddie business…well, it was beginning to get out of hand. Badly.

Nothing wrong with wanting things, true. Unless they were things you couldn't have. And it wasn't as if he was going to act on his impulses, even if they were threatening to melt down his brain. Not to mention other things. He'd learned his lesson on that score, boy. Still, it would just make things a helluva lot easier if she'd find herself interested in somebody else. Somebody solid and steady who'd be there every night for her, who could be a real husband to her.

Who'd love her the way she deserved to be loved.

All Maddie could think about through supper was her conversation with Cal. That, and the strange way Ryan was acting. The whole time they were at the table, he kept looking at the children like he was trying to memorize them.

But he barely looked at her at all.

When Noah and Katie Grace finally finished and went off into the living room to watch their half hour of TV before bed, she got to her feet and started snatching the dirty plates off the table. "Are you really that ticked with me for going out to your brother's?"

Ryan looked startled. He rose as well, taking the plates from her and scraping them before putting them in the dishwasher he'd had installed just last week. "Why would I be ticked? Where you go is none of my business."

Except she'd never seen a man scrape plates with such vigor before.

"Not even to Cal's?" she asked mildly.

"Like I said. None of my business."

She stood on tip-toe to get down a container for the leftover cheese. Just before the whole shootin' match came down on her head, Ryan came up behind her and fetched it for her, close enough that their bodies touched, just for a second. Just long enough for her hormones to start having a hissy fit.

"Heaven knows why I'm telling you this," she said as he walked away, "but I swear to you, nothing's going on. I like Cal, but I'm not attracted to him."

"Maddie," he said, facing her. And the stark longing in his eyes almost knocked the wind out of her. "I do not care if you and my brother see each other."

Then he went back to his task, leaving her standing there winded and confused. Okay, obviously he wasn't longing for her—no hissy-fitting hormones on that side of the room, far as she could tell—but if not her, what? Or who?

Cal was right. Ryan needed to move on, let another woman in his life. Not Maddie, though. But somebody. Maybe he was acting weird because being around her kids had loosened something inside him, making him realize just how much he'd sacrificed for his career. Made him realize…

Standing at the sink, Maddie sucked in a breath. Maybe, just maybe, she'd been led here, to Haven, to Dr. Ryan Logan's house, to somehow save him from his own loneliness. So…surely there had to be at least one single woman around selfless enough to be a country doctor's wife?

"Hey," he said. "You okay?"

With a smile that didn't feel all that bright, she met his gaze.

"Just fine," she said, wiping her hands on a dishtowel. "Now—you any good at carving jack-o'-lanterns?"

Another week passed before Ryan finally got around to asking Hank about Thanksgiving. Not that his heart was in it. But *Maddie's* heart was set on having all the Logan brothers sitting around the table, so Ryan figured he may as well humor her. Just as he'd humored her by helping to carve pumpkins and handing out candy to trick-or-treaters while she took the kids out.

Somebody had given Maddie a tiny peapod costume for Amy Rose. Ryan had never seen anything so cute in all his life as those great, big, solemn eyes staring up at him from inside that ridiculous costume. And judging from Maddie's sparkling eyes when they got back, she'd had nearly as much fun as the kids.

So he liked seeing the gal and her kids happy. So, hey, if it rang her chimes to get up at 5:00 a.m. to stuff stuffing up a turkey's butt, who was he to stand in her way?

Hank wasn't in the motel office. Ryan went back out, listening for signs of life. After a second, he zeroed in on some scraping or something coming from one of the cottages, down by the lake. Couple minutes later, he found Hank up on a roof, dislodging old shingles.

Balanced on his knees, a cigarette dangling from his lips, his brother shielded his eyes from the sun for a moment, then attacked the next layer of shingles. Despite the near-freezing temperature, he wasn't wearing a jacket.

"What the hell are you doing here?"

"Nice to see you, too, Hank. Maddie wanted me to ask you something."

"Ever hear of the telephone?"

"I was in the neighborhood. And what the hell are *you* doing smoking?"

Hank plucked the cigarette from his lips and waved it around. From the looks of things, he hadn't shaved in two or three days. "Think of it as a relapse. So Maddie's still living with you?"

"I think *living at my place* is a better way of putting it, but yes. For a while." He paused. "She's been working for me, in the office. In trade."

"Mmm," Hank said, then stubbed out the cigarette on the roof with the toe of his workboot. "So what does she want?"

"To invite you to Thanksgiving dinner."

Hank stared down at Ryan. "You're not serious."

"What I am has nothing to do with it. She's hell-bent on seeing the three of us sitting around the same table—"

"Forget it."

"No, I'm not forgetting it. And neither are you. It's two lousy hours out of your life, such as it isn't. Pencil it in."

Hank gave him a long, assessing look, tossed the crowbar

he'd been using onto the grass beside the cottage, then jumped down off the roof. Aluminum clattered as he telescoped the ladder, then grabbed it with one hand. "You know," he said, tramping back toward the office, "if I didn't know you better, I'd get the feeling this means an awful lot to you."

"It means a lot to Maddie, which is what's important here. I gather it's been about as long for her as it has for us, having a real holiday."

"Holidays." Hank snorted his disgust. "They're such bull—"

"Get over it, Scrooge."

Hank threw down the ladder and whipped around, his expression thunderous. "I don't do holidays, remember? Especially this one. And I'm sorry if your woman's hurt by that, but *she'll* get over it." He started to walk away, but Ryan grabbed his brother's arm and yanked him back around.

"One, Maddie's not *my* woman," he said in a low voice. "And two, I don't give a damn right now about your baggage, which is getting pretty worn out after two years, don't you think?"

Hank twisted free of Ryan's grasp, then got right up in his face, his fists clenched. "Says the man whose girlfriend walked out more than five freakin' years ago! *Walked* out, Ryan! As in, she was still alive *to* walk."

For what seemed like an eternity, his brother's raw pain reverberated through the woods around them. Ryan hauled in a ragged breath, then braced his hands on his hips, his gut cramping at the anguish blazing in Hank's dark eyes...and the brutal truth of his brother's words.

"Maddie will want to know why you're not coming."

Hank swore, then stomped back to the dumped ladder and snatched it up. "Tell her...actually, I don't give a damn what you tell her. Just as long as everybody leaves me the hell alone."

By mid-November, the colorful, brisk days of fall succumbed to a bleak, bitterly cold early winter. But the weather was the least of Maddie's concerns. She was far too busy trying to find a good woman to steer in Ryan's direction.

Not that she was having much luck.

There'd been Marybeth Reese, the lawyer's secretary who'd called that day everybody thought Sherman was having a heart attack. When Maddie met her in the grocery store, she thought she saw possibilities. But after inviting her over for coffee and seeing how the woman jumped every time one of the kids did something, she changed her mind.

And Tree Sutherland, who ran the gift shop, had looked promising until Maddie decided the funny, pungent odor coming from the back of the shop wasn't incense.

Then, in rapid succession, Maddie disqualified Charmaine Chambers, Ruby's new waitress, who was pretty enough but running short in the brain-cell department; Laura Raley, who ran the bakery, because she always looked like she was on the verge of tears; and Billie Mertz, the librarian. Lord, but the woman could talk your ear off.

Unfortunately, the pool was drying up fast. But at least she wasn't thinking about Ryan so much. Well, she *was*—she'd have to be, wouldn't she, if she was trying to find him a girlfriend?—but not in that "serious trouble" way.

Or so she told herself, at least twenty times a day.

Maddie pulled up alongside the convalescent home where Ned had gone after his release from the hospital, then sat in the car, frowning and picking at a ragged fingernail. Something must've happened when Ryan asked Hank about Thanksgiving, something that went beyond his brother's flat-out refusal to come. Because ever since, Ryan had been more withdrawn than ever.

On a sigh, she got out of the car and headed toward the entrance.

There just had to be a woman out there who'd love him enough to rattle loose whatever was keeping him from having a full life. Somebody who didn't come with three kids and— she thought wearily as she opened the door to Ned's room— a crotchety old great-uncle-by-marriage.

"I want to go home, dammit!" he yelled at Maddie before

she even got all the way inside. "A body can't even take a leak around here without somebody or other gettin' in my way!"

With another sigh, Maddie set the day's food offering on a table beside his bed. As usual, he was sitting in a chair facing the TV in his room, dressed in overalls and a wrinkled plaid flannel shirt. The home made sure his clothes got washed, but ironing was another matter altogether. His hair was combed today, though, at least. "Well, you can't go home, Uncle Ned," she said. "You still need looking after. Besides, your house isn't fit to raise pigs in."

He cussed. Something he did a lot of. Except when she brought the children. He was real good with the children. Especially Amy Rose.

"Nothin' wrong with my house," he muttered.

"Everything's wrong with your house. You know it. I know it. So can we please stop rehashing this conversation?"

To her complete shock, the old man's eyes brimmed with tears. "The food here isn't worth giving to pigs, either," he said, which she might have found funny if he hadn't looked so miserable. She could just imagine what he'd been eating when he was on his own. At least he seemed to be mending pretty good. It was going to take a long while before he got back to normal, if indeed he ever did, but for a seventy-five-year-old man he was doing okay. According to the nurses, he was hell on wheels in that walker of his.

"Ned, I'm sorry. You cannot go back to that shack."

"Then can I come home with you?"

She nearly lost her breath. Granted, he was desperate, but...here she thought she'd have to fight tooth and toenail to convince him to come live with her and the kids, and bless his heart, he thought of it all on his own. Except...

"If I was in my own place, I'd sign you out this minute. But I'm still living with Dr. Logan for another six or seven weeks at least. It's not my house to offer." She reached over and tucked her hand around his. "I'm sorry. I wish there was something I could do."

He looked at her like a little boy who'd just found out Christmas had been cancelled, then nodded.

She reached around to fetch the plate of blueberry muffins she'd made, handing one to him. "It's not so bad here, is it? I mean, the staff seems nice and all. And you've got your own room...."

"Never been in a hospital my entire life," he mumbled, picking apart the muffin and spilling crumbs all down the front of his shirt. "Now I can't seem to get out of one."

"This isn't a hospital, Uncle Ned—"

"Might as well be," he snapped, then shoved a huge bite of muffin into his mouth, half of which landed in his beard. Chewing slowly, he glanced around, sadness drooping his features. "Only real fear I ever had was being left to die in a place like this."

Well, Maddie's heart couldn't have hurt any more if somebody had tried to cut it right out of her body. She leaned over to pluck the biggest of the crumbs off his front, then stood, dumping them in the garbage before going to his closet and pulling out half a dozen or so wrinkled shirts. Honestly, what was she going to do with the men in her life, none of whom she could help in the way they most needed it? She yanked the last shirt off the hanger, thinking there was nothing worse than being a fixer who can't fix a doggone thing.

"Thought I might take these back and iron 'em for you. Can't be comfortable, wearing them all creased like that." When she got to the door, though, she turned around, opened her mouth, and heard herself say, "I'll see what I can do about getting you out of here, okay? I can't promise anything," she added when his face brightened. "But nothing ventured, nothing gained, right?"

"It'd only be for six weeks. Maybe even a little less, if I can get that house before the New Year."

After chewing over how to approach Ryan about Ned for the better part of the afternoon, Maddie decided to just come right out and ask. The baby was asleep; Ryan was outside, raking leaves from the pair of huge sycamores that dominated the front yard, a task he'd been tending to in fits and starts over the past week. At the other end of the lawn, the kids were jumping in the one pile of leaves he'd designated as theirs, occasionally dumping wads of leaves all over each other.

Now he leaned on the rake handle, his blue eyes a stark contrast to all the beiges and browns around him, the flanneled sky overhead. A few stragglers drifted down like a crackly, tawny snow, occasionally bouncing off his head and shoulders. He didn't seem to notice.

He also hadn't said anything yet. She licked her lips and wrapped her arms around herself, the fabric of her old, sorry coat scratching her ungloved fingers.

"And I know I have no right to ask this of you since you've already had enough to deal with, what with me and the kids hanging on forever, but his insurance won't pay for more than a couple weeks, and he just can't go back to his own place."

Okay, so that wasn't exactly the truth. Although she didn't exactly know for sure that it wasn't. It was just that saying Ned simply didn't like being there didn't seem like a compelling enough argument, somehow.

Oh, Lord—why didn't he say something?

"He could stay in that downstairs bedroom, especially as it's got its own bath…"

"Maddie."

"What?"

"Ned's a veteran. Uncle Sam covers all his medical expenses."

"Oh." Her face flamed. "I'm sorry."

"For what? Telling me a story? Or for wanting to help Ned out?"

"For sucking you more and more into my affairs. I should be able to—"

"You should be able to feel you can ask for help, Maddie." He resumed his raking, calmly, quietly. As if nothing or nobody was going to ruffle his feathers. "Without being afraid to. I don't have a problem with Ned staying here."

"Oh. Thank you."

"You're welcome," he said, not even bothering to peer out at her from inside his shell. Across the yard, a laughing Noah dumped more leaves on Katie Grace, who was giggling so hard she could hardly stand up.

All "confuzzled," as Grace used to say, Maddie started to walk away, only to hear Ryan say, "By the way—it's time for your six-week postpartum checkup."

She turned around, blushing all the harder. "Do you really think I need—"

"I figured you'd probably be more comfortable with Ivy doing it than me," he said to the leaves.

"Oh. Yes. Um, thank—"

"You're welcome," he said mildly. Like they hadn't been talking about poking around her inner workings. Of course, he was a doctor. Still, he didn't have to sound so... so...*detached* from it all. And why did she care so darn much?

Why?

The kids' giggles caught her attention again, just for a moment, just enough to enable her to act without thinking. Her heart pounding, Maddie scooped up an armful of leaves from a nearby pile...and dumped them over Ryan's head.

"What on earth—?" He spun around, leaves going every which way.

"Tag!" She poked him and took off across the yard. "You're it!"

Not that her short legs would do her much good if Ryan came after her, she realized as she dashed through one of the leaf piles. She glanced over her shoulder and squealed.

Oh, Lord—he was coming after her all right, huge wads of leaves fisted in both hands. And judging from the look on his face, he was going to make her pay but good. Laughing breathlessly and waving to the kids gawking at her as she zipped past, she took off around the house, squealing again when she heard Ryan's boots pounding behind her. She ducked behind a sixty-foot spruce in the backyard, pretending to be trapped, laughing, laughing...only to dodge him at the last second, sprinting back around to the front, Ryan hot on her heels.

And he was laughing, too.

"Come back here, you little twerp!"

"Who you calling a twerp?" she hollered back, only to let out another yelp when he got close enough to shower her with leaves, some of which got into her mouth. Now laughing and sputtering, she stopped just long enough to re-arm, taking off again…and tripped right over a leaf-smothered tree root. Too close to stop, Ryan plowed right into her, knocking both of them down.

They landed with a *whoomph,* panting and laughing so hard, Maddie's lungs screamed for air. She was vaguely aware of the kids beside her, Katie Grace's sweet little face right in hers, asking if she was okay.

She was, however, extremely aware of Ryan's leg straddling hers, his leaf-speckled face inches away, the way the skin crinkled up at the corners of his eyes, even as his laughter wound down. Then concern flared in his eyes.

"Oh, Lord, Maddie—are you all right?"

"Uh-huh," she said, although she did wonder if maybe she'd hit her head on the root because, frankly, her entire thought process had shut down. For all she knew, she could have a dozen broken bones. All there was, right at this moment, was his body on top of hers, strong and solid and warm and *safe,* his fingers gently brushing leaves from her hair, his breath puffing over her face.

And something in his sweet blue eyes that made her heart foolishly want to believe in dreams again.

Then she squinted at his…face…

"Eeek! There's a spider in your eyebrow!"

Ryan bolted to his knees, swiping at his forehead. Then he frowned at his hand. "Got it."

"Lemme see, lemme see!" the kids said, barreling right over her in their excitement to see dead bug guts, only to make disgusted "ewwww" sounds when Ryan showed them. Then, their attention span all used up, they took off again to the other side of the yard.

Slowly, Maddie propped herself up on her elbows, chuckling at Ryan's continued scrutiny of his inadvertent victim. "Only you would feel sorry for a spider."

Ryan brushed the spider's remains from his palms, then looked down at her, his expression ...wistful? "Only you would dare to start a game of tag with a man who'd almost forgotten how to play."

She pulled herself all the way upright, hugging her knees with one arm while picking bit of leaves out of his hair with her other hand, like it was the most natural thing in the world. Like her entire insides weren't just a'shimmyin' and shakin' for all they were worth.

"Thought maybe it was high time somebody jogged your memory."

Her breath caught as Ryan sighed, then slowly—oh, so slowly—traced one warm knuckle down her cheek.

"We're bad news for each other, Maddie Mae."

She hesitated, her gaze briefly meeting his before returning to his hair. "Why?" she said, barely able to keep her voice steady what with all this shimmying going on inside her. "Because I make you laugh?"

"Yes. Because you make me laugh."

Suddenly exasperated, with him, with herself, with the world at large, she sprang up, brushing leaves off her butt as she walked back to the house. And this time, she didn't stop until she was all the way inside.

Chapter 10

The next ten days passed in a blur, what with getting Uncle Ned settled in and it finally hitting Maddie that she'd never done an entire Thanksgiving dinner on her own before and just how much work it was going to be. She didn't have much time to think about anybody, let alone a certain blasted doctor who was wreaking havoc with her good sense.

But if she'd learned anything from her experience with Jimmy, it was that there was no sense in getting moony over a man who wasn't any good for you. And at least she'd had youth to blame then. At seventeen, what did she know? But she wasn't seventeen now.

Unfortunately, since her heart seemed determined to fight her brain on this issue, Maddie became more determined than ever to jar Ryan Logan out of his stupor and get him dating again, so she and her wayward heart could get on with her life. Of course, finding somebody for Ryan and getting him to actually go out with that somebody were two entirely different things.

But you never knew.

Thus she took it as an encouraging sign when she walked

into the kindergarten classroom for Noah's parent-teacher conference and realized, oh, for pity's sake—she'd completely forgotten about Taylor McIntyre, Noah's teacher. Attractive, thirtyish, ringless, not to mention intelligent, friendly and in a service profession herself. What more could anybody want?

So when Maddie discovered that Miss McIntyre wasn't planning on going home to Texas for Thanksgiving…well, it would have just been downright inhospitable on her part not to invite her to dinner, wouldn't it?

Maddie then swore to herself she'd back off and let nature take its course.

She also swore to herself that she had no right to get upset if it did.

When the alarm shrilled at five-thirty on Thanksgiving morning, Maddie jumped, groaned, then lay there pressing her pounding heart back down inside her chest, wondering what on earth had possessed her to plan dinner for one o'clock? And of course, Amy Rose, who *had* been sleeping through the night for some weeks, decided last night that waking Mama up every two hours was much more entertaining. Yawning so widely her jaw popped, Maddie hiked herself up on one elbow, listening, but all she heard was Amy Rose's soft, even breathing.

Great. *Now* she slept.

Maddie's breasts ached a little with wanting to feed the baby, but having done so no less than four times during the night, she figured playing cow could wait until she got this dang turkey in the oven. Stumbling around the bed, she stripped off her nightgown and yanked on the same pair of jeans and sweatshirt she'd been wearing yesterday, not bothering to put on a bra (she'd stopped leaking a month ago and besides, she didn't figure the turkey would much care) or run a comb through her hair. She did, however make a quick sidetrip into the bathroom to do her business and brush her teeth, although she didn't suppose the turkey would much care if she had morning breath, either.

By this time, she could pretty much keep both eyes open

simultaneously, although she still hung on to the banister more tightly than usual as she descended the stairs—

Was that coffee she smelled?

Telling herself exhaustion was making her hallucinate, she pushed open the kitchen door, only to let out a yip when she found Ryan sitting at the table in the semidarkness, sipping his coffee. Thank goodness he hadn't turned on his music. Mozart this early would've sent her right over the edge.

Tucking her arms over her midsection against the early morning chill, and ignoring the coffee she couldn't have as long as she was nursing, she glowered at the shadowy male shape in front of her. "Ryan Logan, you don't have the good sense God gave you. What in tarnation are you doing up at this hour?"

"Figured you might need help getting the turkey into the oven...*damn* it, Maddie—" His hand shot up to shield his eyes from the sudden glare when she switched on the overhead light. "Warn somebody before you do that."

"Serves you right for scaring me half to death." She shuffled over to the counter and grabbed the cutting board, which slipped from her hand, making a godawful clatter against the Formica. "And why, exactly, do I need help getting the turkey in the oven?"

"Maybe because the damn thing's bigger'n my truck. There's no way you can lift that without spraining something. How much does it weigh, anyway?"

"Twenty-three pounds," she snapped, dragging celery, onions and mushrooms out of a crisper drawer. "Although I don't suppose it occurred to you how it got in the refrigerator to begin with. Not to mention into the grocery buggy—" she slammed down the celery "—from the buggy into my car—" and the bag of onions "—and finally, from the car to the kitchen." She jangled open the utensil door, rattling around inside it for a good five seconds before she found the knife she was looking for.

After a pause, Ryan said, "And here I always thought you were a morning person."

"Long as it's dark, it's still night in my book."

Ryan slowly got up from the chair, stretched, then lumbered over to the refrigerator. "I hate to point this out, but this whole shebang was your idea."

Maddie decided not to tell him he was losing points fast. Except then a glass of orange juice appeared in front of her.

So she stopped banging and clattering long enough to gulp down the juice, which she had to admit perked her up some. Then she flicked a glance in Ryan's direction as he hauled the enormous bird out of the refrigerator, deciding maybe letting somebody else wrestle with a dead bird that weighed nearly as much as her three-year-old wasn't such a bad idea. With her luck, she'd probably have ended up on the floor pinned underneath the dang thing, where nobody would have found her for hours, soaked in turkey juice and breastmilk.

"Okay, fine," she said. "You can help." Then she waved the knife at him. "But as soon as this bird's in the oven, you're to go right back to bed, you hear?"

"Only if you don't need me to help with something else."

"Trust me," she said, knife now whomping against wood as she sliced celery, "the best thing you can do for me is stay out of my way. If I'm going to make an idiot of myself, I'd rather do it without an audience, thank you."

He thunked the still wrapped turkey into the sink, fumbled in the nearby drawer for a pair of scissors to slit the plastic. "Thought you said you knew what you were doing?"

"In theory, yes. I helped Grace do Thanksgiving every year I was there. Just never handled the whole thing on my own."

Ryan discarded the shredded turkey wrapper in the garbage, then frowned at her. "Then how come you're doing it now?"

"I told you. As a way of sayin' thank you."

"And?"

Her brows lifted but she didn't lose her rhythm. "Who says there's an 'and'?"

Underneath his sweatshirt, his shoulders hitched as he removed the neck and package of giblets from assorted turkey orifices. "Just figured there was in your case."

She thought on that a moment, then said, "Okay. I guess

Saving Dr. Ryan

I see this as kind of a rite of passage. Doing Thanksgiving officially makes me a woman.''

"I'm supposed to run cold water over this, right?"

"Hey. You've done this before."

"Just this part. With my mother. Nobody else'd get up this early. Past this point, I'm clueless." Then he said in a low voice, "And by the way, I'd say you've officially been a woman for some time, Maddie."

She froze. Here she stood at five-thirty-something in the morning, braless, showerless, her hair looking like an abused doll's, and unless she was sorely mistaken, the onion-and-raw-turkey-scented air was crackling with sexual electricity.

Of course, she could be hallucinating, being still half-asleep and all. After all, only a blind man would want her in her present state.

"And here I wasn't sure you even thought of me as a woman, Dr. Logan."

She could feel his gaze searing the side of her face. Then he reached over to get the foil roasting pan she'd picked up when she bought the turkey. Several more seconds passed while he loaded fowl into pan, washed his hands.

Maddie just kept on chopping.

Except she started at the touch of Ryan's fingertips on her chin, gently turning her face to his. And before she could catch her breath…he did.

His morning whiskers tickled a little, but in a nice kind of way. But his lips…oh, my. Oh, my, my, my… And oh, was she ever glad she'd brushed her teeth.

Then it was over, and he was walking away, and all she could do was stand there, staring stupidly at his back.

"Ryan?"

When he reached the door, he twisted back, his hand clamped on the frame. He looked…shell-shocked. "Holler when you're ready for me to put the bird in the oven," he said. "I'll be in my office."

Her mouth twisted, Maddie frowned at the window at the lightening sky.

This did not bode well for the rest of the day.

*   *   *

What the blue blazes had just come over him?

Ryan jerked back his desk chair and crashed into it, then rammed his head into his hands.

Hey, Logan—it was just a kiss.

Yeah, well, he could tell himself it was *just a kiss* from now until Doomsday but that didn't change the fact that he *had* kissed her, and he had *wanted* to, and God help him, he wanted to again. And again. And maybe a hundred thousand times more after that.

On a groan, Ryan dragged his hands away from his now pounding head long enough to peer at the calendar on the back of his desk. Ever since their tumble in the leaves, he'd ordered his errant longings to lie down and shut up. And every…damn…time he'd hear her laugh or see her smile or catch a whiff of her scent in a room she'd just been in, those errant longings reared their horny little heads and laughed themselves stupid. New Year's was five weeks away, give or take. Five more weeks of having Maddie around where he could see her and smell her and want her…

He'd go insane. Completely, out-of-his gourd, insane.

Of course, if he'd managed to exercise any sort of control back there in the kitchen, he might have had half a chance of retaining some semblance of sanity. But *nooooo,* he had to *kiss* her.

And he thought her baby was a lip magnet.

A slight noise made him look up to see Mama Lip Magnet standing in his doorway, arms crossed, brows dipped, looking half-perplexed, half-pissed. Make that three-quarters pissed. If he'd ever entertained the slightest doubt about her not being a child, that expression alone would have cured him of his misconception.

If the way she kissed hadn't already.

"Turkey time?" he said, hoping against hope this was all a bad dream.

"Depends if you're talking about the one in the kitchen or the one sitting here in front of me."

He sighed. "I suppose I had that coming."

"Yes, you did. You want to explain what that was all about?"

"I..." Frowning, he shook his head. "No."

"No, you don't? Or, no, you can't?"

"Either. Both."

"Men," she muttered, spinning on her heel and tromping down the hall.

Long about ten o'clock, Ivy called. "I'm so sorry to do this to you at the last minute, but I can't come."

Maddie practically fainted. "Oh, no, Ivy...don't say that. I *neeeeed* you."

After a long silence, the midwife said. "That sounds ominous."

Oops. "Um, I could just really use the moral support, is all. Besides, who's going to pick up Mildred?"

"Oh, I can bring Mildred, don't you worry about that, but..." She lowered her voice. "Dawn showed up out of the blue a few minutes ago—"

"So bring her. What's the big deal?"

"Cal."

"Oh, for heaven's sake—that was, what, ten years ago? And nothing even happened, did it?"

Ivy sighed. "I know, but..."

"He's a big boy, Ivy. I'm sure he can handle being with his ex...whatever she was for a couple hours. Besides, it's not like you've got fixings for Thanksgiving dinner in your house, since you're supposed to be having it here—"

"She's apparently *engaged*," Ivy said in an even lower voice. "And he's *with her*."

Maddie stopped zipping long enough to think about this for a minute. Then she flapped her hand and said, "Unless the man has fleas, bring him along, too. Like I said, Cal will just have to cope. Or if he is carrying a torch, maybe that will cure him."

Just like she was having to cope with thinking about Ryan and his kiss when she didn't want to be thinking about Ryan and his kiss and shouldn't be thinking about it because she was a grown woman and grown women didn't hyperventilate over a single kiss.

Not even grown women who'd only been kissed by one other man their entire lives.

"If you're sure…"

"I'm sure. So we'll see you at one." That crisis was no sooner resolved, however, when Noah called from the living room.

"Mama! Katie Grace just barfed all over the floor—!"

"When the hell you plannin' on servin' this meal, gal?" Uncle Ned came thumping into the kitchen, effectively blocking her exit. "I'm like to starve to death—"

"Have a roll or something. That'll hold you until one—"

"*One?* I'll be dead by then!"

Maddie tamped down the urge to bonk him one with her wooden spoon. "I sincerely doubt that, old man. Besides, I fixed you oatmeal an hour ago."

He screwed up his face. "Oatmeal! Tryin' to poison me, more like! Bacon and eggs, that's what I need! A *man's* food, not this sissy stuff—"

"*Mama!*"

"I'm coming, I'm coming!"

She shoved past Ned and out of the kitchen, only to run smack into Ryan, who was already carting Katie off to…well, she had no idea what he was going to do with her, and right now, she didn't much care.

"Looks like she got into a bag of cookies or something," Ryan said, looking at her, but not quite. "No fever, no pain. Just ten gallons of half-digested Oreos all over the living room floor. You go on back to whatever you have to do, we'll be fine."

Gee. Oreo barf in front of her, Uncle Ned behind her. What a choice.

Why was it again she'd thought this would be such a good idea?

The rest of the morning passed with relatively few additional traumas, however, so that by the time the guests started to arrive at twelve-thirty, Maddie—in a new beige turtleneck sweater and matching leggings—actually felt more or less in control. The turkey was out of the oven and "resting," the gravy was made, the mashed potatoes were done (and not too lumpy), and everything else was either finished or ready to go.

And the table…well, it did look pretty darned good, if she said so herself. Even if the chairs didn't all match. But with the lace tablecloth and Ivy's mother's china and a new set of Oneida flatware Ryan had bought at the Wal-Mart…

"Eat your heart out, Martha Stewart," she muttered under her breath as she set two of those pretty floral tubs of margarine on either end of the table.

"I don't know which I like more," Ryan said behind her, making her jump. Again. She turned to find him leaning against the wide doorway between the dining room and the living room, his hands stuffed in his khakis' pockets, wearing a blue shirt a bit darker than his eyes. He wouldn't exactly meet her gaze, but at least he was smiling. Sorta. "The way it smells in here, or the way it looks."

She beamed. Well, shoot, she couldn't help it. Then she looked back at the table, frowning a little. "You think folks'll mind the plastic cups?"

"With all that food you've got in there," Ryan said, nodding back toward the kitchen, "I somehow doubt anyone's going to notice."

Silence jangled between them for several seconds.

"I really am sorry for what happened earlier this morning," he said.

Which is where she should have said, "Don't worry about it," or "Me, too" or something equally reassuring. Instead she opened her mouth and out pranced, "Well, I'm not."

Took her a second or two to realize the loud booming in her head was the sound of her heartbeat. Or maybe it was Ryan's, since, judging from his poleaxed expression, his heart was probably chugging along quite nicely, too.

"I m-mean," she said, wondering what on earth was going to come out next since she didn't have the slightest idea what she meant by that, "um, it's, uh, just been a long time since I've been kissed, is all."

Then she tried a "see—nothing to worry about!" smile.

"Hot damn, it sure smells good in here!" boomed from just outside the dining room, making both of them jump. Looking taller than ever in jeans, an open-necked flannel shirt and a corduroy jacket, and grinning as usual, Cal clapped Ryan on the shoulder, then strode over and gave Maddie a big hug. And a bunch of yellow and bronze chrysanthemums.

Out of the corner of her eye, Maddie caught Ryan's glower.

"Cal! These for me?"

"Well, they sure aren't for anybody else, sugar." He gaze drifted to the table; shaking his head, he let out a low, long whistle. "If this doesn't bring back memories, I don't know what does," he said softly. His lips moving, he counted the places, then frowned. "Eleven places? Who all did you invite?"

"Oh, we're having a couple extras," she said casually, fiddling for the hundredth time with the centerpiece she'd pulled together from the backyard.

And wondering for the hundredth time if a person could die from good intentions.

Some three hours later, she was still wondering.

"All in all," Ivy said, handing Maddie the turkey platter to dry, since the dishwasher was too full to cram in one more thing, "I'd say it didn't go too badly."

Maddie just managed to tamp down a semihysterical laugh. "Other than Cal and your daughter's fiancé nearly coming to blows, you mean?"

"Every holiday needs some entertainment. And Hank showed up," she added softly.

"For what? Twenty minutes?"

"It's a start, honey. No, actually, it's a miracle. One you can take full credit for."

Suddenly too tired to move another inch, Maddie set the platter on the counter and collapsed into one of the kitchen chairs, smiling when Katie Grace came over and crawled into her lap. It had been a day and half, that was for sure. She smoothed down Katie's flyaway hair before resting her cheek on her daughter's head. On the positive side, she'd pulled off the cooking part of things without a hitch (even Ned, she noticed, had eaten too fast to grouse about anything). Katie was fine after the too-many-cookies-in-the-tummy episode and there'd been no further child-related disasters, and Amy Rose had gone down for her afternoon sleep, good as gold.

Then there were the negatives.

The Hank business, for one thing. True, he showed up, halfway through dinner. But how much of a miracle that was, she didn't know, seeing as he barely said three words to anybody—other than to compliment Maddie on the meal—and then left before dessert.

As for her big plans for Ryan and Noah's teacher…well, the one thing she hadn't taken into account was Cal, who moved in for the kill before Ryan even got a chance to say "hi." Not that it wasn't perfectly obvious to everybody in the room that Cal only made eyes at Taylor for Dawn's benefit. Or—more likely—Dawn's boyfriend Andrew. Who she'd caught tsking at the plastic cups.

And yes, Ryan did get called away.

About ten minutes before Hank arrived.

Aware that Katie Grace had become a snoring lead weight in her lap, Maddie struggled to her feet, whispering to Ivy that she was just going to lay her down for her nap, she'd be right back.

There really was no accounting for how balled-up she felt inside. Wasn't like she didn't know how messy life could be, or how often plans fell apart. And Ryan had warned her that he'd probably not be able to stay. It was just…

Her unformed thought fizzled out on a weary sigh.

As Maddie passed by the living room, she caught sight of Noah and Uncle Ned sitting side by side on the sofa in front of a football game on TV. Their faces were creased in almost identical scowls; their arms both crossed tightly across their chests. Mildred Rafferty, all gussied up in a frilly blue dress that Maddie guessed was a good thirty years old, sat primly in the wing chair nearby, waiting for Ivy to take her home. The old woman asked a question about what was going on; Ned swatted at her, told her to hush until the commercial. As Maddie headed upstairs with Katie, she heard Mildred tell Ned in no uncertain terms he was a rude old man and should be ashamed of himself.

Maddie glanced over the banister just in time to see Ned's scowl deepen even further.

When Ryan got back around ten, damned if Maddie wasn't mopping the kitchen floor, of all things. Just the thought of it made him tired.

"It's amazing how much mess a body can make just cooking a single meal," she said, her voice more gravelly than usual. Then her mouth pursed as she scrubbed the life out of one particular spot near the stove.

"Um…that's been there ever since I can remember," Ryan said.

"Then it's high time it came off." She glanced up, swiping her hair out of her face with the back of her hand. "For heaven's sake—sit down before you fall down."

He didn't argue. Couldn't have if he'd wanted to.

"Hank came," she said quietly, and Ryan nearly jolted out of his skin.

"You're kidding?"

"Nope. Didn't stay long, though." She squatted down, scraped at something with her thumbnail for a second or two, then stood again. "Maybe next time he'll actually make it all the way through dessert."

Before Ryan had a chance to wrap his head around this bit of news, Maddie said, "You were gone a long time. What happened?"

Ryan let a yawn come, then knuckled the hollow at the base of his neck. "Took longer than I expected, too. Had to go out to Sam Frazier's. Widower with six kids, has a farm out near Cal's place. One of his cows kicked him hard enough to break his leg. His oldest girl, Libby, was the one who called me. The break was far too complicated for me to set here, so

I had to get him to Claremore as well as find somebody who could keep an eye on the kids, since Libby's only twelve herself.''

Big gray, empathetic eyes fastened to his. ''And how old's the youngest?''

''A toddler. Two, maybe? Jeannette, his wife, died from a freak aneurysm last year. She was my age. Sat next to me in Mr. Fry's Biology class in high school, in fact.'' A strange ache spread through his chest. ''She and Sam'd been sweethearts since they were kids.''

''That's so sad.'' Her brow creased, Maddie let out a sigh, then, shaking her head, went to rinse the mop in the sink. ''Still. I bet it's a comfort to that poor man, thinking about the time he *did* get to spend with his wife.''

Ryan slouched back in the chair, his hands clasped on his stomach, watching Maddie's strong, slender back as she wrung out the mop, the way her tiny hands soundly gripped the handle when she slung it back out onto the floor. ''You've got a real romantic streak, don't you?''

A beat or two passed before she said, her words coming out in breathless clumps as she scrubbed, ''Depends on…what you mean…by 'romantic.' I sure don't think of love…in terms of candy and…flowers and a fantasy world…where everything is perfect.'' She hauled up the mop to slap it against the floor a few feet farther away. ''To me, love—true love—is…carin' enough for somebody to…ride out the bad times…together, as well as…the good.'' She stopped, panting slightly, swiping the back of her wrist across her cheek. ''Love means not being afraid to let somebody else see your flaws. And being able to live with somebody else's.''

''In other words, being willing to hang on to the bitter end?''

One eyebrow lifted. ''It means not bailing at the first sign of trouble, that's for sure. It also means having the courage to be honest with somebody you love when the path he's chosen isn't doing him any favors. Which is where I made my mistake with Jimmy,'' she said, a split second before the conversation veered off into a direction Ryan did not wish it to go. "There's a difference between sticking by somebody and silently watching him destroy himself. I told myself I was just trying to keep the marriage together, for the sake of the kids, you know? Instead, all I was doing was contributing to its demise." On a short, humorless laugh, she picked up the mop, plopping it back into the sink. "A mistake I won't ever make again, believe you me."

Again, he watched her back muscles bunch and shift through her baggy sweatshirt, tenderness flooding through him like irrigation water through a parched field.

"For what it's worth," he said to her back, "I don't think I've had a Thanksgiving dinner that good in twenty years."

Her movements hitched for a second, then she continued wringing out the mop. Not until she'd leaned it against the counter to dry did she finally say, "What you got of it."

Tired or not, Ryan didn't miss the edge to her voice. "I warned you—"

"I know you did." She leaned back against the counter, her arms folded over her ribs. "And I'm sure that man and his children were grateful to you, for being there and getting them through that."

"But you're still ticked."

She blew out a sigh. "Not because you had to leave. And certainly not because you're devoted to your patients." Her brows nearly met, she frowned so hard. "It just…doesn't seem right, somehow, that you don't have any life of your own."

"This *is* my life, Maddie."

"But it doesn't have to be. Not this way. Not all day, every day, never knowing from one minute to the next whether you'll even be able to finish a meal or get a solid night's sleep."

Irritation began to creep in, souring his earlier feelings. "That's the lot of a country doctor. You know that."

"I also know about the other doctors who've been after you about going into that clinic with them. Ivy told me," she added at his lifted brows. "So it's not like you don't have any options. For whatever reason, you don't *want* to make your life easier. Habit, is all this is, and don't try denying it.''

His arms tightening across his chest, Ryan hooked Maddie's gaze in his. ''When these people call, they expect to get *me.* Somebody they know and trust. I've got no right to go changing the rules on them.''

''You know these other two doctors?''

He frowned harder. ''Well, yeah…''

''You trust 'em?''

''They're both fine physicians. What are you getting at?''

''That maybe you should give your patients some credit that they can learn to trust 'em, too. That maybe you taking a night off once in a blue moon wouldn't bend folks out of shape as much as you think it would.''

''And maybe how I live my life is my business.''

Gray eyes met blue, unflinching. ''Yes, I suppose that's true enough. But like I said. From now on, I see a problem, I say something about it. You're free to listen to me or not, I really don't give a flying fig. So…are you hungry? 'Cause if you are, I could warm up some leftovers—''

''*Dammit,* Maddie!'' He rocketed from the chair, even though he had no idea where to go after that. ''No, I'm not hungry! And if I am, I can fix myself something to eat!''

She recoiled slightly, something like hurt swimming in her eyes for a moment before she took off for the door. Remembering all over again why he preferred living on his own, Ryan cut her off, her shoulders tense under his palms when he turned her around. She met his gaze, angry tears glinting in her eyes.

''I'm sorry, Maddie,'' Ryan said on an exhaled breath. ''I didn't mean to yell. What with everything that's happened today, I'm just on edge, is all. But for crying out loud, honey—your debt is long since paid. You've got to move past this thing you have about putting everybody else's needs ahead of your own.''

Maddie let out a choked laugh. ''Look who's talking!''

He felt his mouth twist into a wry smile. ''Okay, point taken. But it's different for me—''

"No it's not. You forget I've been watching you in action for more than two months now. You *thrive* on taking care of other people, same as me. It's just that all I can do is cook and clean and maybe stick together a few branches to make a centerpiece. Making a home is all I know how to do. All I *want* to do—"

She clamped shut her mouth and twisted away, hugging herself and shaking her head.

"Maddie?"

For the space of several heartbeats, there was no sound except for the *chink-chink-chink* of the sweep hand of the clock, the hum of the refrigerator. Then finally she turned back around, her mouth twisted.

"See, when I got married, I was still all wrapped up in fantasies, about what love was supposed to be, about what married life was supposed to be. Only as we all know, it didn't turn out that way." She looked down at the toe of her shoe, then back up at him. "So I guess I was putting too much on this one dinner. I just wanted it to be perfect."

Ryan didn't completely understand, but since the next line was clearly his, he came up with, "It's not up to you to fix the world, honey."

"I don't want to fix the world any more than you want to take care of everyone in it! I just wanted to have a nice holiday for once in my life!"

She sucked in a sharp breath, apparently startled at her own vehemence.

Ryan leaned back against the counter, bracing the edge in his hands. "Like the ones you used to have with your foster parents?"

Her gaze jerked to his. Then she nodded.

"That's not such an unreasonable thing to want, honey."

"I wonder," she said on an exhaled breath.

"So tell me," he said, because clearly his brain wasn't firing on all cylinders, "did part of your wanting things to be *perfect* include inviting Noah's teacher to dinner?"

He could see her pulse kick up in the hollow of her throat.

"I told you," she said at last. "She just didn't have anywhere else to go—"

"And her being single didn't have anything to do with it?"

Out went that damn chin. "Of course not."

"Right. Maddie, I've been on the receiving end of far too many matchmaking attempts not to recognize them a mile off."

Finally, on a sharp sigh, she said, "It was just a thought. Forget it."

"I intend to. Besides, I don't need anybody but—"

You.

The word caught in his throat like a chunk of wood, while farther down his heart hammered ferociously, desperately, against his rib cage—a prisoner trying to escape its cell.

"Myself," he finished, finally, somehow.

She apparently found that humorous. "Oh, for heaven's sake, Ryan—anybody with one eye and half a brain can see how lonely you are."

He nearly reeled. "*Lonely?* Hell, who's got time to be lonely?"

Silence stuttered between them for several seconds before she turned to go, only to turn when she reached the doorway. "Ask yourself why you kissed me this morning," she said, "and I think you'll find your answer."

Chapter 11

This time, Hank was in the motel office, standing behind the counter at his computer, his expression pretty much matching the stormy weather outside. Not to mention the Wagner opera blasting from inside his apartment. His dark eyes darted to Ryan when he came in, then back at the computer screen as he steadily clicked away at the keyboard with one hand.

"Wipe your feet. I just vacuumed."

"Yes, mother." Ryan plopped his soaked hat on the coat-rack by the door. "Weather's sure a bitch today."

Hank grunted, then said, "I take it you didn't come by to give me a weather report."

"No." Already roasting—why'd Hank have the heat cranked up so high?—Ryan unbuttoned his shearling coat. "Heard you stopped by yesterday."

Underneath a plaid flannel shirt worn open over a button-front T-shirt, one broad shoulder hitched. "Figured long as Maddie'd gone to all that trouble..."

"Shame you couldn't've stayed longer, though."

Hank's hand stilled over the keyboard. "I couldn't hack it, Ry," he said, not looking at him. "I tried, but—"

"S'okay, don't worry about it."

That got a sharp nod. Then Ryan said, "But I didn't come about that. Actually, I was wondering if you might be able to help me with something."

Hank lifted his head, guarded interest hovering in his eyes. "Such as?"

"Seems Maddie lost contact with her last set of foster parents after she got married. All I know is their name and that they lived at the time in Fayetteville, Arkansas. Not much to go on, but—"

Hank's eyes narrowed. "She ask you to look them up for her?"

"No. I get the feeling there was some misunderstanding or other, that she hasn't gotten in touch with them because she's afraid to."

"Which you naturally took as an open invitation to go sticking your nose in where it doesn't belong."

Ryan thought of his and Maddie's conversation in the kitchen the night before and felt his mouth torque into a grimace. "It's the least I can do."

Hank's dark brows lifted at that, but all he said was, "Well, if they're still there, you could start by trying the Fayetteville phone book."

"Which is not something I'm likely to trip over in Haven, am I?"

His brother resumed his infernal key-clicking. "It is if you know where to look, smartass. What's these people's name?"

"Idlewild. Grace and George."

More clicking, more scowling. A couple more taps…then Hank twisted the monitor around. And there it was: a White Pages listing for George Idlewild in Fayetteville, Arkansas.

"That was too easy," Ryan said, entering the number into his cell phone.

"Which should probably tell you right there," Hank said, "to watch your butt."

"Maddie Kincaid," Ruby whispered down from her perch atop a ladder, her hands full of silver tinsel garland, "you are one crazy woman."

Rooting through a box of Ruby's Christmas decorations for the diner—being the day after Thanksgiving, with most folks gone over to Claremore or even to Tulsa to shop, the place was nearly empty—Maddie glanced over at the back booth where she'd parked Mildred and Uncle Ned, who'd actually been having something like a civil conversation for the past ten minutes or so over bowls of Ruby's turkey noodle soup. Noah and Katie Grace were in the kitchen with Jordy, who had put them to work doing heaven-knew-what, and the baby was sound asleep in her baby seat right next to Mildred in the booth.

"Yeah, I've heard that before," she said with a grin that wasn't as forced as it might have been an hour ago.

It had been some morning, one she wouldn't wish on another living soul. She'd promised to take Mildred over to the Wal-Mart before she remembered that the kids didn't have day care or school, so they'd have to go along. Then Uncle Ned had made so much noise about never getting out anymore, she'd had to take him, too, walker and all. Add the awful weather to the mix, not to mention the fact that most of Eastern Oklahoma had had the same idea, and Maddie was frankly surprised she had any brain cells left.

"Where you want this?" she asked, holding up a green and gold foil Merry Christmas sign.

"That goes right in the window, over the center booth." Maddie trooped over as Ruby stapled a swag of tinsel to the ceiling, then carefully lowered her ample form to terra firma in order to drag the ladder over to the next spot. She positioned the ladder, wiggled it with her hand to make sure it was steady, then closed the distance between herself and Maddie and whispered, "I like to fell over when I saw you bring those two in together."

Maddie looked over at the elderly couple again, then back at Ruby. "Why?"

"Obviously you don't know."

"Obviously I don't know what?"

"Only that Mildred Jones—well, she was a Jones before she got married—was Ned McAllister's big love, once upon a time."

Maddie blinked. "You're kidding?"

"Uh-uh. Not that I think she ever knew, seeing as she'd been in love with J.T. forever."

"Oh, my word." Maddie had to fight to keep from staring at them. Then she wrinkled her nose at Ruby. "How come the doctor never said anything?"

"Probably because he didn't know. Few people did. Like I said, Mildred wasn't aware of Ned's feelings, far as I know. And Ned never *told* a living soul."

"Then how do *you* know?"

"From my mama, who heard it from my grandma, who used to clean for Mildred's mama, back in the dark ages. See, when Ned got out of the service and came back here to live, oh, that must've been going on…Lordy, was it really thirty years ago? Anyway, I guess that got Mama to thinking about him and what Granny had told her, that she'd sometimes see Ned walk by Mildred's house when he didn't figure on anybody seein' him. Once he even apparently left a bunch of flowers with no name tag or anything, 'cept Granny saw him skeddadling away from there." She laughed softly. "Hard to think of that old codger wearin' his heart on his sleeve for a gal, isn't it?"

Well, Maddie very nearly just sat right down in the middle of the floor and started crying at that. Honestly—between that poor Sam Frazier losing his wife, and her own convoluted feelings about Ryan, and now hearing of yet another love-gone-awry story…she simply wasn't sure how much more buffeting her poor bedraggled emotions could take, and that was the God's honest truth.

"Honey—you okay?"

Maddie willed the stinging behind her eyelids to stop, pasted a smile on her face and nodded. "Just tired out after yesterday, is all."

"How'd that go, by the way?"

Maddie gave Ruby the *Reader's Digest* version of the day,

leaving out all the parts she didn't want to either think about or discuss, if not both. Which pretty much left Ryan out of the discussion altogether. Then she said, since she'd been talking about how she'd made too many pies and they'd be eating pumpkin and apple pie for a week, "By the way, I was wondering if you might be interesting in having me bake some pies for you?" (She only put forth this idea since Ruby had once confided how much she and Jordy both hated to bake.) "Sadie Metcalf paid her bill in put-by peaches this month. And I've got a whole bushel of apples the Andrews brought over a couple weeks ago. Real nice green pie apples. Seems a shame to let them go to waste, especially since the doctor said I could do anything I liked with them."

Ruby cocked her head at her. "You make good pies?"

"Ruby Kennedy," Maddie said with the first real grin she'd had all day, "I make *great* pies. Just ask Ryan."

She didn't even catch her goof until she realized Ruby's dark-eyed gaze was glued to the side of her face. When she looked up, Ruby said, "Ryan?"

Blood rushed to Maddie's cheeks. Only before she could think of a single blessed thing to say that wouldn't just get her into more trouble, Hootch Atkins ambled in, on the hunt for coffee. With a laugh, Ruby told him to go on ahead and help himself. But when he spotted Maddie, he got this moony expression on his face.

"C'n I get you a cup of coffee, too, Miss Maddie?"

She smiled for him, but politely declined. Ruby just rolled her eyes.

It was nearly two-thirty by the time she dropped off Mildred and then got everybody else back home. Even Noah didn't protest a nap today (for which Maddie said a silent prayer of thanks), Amy Rose was still asleep, and Ned—more subdued than she could recall ever seeing him—had wandered off to his room. For which she sent up a second prayer of thanks. Frankly she wouldn't mind a nap herself this afternoon. Much as she loved doing for people, she wasn't averse to a half-hour to herself now and again. Or even fifteen minutes.

But first—her mouth twisted at the sight of all the blue plastic bags littering the kitchen table and counters—she had to put away all this *stuff.*

She pushed herself through her tasks in record time, then drifted out to the living room. The baby, bless her heart, was still snoozing in her seat, set in a spot on the floor where the drafts couldn't get to her, her little paper-thin eyelids fluttering in a dream. With a somewhat contented—and exhausted— sigh, Maddie collapsed onto the sofa.

She awoke with a start a little later, disoriented and fuzzy. Bolting upright, her gaze zipped to Amy, who was scrooching up her face the way she did when she was cranking up for her next feed. But then Maddie heard noises from the kitchen and figured she'd better check in case one of the kids was trying to help him or herself to something they shouldn't.

She scooped the baby out of her seat, talking nonsense to her as she carried her to the kitchen, where she found, not the children, but Ned, glowering at usual and banging cupboard doors while hanging on to the walker.

"Need help finding something, Uncle Ned?"

He jerked, nearly knocking over the walker. "Dammit, woman—why you have to sneak up a on a body like that?"

"I didn't sneak and you watch your language, old man. I'm not gonna have a cuss word be the first thing out of my baby's mouth."

"Sorry," he grumbled. "Didn't know you had her with you. Where are those cookies you bought today? Can't find 'em anywhere."

On a bemused sigh, Maddie walked over and lifted the top off the cookie jar.

"Oh," Ned said, reaching inside.

"What am I gonna do with you?" she said softly, one- handedly putting the kettle on for tea. Uncle Ned did like his tea. Or maybe it was he just liked having somebody to make it for him. In some ways, he was just like a little boy. But then, she thought with a wry smile, most men were.

Today, especially, there was something about him...an unsettled look in his eyes, the way his whole body seemed to droop, that just tore at Maddie's heart. She didn't dare press him, though. If he felt like confiding in her, she'd be there. But it'd probably been a long, long time since he'd opened up to anybody. If ever. He might not even know how.

The kettle shrieked, startling both her and the baby, who was now trying to suck on Maddie's jaw. So she didn't lollygag about fixing Ned his tea and carting it over to the kitchen table, where he'd planted himself, along with a half-dozen oatmeal cookies.

"You fixin' to feed her?" he said, nodding his thanks for the tea.

"Uh-huh." She reached over to get a napkin, handing it to him to put underneath the cookies. "You mind if—?"

"No, no. You go right ahead."

So Maddie settled herself and her daughter, carefully arranging herself and the baby so that there was nothing showing. When she looked up, though, she nearly gasped at the sight of tears cresting on Ned's lower lids.

"Uncle Ned!" With her free hand, she reached over and grabbed his. "What's wrong?"

No answer.

She hauled in a deep breath and said, "Tell me about Mildred."

His heavy brows flicked up in surprise, but he didn't say anything for a good half a minute, maybe even longer. "How do you know about Mildred?" he finally asked, but she sensed more relief than irritation in his voice.

"Does it matter?" she asked, hoping like heck it didn't.

Slowly he shook his head.

Then he started to talk.

Ryan heard the voices in the kitchen when he came in. Ned's, rough as a pitted road. Then Maddie's, rough, too, but more like a kitten's tongue.

He'd gotten used to hearing other voices in his house. Maybe he wouldn't go so far as to say he *liked* it, but he was used to it. These voices, though…he strained to hear the overtones as he walked back toward the kitchen.

Once at the door, however, he stopped. Ned's back was to him, Maddie sitting close enough to hold his hand. That alone was cause for amazement, since Ryan couldn't imagine Ned McAllister letting anyone touch him like that.

But then, this was Maddie they were talking about.

A tiny crease marred the space between her brows as she sat there, so intent on whatever her uncle was telling her, she didn't notice Ryan right off. Amy Rose had fallen asleep in her other arm, at an angle that couldn't have been comfortable. But either Maddie didn't mind or didn't notice, focused as she was on whatever was going on with Ned.

A pang that was equal parts longing and envy shot through Ryan.

She gave Ned's hand a squeeze, then let go to shift the tiny weight in her arms, her gaze catching Ryan standing there. If his presence startled her any, she didn't let on. Instead, her lips curved in a gentle, welcoming smile.

The kind of smile a man might expect—hope—to see on his wife's face at the end of a long day.

"This could be yours," whispered through his brain, his heart, his aching, traitorous body.

What a fool. What a dadblamed fool. But why? Why should this tiny scrap of a woman be setting him on fire like this?

"Ask yourself," Maddie'd said, *"why you kissed me this morning, and I think you'll find your answer."*

Telling himself he'd only be interrupting something private between Maddie and her uncle, Ryan forced himself to walk away.

Telling himself that maybe Maddie was right, maybe he did need to start claiming some control over his so-called life, he went to his office and dragged over the local phone book, such as it was.

Telling himself it would do him good to maybe get out for a couple hours, he looked up Taylor McIntyre's number.

Telling himself he hadn't just gone over the edge, he dialed it.

* * *

Ned lowered himself into the chair in the downstairs bedroom and clicked the remote to the small TV Maddie had found for him at a yard sale. Supper would be in about an hour, she'd said. Leftovers from yesterday, he supposed, but that was okay. His niece was a damn good cook. She even fixed vegetables so he could eat them and not gag.

He reached up to scratch his face, thinking maybe it was time to ditch the beard, thinking about how good that turkey and homemade gravy was going to taste, about how he wasn't quite as fired up about going back to his own place as he'd thought he'd be. Funny how easily a body gets spoiled. Take having a TV, for instance. All those years without, and now... Not that there was a whole lot on worth watching, but he found some of the talk shows entertaining. Never knew there were that many stupid people in the world.

He frowned at that, lowering the volume in case the kids were still napping. If anybody'd said he'd feel much better for confiding in somebody about his feelings for Mildred, he'd've told 'em in no uncertain terms where to get off. But, you know, secrets were bitches to carry around, even ones that didn't hurt anybody. And he appreciated how Maddie had only said he oughta *think* about telling Mildred how he felt, not that he *should,* like most women would, most women being convinced they had a direct link to God. But when he'd said no, he didn't think that'd be a smart idea, she'd backed right off, swearing she'd never breathe a word to anybody, especially Mildred. Ned saw no reason not to believe her. She was a good gal, that Maddie.

And he'd bet his hide she didn't know he'd caught that look in her eyes when Ryan came to the kitchen door. She probably didn't even know Ned knew Ryan was there, but he'd gotten real good at being able to see who was comin' up behind him in his eyeglasses' reflection. And unless he was sorely mistaken, she felt the same way about Ryan Logan as Ned had always felt about Mildred Jones. *Rafferty,* he corrected himself with a sneer. 'Course, J.T. had been gone for nearly twenty-five years. Still, women like Mildred...well, he couldn't very well fault her for being a one-man woman when there had only been one woman for him all these years.

Not that he hadn't fooled around now and again, when he was in the service. Pining away for a woman he couldn't have had never been on his agenda. But none of those other gals made him feel all warm and sappy inside like Mildred had. None of them had made him feel much of anything, actually.

So why hadn't he taken the damn bull by the horns after J.T.'s death? Oh, not right away, that would've been unseemly. Besides, he imagined she was hurting pretty bad at that point. But a couple years later, when her grief had dulled some… What had scared him so much, that he wouldn't take a chance on just letting the woman know he was there, if she needed somebody? That he cared? After all, he hadn't been the same know-nothing spawn of a pair of drunks he'd been before he went into the service. He'd been decorated for bravery, dammit, twice in Korea and once, much later, in Nam.

Yet he hadn't had the guts to go after the woman he loved.

And now…now it was too late.

Ryan couldn't remember the last time he'd followed through on an idea as dumb as this one. And he hoped to hell it was a long time before he ever did anything this dumb again.

Oh, he'd done his best to convince himself, for the week or so between when Taylor had accepted his invitation to go out to dinner and tonight, that maybe once he got going, he wouldn't feel like such an idiot. Just as he tried to convince himself that Maddie hadn't looked funny when he told her he'd asked Taylor out.

They'd been in his office. Maddie was just putting stamps on a couple billing reminders, a necessary evil out here where so many patients, being largely self-employed, were uninsured. She always added a personal, handwritten note on the bottom of the delinquent bills, encouraging folks to give Ryan a call if they were having trouble, to see what they could work out. That way, she said, they'd understand they still had an obligation to pay him for his services, while still letting them know he understood everybody had difficulties from time to time. More often than not now, they did call and set up some kind of payment schedule, rather than just letting the whole thing slide.

And he had Maddie to thank for that.

Just as he had Maddie to thank for this.

"Isn't this what you'd had in mind?" he'd asked.

"Well, yes. I'm just…surprised, is all. I honestly didn't think you'd do it."

"Well, I did."

"I can see that."

"So you should be happy."

"I am. Really. It's just going to take a minute to wrap my mind around it."

Then she'd said she thought she heard the baby crying and left the office, abandoning the stamped envelopes on his desk. By unspoken mutual consent, neither of them mentioned his upcoming date for the rest of the week. Although he noticed Maddie's conspicuous absence when he came downstairs in his sports jacket and tie. Lord…how long had it been since he'd worn those?

By that point, his stomach had been in more knots than when he'd gone on his first date with Roberta Whitson in the eighth grade, an experience that traumatized him so much he didn't ask a girl out again until his junior year.

And now, pulling up in front of Taylor's small rented house at the north end of town after what could only be described as a bizarre evening, he was hard pressed not to berate himself for being the stupidest man on the planet.

Not that Taylor seemed to corroborate his opinion of himself. In fact, she was as gracious as Ryan supposed a woman could be who'd just spent the past two hours sitting in Dixie Treadway's Day-Glo yellow kitchen while Ryan tried to talk Dixie's eighty-five-year-old mother, Gertie, who had what Dixie liked to euphemistically call "spells," down out of the Treadway's hayloft.

The call had come halfway through their meal. Gertie was okay when she took her medication, but sometimes she'd pull a fast one on Dixie and her husband Willy and they'd find the pills stashed in odd places, like in the bottom of the sugar bowl. That's when the trouble started.

And Ryan seemed to be the only person she trusted at these times.

Sometimes it only took him a few minutes to calm the old woman enough to bring her back down to earth. Sometimes it took a lot longer than that. He'd explained the situation and offered to take Taylor home first, even though that meant losing an additional hour before he could get out there, but Taylor had insisted she didn't mind going along. Or having her dinner interrupted.

"Believe me," she said in her soft Texan accent, huddled against a brisk wind as he walked her up to her front door. "You don't have to apologize." She held up her foam container. "And at least I got a doggie…thing." As they went up her porch steps, she asked, "But why isn't that poor woman somewhere where she could be looked after twenty-four hours a day? That must be a tremendous burden on her daughter and son-in-law."

"Two reasons. They'd have to sell their farm to afford it, for one thing. And Dixie can't stand the thought of 'putting her mother away,' as she calls it. It would break her heart to do that to Gertie, even if they could swing the expense."

Taylor looked away, a half smile tilting her lips. "What a remarkable woman," she said softly, then looked back at Ryan. "Although no less remarkable than the doctor who'd drop whatever he was doing in order to ease the fears of an old, mentally ill woman."

"I am so sorry—"

Taylor laughed. It was a very nice laugh, low and warm. And she certainly was pretty enough, with her green eyes and red hair. She just wasn't…for him.

"So you've said," she said, her eyes twinkling in the porch light. "But you've just driven home why I'll never get involved with a man who's already married to his career. I tried that once. Discovered, much as it embarrasses me to admit, that I've got a real problem with sharing my man with all and sundry.''

Curiosity dulled her comment's sting, at least enough for him to ask, ''Then…why did you go out with me?''

She shrugged. ''It's a small town. Pickings are slim and dates are few and far between. At least, dates with men I'd want to spend more than ten minutes with,'' she added with a light laugh. ''So when one of the town's most eligible bachelors calls me up and asks me out…well, I'm not that much of a fool.''

Ryan felt a grin pull at his mouth. ''Should I be flattered?''

''Oh, immensely.''

He chuckled, then asked, ''So…who are the town's other eligible bachelors?''

''Your brothers, of course.''

''Of course.''

Then she said, ''But tell me something—why did you ask *me* out? It was perfectly obvious from the minute you picked me up your heart was not in this date.''

Ryan's brows lifted. ''Now, that's not true—''

''Yes, it is.'' Funny, she looked a lot more amused than ticked. Then she slanted her head. ''Word is that you haven't dated in quite a while, Dr. Logan. So why now? And why me?''

''Because…because I thought it was time. And…''

''And…?''

He gave a half-laugh. ''Because you're very pretty and nice and a friend of mine thought it would be a good idea…and *damn* I'm not any good at this.''

''Actually you're doing fine. Too bad you're doing it with the wrong person.''

He frowned. ''The wrong person?''

Despite the freezing temperature, she crossed to the porch swing nearby and sat down on it, yanking down her coat to cover her knees. ''Frankly you could have knocked me over with a feather when you called. I would have thought, judging from my observations a week ago at Thanksgiving dinner, that you and Maddie Kincaid had…how shall I put this? Feelings for each other? But then I thought, well, maybe I was mistaken. But I wasn't, was I?''

Ryan stood there like a bump on a log, then said, ''There's nothing…romantic going on between Maddie and me, if that's what you mean. I certainly wouldn't be out on a date with another woman—if you can call what we just had a date—if I was.''

Her eyes narrowed; she clutched her coat collar, scrunching it up higher around her neck, then rose from the swing, fishing for her housekey in her purse.

''But there won't be another date, will there?''

After a tense couple of seconds, Ryan shook his head. ''No. Please understand, though…this has nothing to do with you.''

Her key in her door, she turned, her eyes crinkled with laughter. ''You know, that's the first time a man's said that to me that I actually believe him. No, Dr. Logan, I'm not hurt at all. Except that it pains me greatly to see such an honest man lying to himself.'' She opened the door to her house, then leaned over to kiss him briefly on the cheek. '''Night.''

Well. So much for that.

When he arrived back home ten minutes later, Maddie was sitting cross-legged on the sofa, nursing the baby and watching some legal drama on TV. She looked up when he came to the living room door, her expression unreadable.

''Well?''

''Well, what?''

She huffed a sigh. ''How'd it go?''

''It didn't. Ended up spending most of the night out at the Treadways'.''

That little crease nestled between her brows. ''Gertie again?''

''Yep.''

''She okay?''

Ryan shrugged. Maddie nodded, then said, ''Maybe I'll drive out there tomorrow, take them some of that banana bread I made.''

''They'd like that.'' Then he said, ''It didn't work out. With Taylor and me.''

"Oh." Maddie forked her hand through her hair, making the layers shiver and shimmer in the light from the table lamp. Amy Rose's little hand jerked up, batting her mother's breast. "Any particular reason?"

His throat suddenly dry, Ryan stared at Maddie for a long moment, then shook his head. "Just...don't be getting any more ideas about trying to fix me up with anybody else, okay?"

"Okay," she said. Which should have meant he'd won that round, right?

So how come he felt more like he'd lost?

Chapter 12

By the middle of December, Noah had lost his first tooth and Amy Rose cut hers; Katie Grace learned all the words to "Jingle Bells," which she would sing for anybody at the drop of a hat; Maddie found herself in the pie-baking business, since apparently Ruby's customers couldn't get them fast enough; and Mildred Rafferty, who had broken her wrist when she slipped on a patch of ice on her way to her mailbox to send in her *TV Guide* payment, had come to stay with them for a little while, at least until she could do for herself again. At Ryan's insistence.

Maddie, who was way too full of the holiday spirit to let anything get her down, saw this as one of those "lemonade out of lemons" kind of things—

"Oh, for the love of heaven, Ned McAllister—stop your infernal fussing!"

—or maybe not.

Maddie tried to keep a straight face as she mounded sliced apples in the crust-lined pie plate, letting Katie Grace pat down the lumps and bumps with the back of a wooden spoon, followed by Noah's sprinkling a premeasured mixture of brown sugar, cloves and cinnamon on top (neither kid any the worse for wear from the flu they'd gone through the week before). Mildred, her arm in a cast and sling, had been sitting at the table, entertaining Amy Rose in her swing. But when she got up to fetch more cinnamon for Maddie, she nearly collided with Ned in his walker, asking if she needed any help.

"The only thing I need, old man, is for you to get out of my way before you make me fall and break something else!"

They were quite a pair, these two.

In the middle of all this, Ryan wandered into the kitchen, his very presence making Maddie's breath hitch inside her bony chest. Considering that three months ago he'd been living completely alone, he was being a very good sport about not being able to turn around in his own kitchen without tripping over somebody.

"Rrrrr-oooowwww!"

Or something. Well, how much sense did it make for one of them to make the trip out to Mildred's trailer every day to feed her cats when they could just as well bring them here?

Gamely, he ruffled kids' hair and unruffled the cat's feelings, let Amy Rose poke her finger in his nose, and told Ned he wasn't doing Mildred any favors by trying to do everything for her, to which Mildred said, "Hallelujah."

Then he got what he apparently came into the kitchen for—a cup of coffee—coming to stand next to Maddie. But not too close.

"Apple?" he said.

"Uh-huh." Feeling warmer than she should, she swiped her cheek with the back of her hand.

"Any chance one of them is for us?"

"Yep. This one."

"You just made my day, Maddie Kincaid," he said, then added, "you feeling all right? You're looking a little flushed."

Her heart jerked, making her fingers do the same, making her have to redo the fluting on the pie crust. "Just the heat from the oven,'' she said, trying to ignore the four sets of eyes glued to them.

''Oh. Okay. Well. I'll be in the office if anybody needs me.''

Then he left, taking his scent and warmth with him.

And finally, inevitably—Maddie sighed at this—her heart.

Yep. It was official. Despite all the promises she'd made to herself, despite everything she knew to be true, Maddie Kincaid had fallen head over heels in love with Ryan Logan.

On the surface of it, nothing had changed between them since his date with Taylor, even though she'd been far more relieved than she had any right to be that there wouldn't be a second date. But one night about a week before, they'd just sat down to dinner, and she passed him the biscuits. And when he took one, nodding his thanks, his gaze brushed hers…just barely…and *boom*. There it was. The truth of her feelings, blowing raspberries at her.

This time was so different from her only other experience she'd nearly missed it. With Jimmy, falling in love had been like that first incredible swoop down on a roller coaster— she'd been almost unable to breathe with the wonder and exhilaration of it. But with Ryan, the feelings had snuck up on her, all soft and sweet, like the sensation of holding a child's hand or smelling cookies baking or the way the air feels after a spring rain. This time, falling in love was more like a gentle warmth spreading through her, all the way out to the tips of her fingers and toes, all the way down to the most secret parts of her.

She could only imagine what it would be like, making love with him.

And since imagining was as far as things were going to get, she had best be about controlling all those feelings. Sweet or not, since it was obvious Ryan didn't return them, they were only going to get her into trouble. Dreams were still a luxury she could ill afford. The longer she stayed, the more likely she was to get hurt. Not because Ryan would ever deliberately cause her pain, but because Maddie knew that once the seed of love had taken root in her heart, it would only keep growing. That's just the way she was.

So all she had to do, she thought as she slipped the next pie into the oven, was get through Christmas. Once they all got into the new house, maybe her dumb hormones would settle down and stop nagging her half to death.

Then she straightened up and her legs gave right out from under her.

"You sure Mama's gonna be okay?" Noah asked as Ryan tucked him into bed, Katie Grace having fallen asleep in her own bed some time ago. Ivy had come right over to pitch in as soon as Ryan told her Maddie'd come down with the same crud that had taken half the town under within the past week, but the midwife had had to leave a little while ago to attend a delivery. Ryan hoped against hope *he* wouldn't be called away, too, since, despite Mildred's and Ned's protests, he wasn't real comfortable about leaving the children in their care.

Ryan sat on the edge of the bed, smiling down into Noah's worried dark eyes. He smoothed the child's unruly hair away from his forehead, the gesture as natural as breathing. "She's gonna be fine, grasshopper. I promise."

"But…she's just lyin' there. Can't you give her some medicine or somethin'?"

Frankly, it had scared the bejesus out of Ryan, too, when the kids had burst into his office, blubbering about their mama being on the floor and not waking up. Of course, by the time he got there, she'd come to and was more embarrassed than anything else about passing out. Except then she'd looked up at Ryan with those sweet silver eyes of hers, glazed with fever, and said, "Maybe I don't feel so good after all," and he'd laid a hand on her forehead and felt her burning up, and worry had flooded right through him until he remembered he'd seen no less than a dozen cases exactly like this, just in the last couple of days.

"Not for this, squirt. All she needs right now is lots of rest so her body can fight this off on its own. That's why she's so still—she's sleeping real hard.''

Still, the trepidation in Noah's eyes tugged at Ryan's heart. Little guy had already lost a daddy; he was probably petrified of losing his mama, too.

"You've never seen your mama sick before, have you?"

Noah shook his head. "Not since she had the baby, anyway."

Ryan smiled. "That's different. It hurts when a lady has a baby, but your mama wasn't sick. And you saw yourself she was just fine right after Amy Rose was born, remember?"

That got a tentative nod.

"Well, I swear, there's nothing for you to worry about. In a couple of days, your mama's gonna be good as new—"

Tears glistening in his eyes, Noah scrambled out from under the covers and into Ryan's arms, nearly knocking the breath clean out of him. The child smelled of baby shampoo and cinnamon and his mama, and Ryan wrapped his arms around the boy and held on tight. He got hugs all the time from his littlest patients, but this wasn't like any of those. This was a hug that was asking for something he wasn't sure he could give.

No matter how desperately he might want to.

He shifted Noah around to sit on his lap; the child slumped against him, completely trusting, provoking a sweet ache deep, deep inside Ryan's chest.

He loved these children, he realized. As much as he would have his—

"C'n you read me a book?" Noah asked.

"I guess I can do that. Which one?"

Thanks to the town library, Maddie made sure the children always had a pile of books on hand. Noah slid off Ryan's lap to reach the stack on the nightstand, taking several seconds to make his selection.

"This one," he said, crawling back up on the bed to lean into Ryan's side.

So Ryan read a story to Ryan, about a little boy who learned to conquer his fear of the terrible "monster" that

lived in his cellar. He made his voice go deep and scary whenever the monster talked, like his father used to do when he
read to Hank and him, and Noah giggled and snuggled closer.
And Ryan's eyes burned, but not from eyestrain, he didn't
think.

By the time he'd finished reading, Noah's eyelids were at
halfmast. Ryan yanked back the covers and repeated the tuck-
ing-in procedure.

"Dr. Ryan?" Noah said on a yawn.

"Hmm?"

"I'm not scared a'you anymore."

The ache sharpened. "Well. That's good." He leaned over,
tickled the boy through the covers. "I'm not scared of you
anymore, either."

Noah's eyes went wide. "You were scared of *me?*"

"Well, sure. Tough guy like you…you had me pretty worried there for a little while."

That got a giggle, revealing the new space between his
bottom teeth. "You're a silly-billy, Dr. Ryan." After another
yawn, he forced out, "Mama said we could go get a Christmas tree tomorrow, but now she's sick." His tiny forehead a
mass of creases beneath his rumpled hair, he picked at his top
sheet for a moment, then gave Ryan puppy-dog eyes. "D'you
think maybe you could take me and Katie to get one instead?"

Ryan felt a clutch in his chest. "Oh, gee, squirt…I don't
know. I've got office hours in the morning, and then hospital
rounds in the afternoon. And with this bug going around, I'm
liable to get a lot of calls—"

"It wouldn't have to take long, I promise! An' you could
take your phone with you so if anybody needed you, they
could call you, right?"

His hands braced on either side of the child's pillow, Ryan
felt the corners of his mouth kick up into a half smile at this
beseeching expression in those huge, dark eyes. For Ryan,
Christmas trees were but distant memories. Remembering
what it was like to be a child at Christmas time was downright
ancient history.

But he did remember.

"I guess they could at that," he said, and Noah's entire face bloomed into a smile. Then he linked his thin arms around Ryan's neck and gave him a hug, falling back onto the pillow with a deep, satisfied sigh.

"Thanks, Dr. Ryan," he mumbled, his eyes closing before the words were all the way out.

And the ache, which by now was threatening to cut off his breathing altogether, only intensified when he peeked in on Maddie in the next room. She was sleeping fitfully on her side, her brow puckered. Once again, she was his patient. But when she'd first come, that's all she'd been. Now...

Now.

He took a step closer, his thumbs hooked in his pockets, not even bothering to deny the emotions welling up inside him at the sight of her.

The children weren't the only ones he'd come to...

The word jammed in his brain, rusty and so long unused, he wasn't sure he knew the meaning of it anymore.

But he sure as hell knew what it felt like.

It felt like...a war raging inside him. Logic versus emotion, fear versus need, the breath-stealing urge to flee versus an equally breath-stealing desire to never leave. Total helplessness versus an almost savage protectiveness, as he watched Maddie sleep, wishing it was him sick instead of her because he couldn't stand the thought of her being in any sort of pain.

He'd do anything for her, to see her happy. To see her safe. Anything.

Blinking, Ryan glanced around the room. Other than this morning when he'd carried her to bed, he hadn't been in here since that first night. For the most part, the room was exactly the same, although she'd hung a decorated grapevine wreath over the bed that she'd gotten at the high school's annual arts and crafts show. But it was vastly different, even so. This was *Maddie's* room now, not a guest room in which Maddie happened to be staying. It smelled like her, looked like her...felt like her.

How long would it take, after she left, for him to stop thinking of this as her room?

Nearby, in the crib someone had donated to the cause when Amy Rose grew discontented with the bassinet, the baby stirred. Ryan frowned. The only major hitch about Maddie's being sick was that she was still breastfeeding. There was little danger of her passing on her illness to her daughter, since her own breast milk provided sufficient antibodies, but whether she felt up to feeding her daughter was something else again. And bottle feeding the baby could not only easily wean her before Maddie was ready, but would undoubtedly be extremely uncomfortable for Mama.

He hated to do this, especially as it looked as though she was finally getting some decent sleep, but...

He scooped Amy Rose up from her crib, his insides twisting a little more at the baby's crooked, trembly smile, at her gurgles of communication. As he changed her diaper, she made little breathy sounds in response to his soft chatter, staring at him as if trying to absorb him. After snapping up her sleeper, he carried her over to Maddie, gently stroking her shoulder. At her daughter's first whimper, however, she came awake enough to understand what was being asked of her. And groaned.

"Sorry, honey. This is one thing I can't do."

After a moment, she nodded, then unbuttoned her nightgown, unmoving, letting Ryan set the baby down where she could reach her mama's breast. He sat at her back while she dozed and Amy Rose took her fill, the baby grinning up at him periodically with the nipple in her mouth until she let go altogether and cooed at him, her tiny hand batting at the air.

Maddie didn't even stir when Ryan removed the baby from her arms. He burped Amy Rose, set her back down in the crib—Maddie had said she was sleeping through to seven now. If he didn't hear her awaken before then, he'd come back in the morning.

But he paused at the doorway, his gaze flicking from mother to baby and back again, unable to staunch the yearning streaking through his veins. It had been a long time since he'd let himself want something he couldn't have. Since he'd given two seconds' consideration to his own needs.

He smirked, shaking his head. Maddie was the romantic, not him, even if her brand of it was more practical than most women's. That didn't stop her from still believing that love was enough.

Which was the major difference between them. Because Ryan knew it wasn't.

She awoke with a start, her skin cool and slightly damp, not knowing whether she'd been out of it for several days or just a few hours. Weirdest dang…whatever it was she'd ever had. The last thing Maddie clearly remembered was taking a pie out of the oven. Or was it putting one in? Then nothing but a blur, sleep alternating with vague images of Ryan or Ivy bringing Amy Rose to her to feed, trying to get her to drink ginger ale and tea or eat chicken broth, which she'd hated from the time she was a little girl. Suddenly this evening, she felt almost completely well. Certainly well enough to shower and change her nightgown. Slipping on her robe, she ventured downstairs to see what all the commotion was about.

The scent of evergreen assailed her before she'd made it halfway down the stairs. That, and one of those three tenor guys, she thought, singing "White Christmas" with a Spanish accent.

"Mama!" Noah yelled out, tripping over boxes and things in his split to get over to her and grab her hand. "We gots a tree! A real live one! Dr. Ryan taked us to Uncle Cal's house an' we got to go out to the woods an' cut one down!"

Still feeling a little fuzzy, her gaze wandered around the living room for a moment until it found Ryan's, which seemed to reach out to hold her steady as surely as if he'd taken her arm. He looked…pleased with himself, she thought. No, he looked downright *smug*. Such an expression seemed at once so out of character and endearing that Maddie had to smile, her heart swelling with something that went way past love.

By now, both kids were pulling her across the room toward the tree, like she might miss it if they didn't get her close enough. As if she could. Goodness—half the living room was

Christmas tree. Out of the corner of her eye, she saw Uncle Ned seated in the wing chair, untangling lights, all the while going on about something to Amy Rose in her baby seat near his feet, who was holding up her end of the conversation with lots of agitated air-batting and burbles.

Then Ryan slipped one arm around her waist to lead her over to the sofa, and she very nearly burst into tears from the gentleness of his touch.

"How're you feeling?"

"Human. I think," she said, realizing just how wobbly her knees still were when she tried to lower herself onto the sofa.

"You'll recover pretty quickly from now on," he said. "By tomorrow, you won't even know you were sick."

"I'll look forward to it." Then she realized what was missing from the scene. "Where's Mildred?"

"Gone back home," Ned grumbled, yanking apart a particularly tangled portion of the lights with more force than necessary. "Said she could do just fine on her own now, didn't need anybody hoverin' over her any more."

Ryan sent Maddie a look which told Maddie pretty much what she'd figured—that Ned had driven her away.

"Look, Mama!" Noah thrust a cardboard box into her hands. "Cal gave us lots of ordaments an' stuff!"

"Oh, my…" She gingerly lifted one of the blown glass houses out of the box, twisting it slowly to get the full effect of the white glitter "snow" on its roof. She looked up at Ryan, then glanced over at the children. "Are you sure these should go on the tree with, um…"

"They made it through the three of us," Ryan said. "I imagine they'll survive those two. We've already discussed it, right guys?"

They both looked up and gave enthusiastic nods. Then Noah said, "We can't touch without a grown-up with us. At *all.* 'Cuz they're glass an' they might break and cut us."

Ryan reached over and picked up another box, stacked on an empty chair. He opened it, handed it to Maddie. It was full of tiny crystal angels, each one in a different pose.

"My mother collected these from all over. Christmas was her favorite time of year."

Maddie smiled, stroking one of the angels with her fingertip. "Mine, too. Although a lot of them weren't exactly memorable."

"Here's hoping this one will be," Ryan said, and she looked up into his kind blue eyes and felt like she was floating above the clouds.

Of course, that could be due to her not being completely well yet.

Then she finally got a good look at the tree, and horror streaked through her, that such a big, beautiful tree had been sacrificed for a few days of pleasure. When she voiced her concerns, Ryan explained that it had been growing in a bad spot and had to be culled, anyway.

"Oh. Well. I suppose that's all right, then."

Then he seemed to realize that it had been a while since she'd eaten anything to speak of so he asked if she was hungry. She was. Starving, in fact. But when she tried to get up, Ryan said, "And just where do you think you're going?" and she said, "To the kitchen, since that's where the food is," and he said he'd bring her whatever she wanted and to sit back down. So she did.

A few minutes later, he brought her a sandwich on a tray, with some potato chips and a glass of ginger ale, although what she really had a yen for was one of Ruby's deluxe cheeseburgers with a large fries and a chocolate shake. However, she kept this thought to herself, not wishing to put anybody out.

Then she lifted her napkin and found a little package underneath, wrapped up in silver paper.

"What's this?"

"Open it and see," he said, wearing one of those goofy grins men get when they're tickled with themselves.

It was a Tim McGraw Christmas CD. Tears sprang to her eyes. "But you hate country music," she said softly, stroking the plastic case over and over.

"Didn't buy it for myself, did I?"

He took the disk from her and slipped it into an inexpensive player they'd picked up the last time they'd gone shopping, and the kids started dancing like fools in front of the Christmas tree, while Ryan laughed and she ate the sandwich, thinking it tasted better than anything she could remember and that she had much to be grateful for.

Then she looked over at Ned, who was watching the children, frowning. Except, as he watched, the frown began to get all smudged, until the only wrinkles left were the ones put there by time and gravity. Then, slowly, he started to clap to the music, spurring the children on in their dancing, as a smile spread across his face like the sun breaking over the mountaintops at dawn.

And Maddie closed her eyes, as if doing so would trap the happiness inside.

Even though she'd only stayed up a couple of hours, by the time the tree was decorated Maddie found herself more than ready to get back into bed. So she didn't protest Ryan's insistence on getting the older two ready while she sat up to give Amy Rose her last feed of the evening. Both her babies came in to say good-night, Noah in particular clearly relieved that she was feeling better. They exchanged more kisses and hugs than usual, then Ryan herded them off to bed, returning not fifteen minutes later. Only he didn't come in at first. Instead, he stood in the doorway, his thumbs hooked in his pockets, something in his expression making her get all fluttery again. Making her wish…

Well. She could just stop that thought right there.

"Mothers aren't supposed to get sick, I guess," she said, smiling.

He looked at her then, his mouth pulled tight. "No. They're not," he said, which is when she remembered that his mother had died when they were all still pretty young and that had been a stupid, thoughtless thing for her to have said.

"Oh, Lord, Ryan, I'm sorry. I didn't mean—"

"It's okay," he said, finally coming all the way into the room to look down at the baby. "She finished?"

"What? Oh, yeah—I guess so." She pushed back the covers to get up, but Ryan took the baby from her.

"Uh-uh. You stay right where you are. Miss Amy and I, we've got our routine down pat."

So she sat, watching him tend to her daughter, his big hands so careful and sure, and the little glow of happiness got all mixed up with the fluttery feelings to the point where she no longer knew whether she was coming or going.

"Thank you," she said after he'd laid the baby down and covered her with a little cotton quilt somebody or other had given her.

Ryan turned, his expression half amused, half something she couldn't quite put a finger on. "For what?"

"For giving us Christmas, for one thing."

A shadow swept across his features, so fast she nearly missed it. "I figured that was the least I could do."

"At least? Oh, my word, Ryan—what haven't you done for us? I can't even put into words how grateful I am to you, for giving us a home when we needed one and being so good to my kids and taking care of them—and me—the last couple of days. For putting up with Uncle Ned and Mildred and her cats. For not complaining about having your home taken over by crazy people." She brought her knees up, hugging them through the bedclothes. "For being my *friend*. And for showing me what a man's supposed to be."

She saw him flush with embarrassment. "I'm not—"

"You are, Ryan Logan. You have the biggest heart of any man I've ever known. Even if you are a big grouch in the mornings and you leave your socks inside out when you take them off and you don't like country music. None of us is perfect," she finished with a grin that probably wobbled a little. "But my babies and I were truly blessed when we were led to come here, to this town. To you. And…and I just wanted you to know that."

Amy Rose snuffled in her crib, trying to get settled. On the landing, the grandfather clock chimed nine o'clock. The sound from Ned's TV worked its way up through old walls and floorboards, his room being directly below Ryan's next door. But Maddie was barely aware of any of that, mesmerized as she was by Ryan's painfully slow progress toward her.

Beneath her ribs, her heart twanged, just as painfully, and although her sickness fever had been gone for hours, now another type of heat seared through her from the effort it was taking to not want something she wanted more than anything in the world.

He sat on the edge of the bed, his expression at once tender and serious. She held her breath, watching him swallow. Saw his hand clench on his lap. Saw an unspoken longing in his eyes, a longing he clearly had no idea what to do with.

"I think…I think I'm the one who's been blessed, Maddie Kincaid," he said, and she thought *Oh, Lord*—it was up to her, wasn't it?

His jaw was prickly where her fingertips rasped against it, his mouth soft. He grasped her hand and held the palm against his cheek, all the while keeping her gaze snared in his. Tendrils of need unfurled inside her, too, a sweet ache, the ageless female instinct to bond her man to her through touch. Not that Ryan was her man, or ever would be. And she knew—since she'd read it somewhere or seen it on a TV show or something—that men weren't wired the same way…

Ryan placed a gentle kiss in the center of her palm, making her suck in a quick breath.

Then he put her hand back on her lap and started to get up.

"No!" she cried out in a strangled whisper, grabbing his arm.

He looked down at her hand, covering it with his own as desire such as she'd never known swirled and trickled and sparked through her. But right alongside the desire came something else—the realization that maybe she wasn't quite as ready to give up on having dreams as she'd thought she'd been.

And that some dreams are worth risking everything for.

"I'm in love with you, Ryan Logan," she said, hope tangling with dread at his stricken expression. But there was nothing to be done for it now. "I told myself I wasn't ready, that I couldn't let it happen. That I *wouldn't* let it happen. But it did, and I am, and no matter what happens, I'm not sorry for it."

With a heavy sigh, Ryan sat back down on the bed, not looking at her. "Oh, Lord, Maddie...this isn't good."

That was her cue, she knew, to ask him *why,* to give him an opportunity to voice his objections. She refused to play into his hand, even though she was nearly dizzy with fear. "Well...I've always believed it's better to tell the truth, to get things into the open. What good would it do either of us for me to keep my feelings locked up inside me—?"

"Maddie, please..." His gaze locked with hers, his expression ravaged with...guilt, she realized. "Don't beg."

Her mouth dropped open. *"Beg?"* she finally got out. "I have never begged for anything in my life. Which you of all people should know. I'm not asking. I'm *giving.*"

A second was all it took, for her to push herself up and thread her arms around his neck, to join her mouth to his, holding her breath that he wouldn't find her too bold. That he would push her away.

So she nearly sagged with relief when he tangled one hand through her hair and kissed her back, when his tongue invaded her mouth and his other hand found her breast—

And then it was over. No mouth, no hand, nothing. Except his breath, coming in tortured gasps close to her ear, his forehead touching hers. The pain edging his words.

"Dammit, Maddie...I'm not supposed to want you like this."

Her heart, which had stopped when he broke the kiss, started beating again. But it wasn't a pleasant feeling. "Says who?"

"Says me."

"Then maybe you should rethink who you listen to."

With a half smile, he backed up enough to study her face, tracing his thumbs over her cheekbones, her nose, her mouth. Which he then covered with his own in a kiss so gentle, so *loving,* tears sprang to her eyes all over again. This time, when the kiss ended, his tormented expression all but extinguished the little glow of happiness she so desperately wanted to keep alight.

"Maddie, honey…no. I'm not what you need."

"And what if I don't agree with you?"

His laugh was sad. "How many missed soccer matches or Little League games or piano recitals or school plays would it take before the kids would hate me? How many interrupted dinners and holiday gatherings, or having to handle a crisis by yourself because I'm not around, would it take before *you* would hate me? Believe me, nobody understands more than I do what it means to want something. But here's where I'm a few steps ahead of you, because I've learned that sometimes, we want the wrong things. Things that might only hurt us, in the end. Do you understand what I'm trying to say?"

She stared into his anguished eyes for a good minute while her heart disintegrated into a fine dust that finally suffocated her little flame…only to have another flare into life in its place, ten times hotter than the first. "Yeah, I understand. You're saying I'm too young to know what I want."

One corner of his mouth twisted. "I'm saying our age difference is bound to influence our perspective on life. Not to mention how we go about making decisions. I have no doubt you know what you want. But I'm not sure you know what you *need.* Or what you'd be really be getting into if we let this…attraction get away from us."

The flame flared higher. On a frustrated growl, Maddie scrambled off the bed, nearly tripping over her nightgown. "Never mind that I've dealt with more in my twenty-four years than most folks do in a lifetime!" She rammed her folded arms over her quaking stomach, willing herself not to cry, not to act like the *baby* he obviously thought she was. "Not to mention that I don't give up easily. I mean, look at how I stuck with my marriage to Jimmy—"

"Yes, let's look at that." Ryan stood as well, his hands on his hips, his expression grim. "That's exactly what I'm afraid would happen this time, that you'd feel obligated to stick something out even if it's not working."

When her breathing was steadier, then said, "So what you're sayin' is, you're pushing me away for my own good."

After way too long a pause, he said, "You don't need another man hurting you, sweetheart."

After another one, she walked over to the bassinet and peered down at her sleeping daughter through a haze of exasperated tears.

"Maddie?"

"What?" she snapped.

"I assume you know I was engaged once before?" When she nodded, he said, "Well, Suzanne thought she was up to handling the demands of my work, too. Only I ended up causing her more pain than I'd ever believed possible. And damned if I'll ever put anybody through that again. *That's* why I'm not married. Why I can't have a family the way other men can. Because it's not fair to ask a woman, to ask any kids I might have, to settle for leftovers."

She twisted around, almost trembling with anger. "But it's okay for *you* to live off them, is that right?"

He shook his head, then left, shutting her door softly behind him.

A second later, Maddie's pillow sailed across the room to whomp against it.

Chapter 13

On the surface, Ryan mused a few days later, frowning at the tricycle assembly instructions spread out on the living room floor in front of him, things seemed downright hunky-dory. Between the fire he'd gotten going in the fireplace and the sparkling, fragrant tree and Maddie sitting cross-legged on the floor surrounded by shimmering bows and ribbons and rolls of brightly patterned wrapping paper, it was an idyllic pre-Christmas scene. In reality, however, their unfinished conversation after Maddie's revelation had been festering between them ever since, like a splinter that had been only partially removed. So when she announced that the Emerson house was ready for them to move into any time, Ryan felt as if somebody'd taken a hammer right to the sore spot.

"Oh?"

"Yeah," she said, scraping the blade of her scissors along a length of emerald green ribbon she'd already tied onto a package, then arranging the resulting corkscrew curl exactly the way she wanted it. She'd said she didn't want the kids to get too many presents, that they'd never had a lot and she didn't figure she'd be doing them any favors by spoiling them with more than they could handle. But there were books and drawing kits and a doll and the tricycle for Katie Grace and a sturdy building block set and a first two-wheeler for Noah. And a giant stuffed Elmo for Amy Rose, three times her size, that Ned had insisted on.

As for Ryan's present to Maddie…well, Ivy had suggested a gift certificate to a nice dress shop over in Claremore, something she couldn't turn around and use for the kids. But what he'd hoped to give her—a reunion with her foster parents— was looking less and less likely, since the message he'd left on the Idlewilds' answering machine weeks ago had gone unanswered. In other words, he couldn't seem to do a single damn thing right these days, could he?

"I suppose that's a load off your mind, then," he said.

She nodded, keeping her eyes on the gift. "I figured I might as well wait until after Christmas, though, seeing as the tree's already set up here and all." She signed a card—To Noah from Santa—and slapped it on the package.

It killed him, that she wouldn't look at him for longer than a second or two. Not that he blamed her, but still. "Maddie…you know you don't have to leave."

She did look at him then, but with the same vexed set to her mouth she got when one of the kids tested her. "You need your life back," she said, dragging the scissor blade down another another length of ribbon. "And I need to get on with mine."

"Look, I know things are a little…strained between us—"

Her gaze zinged to his. "You can't have it both ways, Ryan! We can't go back to the way things were! And I'll be the first to take blame for that—"

"Hey." Ryan reached over and grabbed her hand, tightening his grip when she tried to pull away. "Nobody's to blame, Maddie. And I—"

She pointed the scissors at him. "Don't you *dare* say you're flattered."

"—and I'd like to think," he continued, "that we could

get past this. Moving out is an extra financial burden you don't need right now.''

She jerked her hand out of his, her eyes blazing. But at least she lowered the scissors. ''I'll get by. Ruby's taking thirty or forty pies a week from me now, so I've got that income on top of what you're paying me. And Ned's pitching in part of his pension for the rent and food…''

Ryan never thought he'd live to see the day, but Ned had had all the junk on his land carted off, the shack razed, and had put the property up for sale.

''…so you see,'' she continued, her brow scrunched up as she plunked a book down onto the backside of a piece of wrapping paper, ''everything's working out just fine. Just the way we'd always planned from the beginning, right?''

Ryan took the wrench to the tricycle seat bolt, then looked over at Maddie, feeling more or less like dirt. ''I'm not going to stop worrying about you just because you move out.''

Her back rigid, she struggled to her knees to pile the just-wrapped presents under the tree. Then she looked over at him and said, ''I don't need somebody worrying about me. What I need is somebody who doesn't think I'm clueless—''

''Dammit, Maddie!'' He threw down the wrench, its clatter against the bare floor echoing painfully inside his head. ''This isn't about you—''

''Of course it is!'' She twisted around, her eyes flashing. ''But I get it, okay?'' Twin tears spilled from her lower lashes and streaked down her cheeks. She swiped at them, ducking her head to gather up the rolls of paper, the ribbons, the scissors and tape and tags. ''You don't have to keep rubbing it in!''

Ready to explode with frustration, Ryan reached over and clamped his hand over hers. ''No, Maddie, you *don't* get it! How could you, when I barely do myself?''

She jerked up her head. ''Then why don't you explain it to me?''

He let go of her hand and hauled himself to his feet, rubbing the back of his neck. Damn, damn, *damn*—no matter what he did, what he said, there was no way now to avoid hurting her. Hurting her more. He had to remove the last of the splinter, no matter how painful it might be. But otherwise, the wound would never heal.

He stared at the tree, the beautiful, glittering symbol of *joy* and *peace* and *love* taking up half of his living room, as if it would give him answers. Or at least, strength. Then he turned, finding the courage to meet that steadfast, earnest gaze, his heart breaking for what he was giving up.

"You have no…idea how tempting it is to take you up on your offer, Maddie. *No* idea. And I can't let you leave without…" He placed his hand over his heart, as if that might salve the pain. "I'm not calling a halt to this because I don't love you," he said, his heart cracking even more when her face crumpled in confusion, "but because I *do*. With all my heart and then some. And I can't find it within myself to let you go on thinking your feelings are one-sided, because believe me, sweetheart…they're not. They're not," he repeated on a whisper, his eyes on hers. "But I would be one selfish bastard if I let you love *me*."

For what seemed like an eternity, she simply sat there, silent, the confusion in her eyes giving way to defeat.

His phone rang; cursing the timing, he snatched it off his belt. But when he glanced back where Maddie had been, she was gone.

And now that the splinter had been dug out, he wasn't sure he could staunch the bleeding.

"But I don't wanna go! Katie Grace an' me like it here, don't you, Katie? So does Amy Rose."

The kids' room littered with their Christmas loot—Maddie hadn't counted on all the presents other people would give them—she sat on the edge of Katie's bed facing Noah's grumpy expression, while Katie snuggled on her lap clutching Audrey Anne, her new doll. "A month ago, you loved the new house." *A month ago, my heart wasn't broken.* "And you're gonna have your own room, too—"

"I don't care. I wanna stay here with Dr. Ryan."

''Me, too,'' Katie breathed against Maddie's chest. ''Wanna stay wif Dokker Rine.''

At least the kids had had a good Christmas. For Maddie, however, the past forty-eight hours had been, to put it simply, hellacious. Prior to two nights ago, Maddie would have said that nothing hurt more than unrequited love.

She'd been wrong.

''Well, sweet things, we can't. This isn't our house. But it's not like you'll never see Dr. Ryan again, since he said you can come over and visit any time you like.''

Noah glared at her, his arms tightly folded across his chest. Although, to be truthful, she'd rather see him defiant than scared of his shadow like he'd been before. ''But Uncle Ned's coming with us?''

''Didn't I tell you he was? Now both of you need to get to sleep. We've got a big day ahead of us.''

She tucked Katie and Audrey Anne back into bed before turning to give Noah one last hug and kiss. But when she leaned over, he twisted away. So Maddie plopped herself down on the edge of his bed and took his hand in hers, loving him whether he wanted her to or not.

''I'm sorry, baby. But this really is best.''

His gaze shot to hers, full of accusation for things she doubted he could put into words, even if he'd wanted to. Did he blame her for not being there to protect him from his father, or for being the one who'd sent Jimmy away forever? And now this, taking him—as she was sure he saw it—from somebody who'd been more of a father to him in the past few months than Jimmy had been in the last three years. Tears welled up in Maddie's eyes as she remembered what it was like to be small and helpless and unable to think past your fear and confusion. Or to have any sort of confidence in the future when your past hadn't exactly been filled with a whole lot of bright spots.

She leaned over, laying her cheek next to his soft, smooth one for a moment before placing a kiss right on the little crease between his brows. That he let her was something to be grateful for, she supposed.

"Believe me, baby," she whispered into his hair, "I understand exactly how you feel."

She didn' have much to move, just the few things she'd brought from Arkansas and Ned's belongings and the kids' Christmas presents, mostly, as well as all the paraphernalia that folks'd donated to Amy Rose along the way. But all of that put together didn't weigh near as much as the sadness in her heart. Even when Cal came with his truck to load it all up, his green eyes full of sympathy, and she caught sight of the beautiful maple chest of drawers and a ladder-back rocking chair he said he'd found up in the attic just waiting for somebody to adopt them, the heaviness refused to lift, despite her being deeply touched by his gift.

Ryan wasn't there: he'd gotten a call and was thus unable to help with the move. Frankly, Maddie was just as glad.

All afternoon, folks had been dropping by with food and little housewarming gifts—Maddie now had three coffeemakers—and Ivy and Ruby and Luralene, bless their hearts, had raided their closets and cupboards, donating enough pots and pans and dishes and linens that Maddie wouldn't have to buy much more than cleaning supplies and maybe some new place mats to brighten up the old, scarred kitchen table.

Around which the four women now sat, the older ones yakking their heads off. Luralene—in a lime-green running suit with hot-pink trim—bounced a cooing Amy Rose in her arms while Noah and Katie Grace were out exploring the backyard. Ruby had poked through the food offerings laid out on the bright aqua countertop, finally selecting Didi Meyerhauser's homemade crumb cake.

"Now this woman knows how to burn a pot," she said, coming up with four forks from somewhere or other. "Unlike some people we could name. You got any napkins, sugar?" she asked Maddie, who said no, but there was probably a roll of paper towels around somewhere, just give her a second to look.

She got up, grateful for the excuse to not have to smile for a little while. It was a shame, really, since everybody was being so nice and the kitchen was so cheery and bright and things were looking a hundred times better than she could ever have envisioned a few months ago. Ned even liked his room, had plugged in his TV and settled into the armchair Ryan had said he could have, if he wanted, since he knew how partial the old man had become to it.

Maddie swallowed hard, forcing down a lump in her throat big enough to choke a horse. How ironic, that Ryan's admission of his feelings should actually kill hope instead of feeding it. If he hadn't said he loved her, then she could have reasoned, Oh, well, then—maybe he just needs more time. Maybe one day, he'll feel differently—

Tears burned the backs of her eyes—she was still nothing more than a starry-eyed twit, wasn't she, believing in the power of love to conquer all? Or at least, she had been up until a few days ago. And where the *heck* were those dang towels?

Oh, Lord—how was she supposed to work with him? If she had any choice, she'd quit. But good-paying part-time jobs were hard to come by, not just here, but anywhere. He'd have to fend for himself with his meals again, though. That much of a masochist, she wasn't.

Maddie sucked in a deep breath, plucked the towels out of the box and turned around to find a trio of sympathetic frowns awaiting her.

"The man's a fool, baby," Ruby pronounced, and by the time Luralene and Ivy had said their "amens," Maddie was sobbing her heart out.

The house was almost unbearably quiet.

Ryan hung his truck keys on the hook by the kitchen door, setting his bag down on the small table off to the left. A new bag, one Maddie had ordered especially from one of his supply catalogs for Christmas. When he'd protested the cost, she'd said she and Ned and Mildred had all gone in together to get it, since his old one was about to fall apart.

An odd, rhythmic ticking sound from over the refrigerator caught his attention—the clock, its sweep hand snicking relentlessly toward the end of another day. Had it always been that loud?

He didn't bother removing his boots, even though he found himself walking around the newly washed rag rug in front of the sink rather than over it to turn on his radio. Sure enough, it was on a CW station. Ryan twisted it back, thinking how nice it was gonna be to know the damn thing was going to stay where he put it from now on—

There was a note stuck on the refrigerator, eerily clear of children's drawings and grocery lists and school schedules, telling him that there were still plenty of leftovers from Christmas—ham and sweet potatoes and new potatoes and fresh green beans in garlic butter—so he should be okay for a couple days. It was written on the back of the gas company bill envelope, Maddie's flowery handwriting hiccuping in the spots where the paper overlapped.

Ryan crumpled the note in his fist, tossed it into the kitchen garbage. Then he strode into the living room, where the tree seemed to sneer at him.

"What the hell else was I supposed to do?" he asked it, his voice overloud in the silent, empty room. "I did this for her, you know. And the kids."

But the tree had no answer.

His phone rang. The land line, not his cell. He snatched it up, barked a greeting. After a moment of silence, a rich, contralto voice said, "Dr. Logan? This is Grace Idlewild. You left a message on my machine that you know where my Maddie is?"

By Wednesday, the entire town—and beyond—knew that Maddie had moved out. By Thursday, Ryan—who had clearly underestimated just how much of an impression Maddie had made on the good citizens of Haven—had been made more than aware of just how everybody and his dog felt about that.

"Heard Maddie got her own place," Alden Lancaster said when Ryan went out to see him, just to keep an eye out that his most recent upper respiratory infection didn't turn into pneumonia again.

Ryan slipped his stethoscope off his neck and peered at the old man. "It was what she wanted to do." Well, that was true, wasn't it?

"And I suppose you gave her your blessing?"

"Wasn't up to me to give her my blessing or not. She's a grown woman. She's free to live where she wants to."

Alden just hmmphed at that. And Ruthanne, his prune-mouthed daughter, was even more prune-mouthed than usual when she saw him to the door.

It seemed everywhere he went, somebody had a non-comment to make about Maddie's relocation that said far more than an actual comment would have. What was most aggravating, though, was that their not actually *saying* anything one way or the other—pointed though the observations may have been—gave Ryan absolutely no opportunity to defend his position on the matter.

By Friday, he was grumpier than a bear with a thorn in its paw. So when Ned McAllister called him up and asked if he'd come see him since he'd been feeling poorly for a couple days, for the first time since he'd taken over Doc Patterson's practice, Ryan found himself dreading making a house call.

"You sure you can't make it into the office—?"

"Maddie ain't here. It's her morning over at the day care. So I have no way to get over there." He coughed a couple of times for effect. "Hear that?"

"Yeah, Ned. I hear that."

"Well, it sounds ten times worse in person, believe you me."

Click.

"Must've cleared up within the last hour," Ned muttered, warily eyeing Doc as he folded up his stethoscope and stuffed it back into his bag. Ned was sitting on his bed in his room, that screened-in porch at the back of the new house. It was light enough and all, but a little on the drafty side. Not near as bad as his old place had been, though. "But you yourself heard that cough—"

"Would you mind getting to the point, Ned? I do have other calls to make."

Ned screwed up his face, buttoning his shirt back up. Now he remembered why he'd avoided getting sucked into other people's business all these years. "Fine." He finished with the last button, then planted his hands on his thighs. "I can't believe you actually let Maddie walk away, boy."

Ryan let out a mighty sigh. "Well, that certainly seems to be the sentiment of the week. Although, like everyone else, you seem to have missed the point that she left of her own free will. I told her any number of times she and the kids could stay."

Ned blew out a sigh of his own. It was true, what they said about youth being wasted on the young.

"As what? Your guest? Your housekeeper?"

Well, would you look at that? The man looked downright pissed. "What's that supposed to mean?"

"Oh, don't play dumb with me. You're forgettin' one thing, Doc, which is that I've been watching the two of you for the past month. And you can't tell me you've missed how much that gal cares about you."

"I really don't want to talk about this, Ned—"

"I'm sure you don't. And unless I've gone blind as well as lame, you're crazy about her, too."

His arms crossed, Doc stared at Ned a long time. A real long time. Then he said, "And what if I am?"

"What if you are? What kind of damn fool answer is that? Are you or ain't'cha?"

Doc walked over to where he'd set his bag on the nightstand, frowning so hard Ned thought for sure his face would set that way. "She certainly *makes* me crazy. Does that count?"

But underneath his smart-ass reply, Ned could hear something that set off an echo inside his own head. An echo he had the feeling he couldn't ignore anymore. That maybe he didn't want to.

"Lemme tell you something, boy," he said softly, looking down at hands gnarled and spotted with age. Hands that knew how to fire a gun, to do things Ned still had nightmares about, sometimes. Hands that, at one time, had itched with wanting, just once, to touch the soft cheek of a pretty little redhead with silver-green eyes. He looked up at Ryan, fighting a sudden tightness in his throat. "I was younger'n you when I lost my heart to a woman, a woman who was in love with somebody else. I had no choice but to walk away and let her live her own life. You do have a choice. Don't be an idiot and make the wrong one, because I'm here to tell ya, loneliness is a pain in the—"

"Uncle Ned—is everything all right?"

They both turned; Maddie stood in Ned's doorway with that look women get on their faces when they catch you doing something they told you not to.

"What the Sam Hill you doin' home so early, gal?"

"Only three kids showed up, including Katie. So Didi sent me home." Her arms crossed over her chest. "Which you didn't count on, did you?"

Standing on her porch, Ryan looked a real mess. Good, Maddie thought. Maybe there was some justice in the world, after all.

She stood in her open front door, hugging herself against the cold. "I can't believe Ned did that."

Ryan shrugged it off. "Forget it." Then he looked at her, good and hard. "So. How're you settling in?"

She'd already arranged with him not to go back to work until after New Year's. "Good," she said, trying not to shiver. "You getting enough to eat?" she asked.

He sort of smiled. "Finished off the ham last night." Then he nodded toward her door. "You better get inside before you freeze to death."

"Yeah. I suppose. Well. See you Monday afternoon."

He touched the brim of his hat and turned away. Maddie told herself watching him leave would have been childish and dumb.

And besides, she had an old man to chew out.

* * *

"You've got no right, none, to meddle in my life!"

"Dammit, gal, somebody had to say something—"

"And just what good did you think that would do?" She poured hot water into Ned's mug for his tea, trying to keep her hand from shaking. "Did it ever occur to you that maybe this is between Ryan and me? Or that—" she plunked the mug down on the kitchen table, wincing when the hot tea sloshed over the rim and burned her fingers "—or that this isn't something that's even fixable?"

"Maybe. Maybe not. But you and Doc are the only two people in the world who ever gave a damn about me, and...and it just kills me to see the two of you letting an opportunity pass you by like this."

"Says the man who's let more than a quarter of a century pass by without telling the woman he loves how he feels!"

They stared at each other for several seconds. Ned blinked first. "And you know what?" He slapped his hand on the table and struggled to stand up. "You're absolutely right. I've got no right tellin' you and Ryan how to run your life if I don't have the wherewithal to follow my own advice." He held out his hand, palm up. "So give me your car keys. Seems to me I'm about twenty-five years late for an appointment."

As startled as she was by this abrupt turn of events, Maddie still had the presence of mind to snatch the car keys off the counter where she'd dumped them earlier and hide them behind her back. "You're nuts!"

"I would be if I tried to drive my truck. But the Impala's an automatic, right?"

"Well, yes, but—"

"Then I reckon I don't need my left foot. Right one works just fine. So give me the damn keys."

"Forget it."

He lowered his hand and gave her that blamed puppy dog look again. Lord above, she was growing to hate that look. "Maddie Mae, I'm seventy-five years old. Mildred is seventy-three. Time is of the essence here. Besides, if I wait, I'm liable to lose my nerve." Then he slanted his head at her. "And it's not like you haven't been angling for me to do this for some time.''

He had her there. But there was no way she was letting him drive himself. ''Okay, okay, fine—just…let me find somebody to pick up the kids and keep an eye on 'em for me. Then I guess I'll drive you out there.''

Now that he'd won, Ned sank back into the chair, his cheeks nearly the same shade as his beard. ''What if she says she's not interested? What if she laughs in my face? What if—''

''Welcome to the world, Uncle Ned,'' Maddie said, dialing Ivy's cell phone. ''Fun, isn't it?''

Forty-five minutes later, they pulled up in front of Mildred's trailer. Ned stretched out his neck, fussing with the knot in his tie. Maddie hadn't known he had a tie, let alone a fairly decent-looking sports jacket and pants. They were old as the hills, but it was the thought that counted.

''Ain'tcha gonna ask me if I really want to go through with this?''

''Nope.''

''Oh.'' He peered out the windshield, like he could tell from the way the sun was shining on the side of Mildred's trailer what his chances were. Then he frowned at Maddie. ''Might make it kind of awkward if you're there.''

''I'm not planning on going in there with you, Uncle Ned. I'm strictly the chauffeur.''

''Oh.'' Another peek out the windshield.

Maddie hefted a sigh. ''Uncle Ned. Go on up there, tell the woman you've come to court her, tell her you've come to visit, tell her…well, what the Sam Hill do I care what you tell her? I may as well go on to the Wal-Mart and get some shopping done, I'll come back in an hour. It's not like she's gonna make you sit outside on the steps or anything.''

''Oh. Well, yeah. I suppose you're right.''

''Good.'' She got out of the car, went around to get his walker out of the backseat. ''Now get your ornery backside out of my car and go woo your ladylove before the pair of you ossify.''

His brows shot up, then he let out a loud laugh. She helped him maneuver his long, creaky legs out of the car, emitting a little "oh!" of surprise when he leaned over and brushed a dry kiss on her cheek. "That fool boy don't know what he's missin'," he said, getting himself adjusted in the walker. Then he awkwardly pivoted and slowly made his way up to Mildred's front door.

Maddie waited by the car until she saw Mildred open her front door, her mouth dropping open in an expression of startled delight.

Well, good. High time *somebody* got it together around here.

Ryan almost didn't recognize Suzanne. But then, the last thing he expected was to run into her at the Homeland, where he was trolling the frozen food aisles in search of something to keep him alive.

It was New Year's Eve tomorrow. All day long, the sky'd been trying to make up its mind about whether it wanted to snow, rain or sleet; at the moment, it was a mixture of all three, and now coming up on dinnertime, the roads were becoming more deadly by the minute. And the store more and more crowded. Ryan had already endured any number of curious, matronly stares, to the point where he started flinging things into his basket, just to be done with this infernal shopping and get the hell out of there. So he wasn't exactly firing on all cylinders when he went careening around the corner and crashed his shopping cart right into Suzanne Potts's. Or whatever her married name was now.

He opened his mouth, but nothing came out. No less than ten people stopped whatever they were doing to stare. Until Ryan, taking a page from his older brother's book, scowled at them hard enough to make them rethink their rubbernecking. When he returned his attention to his former fiancée, he noticed twin dots of bright red staining paper-white cheeks.

"Ryan!" She gave a nervous laugh, her thin lips pulling up into a half smile. Her light hair, once worn nearly to her waist, was shorter now, pulled back into a severe ponytail with no bangs or stray waves or anything to soften the austereness of it. Just as she wore no jewelry to brighten her somber outfit of dark pants, sweater and carcoat. Still, even unadorned, Suzanne Potts had the kind of perfectly balanced features and wide, guileless blue eyes that used to suck Ryan's breath right out of him.

Used to being the operative term here.

"My goodness," Suzanne said, her cheeks still flushed. "I don't know why it just never occurred to me that... Well." She cleared her throat.

"So. What brings you home, Suzie?"

A smile flickered across her mouth. "The holidays. It's been a while since the kids and I've been back. Mama and Daddy always came to see us, you know..." She seemed to run out of steam, her eyes darting around as if she couldn't quite decide if it was okay or not to look right at him.

"How...how old are your kids?" he said, sympathetic to her obvious discomfort.

Again, the smile made a brief appearance. "Toby's three and Amanda's just turned two. Mama's sitting while I'm here picking up a few things before it gets any worse out." She jerked her cart over to let several other shoppers squeeze by. "Which I suppose accounts for why half the town's in here right now, too."

Ryan smiled a little. "Yeah. I suppose."

"So." She lifted a hand to swipe back a stray hair that wasn't there. "I hear you're still the doctor of choice around here?"

"Looks that way."

"Are...you happy, Ry?"

Loaded question. "Can't complain. You?"

"Oh...I'm doing okay." She hesitated a moment, then said quietly, "I got divorced last year, though."

"Damn, Suzie...I'm sorry to hear that."

Her mouth twisted. "Don't be. It was...more a matter of rectifying a mistake than anything else." She worried the baby strap in the cart for a few seconds, then dropped it.

The moment dragged on, painfully empty, until she said,

"So. How are your brothers doing?" which was at least enough to get the conversation airborne for a minute or two.

And when they finished saying what little they had to say to one another and wished each other well the way people do who have a history together but no future, and Ryan paid for his groceries and trudged back through what was now a full-fledged snowstorm and got into his truck, it hit him just *how* little they'd had to say to each other, that the sum total of all they'd meant to each other after six years of being a couple could be boiled down to a few stilted sentences.

It hadn't escaped his attention, either, that she hadn't asked him if he was married. For some reason, he found that mildly perturbing.

He'd just put his key in the ignition when a car horn went off beside him, startling him. He looked over to see Suzanne jump out of a blue Lexus, popping open one of those one-handed umbrellas before dashing around both vehicles to his passenger door. Ryan leaned over and opened it for her; smelling of wet wool and something floral, she climbed in, shaking the slush off the umbrella before closing it up and pulling it inside. Then she turned to him, her smile shaky.

"I can't believe you still have this old truck."

He patted the steering wheel. "Yeah, well, I don't figure she's ready to put out to pasture just yet." Then he looked at his old girlfriend and said gently, "What is it, Suzie?"

She blew her breath into her cupped hands, letting them rest against her mouth for a second before saying, "It kind of threw me back there, running into you. Not something I'd planned on, you know? But…being home has given me some time to rethink a few things. And since the opportunity has presented itself…" Her breath left her lungs in a rush. "I just want you to know, Ry, I don't blame you, at all, for what happened. I know it seemed like I did at the time, but I was confused and upset and just plain not thinking straight. Which I don't suppose is much of an excuse, but…" She lowered her gaze to her hand, fiddling with one of her coat buttons. "I acted like an idiot, Ryan. But after…you know…I guess I just freaked. And by the time I realized what a fool I'd been…well. Sometimes, there's no point in going back, is there?''

His heart torqued. Not for what might have been, or what he'd thought he'd lost, but simply…for her. "No. I don't suppose there is.''

"Well…'' She opened the door again, manning her umbrella. "That's all I wanted to say." But just before she got out, she added, "I just hope, for your sake, you made some better choices than I did.''

He was still chewing over what had just transpired when he pulled into his driveway a short time later, a frown consuming his features at the sight of Hank sitting on his porch in a rocking chair nobody ever used any more. His coat was only half on, and he was supporting his left arm with his right, around which he'd wrapped something light colored, like an undershirt or something.

Hank stood when Ryan came up the steps, still supporting his arm and wearing the look of a man in pain who refuses to let anybody in on that fact.

"What'd you do to yourself this time?'' Ryan said, stomping snow off his boots, shaking it from his hat.

"Runaway screwdriver.''

"How bad is it?''

"Bad enough that I'm here.''

They were inside by now, heading straight for the exam room. After Hank shook off his coat, Ryan made him sit next to the exam table—he wasn't looking any too good—then unwrapped the arm, shaking his head at the gash running a good five inches or so along the top of his forearm.

"Nice job.''

"Thanks.''

"Bleeding's stopped, but now I have to open it up to clean it out.'' He grabbed a couple gauze pads and the Betadine. "When was your last tetanus shot?''

"Beats me. Ten, eleven years ago? Guess I should have a booster.''

"Ya think? And I won't bother asking how you managed to do this.''

Hank tried to grin, but it came out looking more like he was being tortured. "Talent."

"Was the screwdriver at least clean?"

"Oh, yeah. I make a point of sterilizing all my tools before I start on a project."

Ryan placed an absorbent pad on the exam table, had Hank set his arm over it to clean around and irrigate the wound. At Hank's first wince through gritted teeth, Ryan said, "You can go ahead and cry, it's okay."

"Hell, no…I want my sucker—" He let out a five-star curse. "Son of a *bitch,* that hurts!"

"And just wait until I stick the needle in the wound to numb it."

"You're enjoying this, aren't you?"

"Just thinking back to that time you put airplane glue in my hair when I was asleep."

"Damn, I'd forgotten that. How old were we?"

"*You* were old enough to know exactly what you were doing. I was old enough to know exactly how stupid I looked with a shaved head."

Hank snorted. "Mama had to cut the pillowcase away, as I remember."

"You *still* think it's funny, don't you?"

"Hell, yeah. *Damn!* How long's that needle, anyway?"

Ryan grinned.

Several minutes later, when the Lidocaine had done its thing and Ryan started to suture the gash, Hank said, "So. You ever get hold of those people you were trying to find? For Maddie?"

As if he didn't have enough on his mind.

"Yes, as a matter of fact—hold still, you idiot!—a few days ago," he said evenly. "The foster mother said she'd be out as soon as there was a break in the weather."

"Does Maddie know?"

Ryan carefully tied the first suture. "No."

Hank's brows lifted, but that was all. Then he said, "She's gone, isn't she?"

"Yep. Few days ago."

"Thought it seemed awfully quiet." Relaxed quite nicely now, Hank watched Ryan stitching up his arm with something akin to interest. "How you feel about that?"

Ryan wasn't sure which surprised him more, the question itself or that Hank seemed to genuinely care about the answer. Determined to keep a neutral expression, Ryan asked, "What's that supposed to mean?"

Hank lifted one shoulder. "Whatever. Although I guess it's easy to get used to having a woman around. One like Maddie, anyway. Gal sure can cook," he said, frowning down at his half-stitched up arm.

Ryan grunted. Hank went on.

"So I guess you're probably relieved that she's gone. Must've been hard to deal with that kind of temptation, day in and day out."

Needle poised in midair, Ryan fixed his gaze in his brother's. Hank smirked. "Oh, I'm not talking about *that* kind of temptation, don't go getting your drawers in a knot. What I'm talking about is the kind of temptation that makes a man forget why he'd rather stay single, that getting involved just sets you up for trouble down the road. And who the hell needs it, right?" He nodded toward his arm. "How many more of those you gonna do?"

Ryan frowned, tying off a stitch. "Two, maybe three. And this has nothing to do with me. It's Maddie I was thinking about. What she needs."

He could feel Hank's gaze riveted to his face. "You are so full of it, you know that? We're all full of it. Oh, we tell ourselves, and women, that we're afraid of commitment, because what can they say to that? But what it boils down to is that we're afraid, period. Of getting dumped. Of being rejected. Of being found…lacking in some way." His heavy brows nearly met. "Of being the one left behind." He lifted his gaze to Ryan's. "The pain's not worth it, Ry. You're better off this way. Damn sight better off."

His thoughts churning, Ryan tied off the last stitch, then dressed the wound. His brother's bitterness over his fiancée's death had skewed his perspective about everyone and everything, a condition only exacerbated by his reclusivity. Not that Ryan didn't understand where his brother was coming from. He just didn't see his situation in the same light.

Nor was he going to get into that with Hank. Not tonight.

Ryan gave Hank his tetanus shot, then said, "You want something for the pain? Cause that thing's gonna hurt like holy hell when the local wears off."

"I imagine I'll live," Hank said, carefully rolling down his sleeve over the bandage. "Can I go now?"

"Not in this storm, you're not."

"I can drive in the damn snow, Ryan. Besides—" he carefully maneuvered her arm through his coat sleeve "—storms mean stranded travelers. With any luck, a few of 'em might even blow my way. Duty first, y'know?"

Yeah. He knew.

Early January saw a series of snow and ice storms that paralyzed most of Arkansas, Oklahoma and a good part of east Texas as well. Nobody went anywhere unless it was a real emergency; Maddie couldn't help but fret about Ryan and that old truck of his, knowing he didn't have the luxury of staying put just because the weather was nasty. Eventually though, the weather cleared, the kids went back to school and day care, and Maddie got back into her work routine. Ryan, however—unfortunately—insisted on tagging along in her head.

More than once, she had to stop herself from taking him dinner, reminding herself the man had survived just fine before she came along; it was highly unlikely he'd starve to death now. Still, she couldn't help but feel—

Stop it, Maddie Mae.

"Somebody here to see you."

She jumped, having not heard Ned's thumping into the kitchen. Glancing over from the pot she was filling at the sink to cook the potatoes in for dinner, she said, "Me? Who on earth would be looking to speak to me?"

"Don't rightly know. Ain't never seen her before."

She turned off the water. "And it didn't occur to you to ask her name?"

"Well of course I asked her name, gal—what do you take me for? But she wouldn't tell me. Said it was a surprise."

By now thoroughly puzzled, Maddie wiped her hands on the dishtowel hanging underneath the sink, forked her hand through her hair, then made her way out to the living room. The woman, a tallish, thin figure in a blazer and nice pants, her blond hair cut short, was standing with her back to Maddie, looking at the Wal-Mart picture of all the kids she'd just hung on the wall the other day.

"May I help you?"

The woman turned. Maddie's breath caught in her throat.

"Oh, my sweet Lord, Maddie," Grace Idlewild said, grinning from ear to ear, even though Maddie caught the tears shining in her brown eyes. "I'd just about given up hope of ever laying eyes on you again. Come here, sweetie," she said, flinging her arms wide. "Come here and let me give you a big old hug."

"You've learned to make real good coffee, honey," Grace said a few minutes later, seated at the kitchen table.

"Thank you." Maddie was still somewhat in a state of shock, a condition she imagined she'd be dealing with for some time to come. Although she hadn't had to fabricate her needing to start the meat loaf, since it was getting on to five o'clock as it was, she was just as glad she had something to keep her mind occupied. "You say Dr. Logan contacted you?"

"Got my number off the Internet White Pages, he said. Left a message on my machine. Except didn't figure he'd call the one time in God knows how many years I'd gone out to Idaho to visit my brother and his wife."

Her back to Grace, Maddie poured a can of tomato sauce over the meat and bread crumbs in the glass bowl. If she didn't have to see her—Maddie had yet to get used to Grace's newly-slimmed figure, her youthfully styled, colored hair—

Maddie could almost imagine herself back in Grace's kitchen in Fayetteville.

"Why…why didn't you call first?"

"You know, I told Dr. Logan this was risky, but he insisted on doing it this way." She hesitated, then said, "Takes a very brave man to do something he knows full well could backfire on him. So my question is…did it?"

Maddie reached over for her salt and pepper. Shook her head.

"Well, that's a relief," Grace said on a laugh, her coffee mug clunking back on the table. "I can't believe you have *three* children!"

Maddie reached up, flicked a tear off her cheek. "S-sure do. A boy and two girls. The baby's just a little over three months old."

"Where are they?"

"Noah's at a friend's house until six. Katie Grace and Amy Rose are both napping. They'll be up soon, I imagine."

"Katie…Grace?"

Nodding, Maddie sank both hands into the meat loaf concoction to smush it all together, her throat tightening when she heard Grace get up and walk over to stand beside her. "Why didn't you get in touch with us, honey? You know we would've helped you out if you needed it."

Maddie kept her attention on the meat loaf. "It's like I told Ry—Dr. Logan. Didn't seem right to ask you and George to bail me out of the mess I only had myself to blame for."

"I see." Grace reached up, pinching a dead leaf off the little African violet Mildred had given Maddie for Christmas. "So you assumed we'd written you off?"

"You didn't exactly hide your feelings about me marrying Jimmy."

"We were concerned for you, honey," she said gently. "You know we'd hoped you'd go on to college, make a real life for yourself. Wait a few years to get married."

"To somebody besides Jimmy."

After a long moment, Grace said, "Would you want one of your daughters to marry someone like Jimmy Kincaid?"

Her words brought Maddie up short. Still, several beats passed before she said, "I'd be tempted to lock her up someplace first."

With a chuckle, Grace looped one arm around Maddie's shoulders. "I don't think there's a woman alive who hasn't felt the pull toward a man like Jimmy. A man who seems to exemplify everything magic and hopeful and exciting. And true love is magic, sugar, no doubt about it. Just not the kind of magic the Jimmy Kincaids of the world seem to think it is. But that doesn't mean you did wrong by loving that young man. And you didn't do wrong by sticking with your marriage when the going got tough, either."

"How do you—?"

"Your Dr. Logan told me what he knew." She lowered her arm, then leaned against the counter. "That man thinks the world of you, Maddie. It's a rare thing to find a…friend like that."

Grace was fishing and Maddie darn well knew it. Her cheeks heating, she sprayed a loaf pan with Pam, plopped the meat loaf mixture into it and changed the subject. "How's George doin' these days?"

After a moment, Grace said quietly, "He's been gone for nearly two years, honey. Went peacefully in his sleep, just two weeks shy of this seventieth birthday."

Maddie's mouth fell open on a soft "Oh" of genuine regret. "I'm so sorry."

"Nothing to be sorry about. We had a lot of wonderful years together." She smiled. "Mixed in with a few not-so-wonderful years, but that's the way it is when you're married—"

"I'm in love with him." The words popped out of her mouth like erupting lava. "Dr. Logan, I mean. I'm in love with a man who…who's completely convinced himself he's doing the 'honorable' thing by pushing me away." Her eyes burning, she finally looked at the one woman she'd always been able to talk to. Would have been able to talk to, she now realized, even when she'd thought she couldn't. "And I have no idea what to do."

The corners of Grace's mouth turned up as she lifted a hand to cup Maddie's cheek. "I could hear the love in his voice, honey. And I wondered what on earth was going on." Then she shrugged. "Unfortunately sometimes the only thing you can do is wait. Other times…" Another shrug. "You gotta light a little fire under their butts."

Maddie smirked. "And how in tarnation do you propose I do that?"

Grace's laugh startled her. Maddie turned to find herself facing an impossibly smug grin. "You know, one of two things is gonna happen here. Either your Dr. Ryan is going to rue the day he left that message on my machine…"

"Or?"

The grin grew broader. "Or he's not going to be able to find words to thank me."

Chapter 14

It turned out that Grace Idlewild had any number of ideas on the subject of male butt-burning, none of which Maddie could bring herself to implement. At least, not right off. Not that she wasn't tempted—it was perfectly clear that Ryan was nearly as miserable as she was, but she didn't think anybody would be any less miserable if the issue were forced. If his mind was made up, it was made up and that was that. So Maddie took the chicken's way out, only going into the office when she pretty much knew he wouldn't be there, otherwise letting things lie, through the rest of January…through February…and March.

And oddly enough, life didn't come to a halt during those long, miserable weeks. Her foster mother stayed with them for a full week before going back to Arkansas, with promises to return in the spring. It snowed three more times, once bad enough to close school, and they had one crazy warm spell where it reached the seventies for three days in a row and all the daffodils started coming up.

Katie Grace turned four and learned to write her name.

Amy Rose sprouted three more teeth, learned to roll from

her tummy to her back, and let Maddie know in no uncertain terms she was done with breast-feeding.

Noah got so caught up with all the new friends he'd started to make, he eventually forgot that Maddie was the enemy.

Ned and Mildred went to the senior citizens' annual winter dance together and were thus declared an official "item."

Maddie borrowed an old Singer from Didi Meyerhauser and made blue and white checked curtains for her kitchen, added custard pies to her repertoire, turned twenty-five without telling anybody and passed the first anniversary of Jimmy's death without telling anybody about that, either.

Ruby and Jordy bought a new sofa and gave Maddie their old one.

Ryan gave her another raise. Maddie figured it was out of guilt, but she accepted it anyway.

And, long about the beginning of April, Maddie suddenly realized the hole in her heart, if not healed, had at least scabbed over enough to stop hurting quite so much. Which meant when Hootch Atkins asked her out for the fourth or fifth time, she accepted, ignoring the little voice in her head that was going, *"Uh, uh, uh…"*

In the weeks and months that followed that first snowy week in January, Ryan diagnosed twenty-three cases of the flu, five strep throats, removed no less than a half-dozen foreign objects from children's assorted orifices—including an adventurous roly-poly from Timmy Frazier's ear—set four broken bones, and lay awake half the night wondering if he was losing his mind.

He also found himself standing in the middle of his empty living room a lot, imagining he could hear Maddie's laughter spilling down the stairs as she gave the kids their baths. Or he'd come home and could almost smell fried chicken or pork roast or spaghetti cooking. Or worse, much worse, he'd find himself looking for her, just to talk to, on those days when he'd had to break bad news to a patient, on those days when his best simply wasn't good enough.

He missed her nagging him.

He missed hearing her country music.

Well, maybe he didn't miss that. But he sure as hell missed *her,* just as he knew he would that day in October when she'd gone out to Cal's. Even though he still saw her several times a week, when she'd come in to work for him, or when he was out on his rounds and would run into her someplace or other. It wasn't the same as having her around, though.

Not the same at all.

But when a man's in a rut as deep as Ryan's, it takes some time before he figures out just how cramped it is in there. Maybe even two—or three—months. And during those two—or three—months, Ryan chewed over Ned's and Hank's words until there was nothing left of them but the truth, which was that he'd been expending a lot more energy these past few years saving his own hide than he had been saving his patients.

There was a shocker. And here was another one: in no way, shape or form was Ryan better off *without* Maddie, no matter what Hank thought.

Only about the time he decided he needed to do something with this revelation, he also decided he needed a haircut. And it was while he was at the barber's that Coop Hastings let it slip that Hootch Atkins had been bragging over at the hardware store that Maddie Kincaid had finally agreed to go out with him.

Maddie had made it crystal clear to Hootch—or so she thought—that he was not to read anything serious into her acceptance, that they were just going out as friends. He'd assured her that was okay by him. And for the first part of the evening—he'd taken her to a popular bar and grill out near Pryor—he'd been a perfect gentleman.

Until about halfway through their meal when it became evident that the man couldn't hold his liquor worth spit. Three beers and the man was drunk as a skunk. And although Maddie knew she could call any number of people to come get her—no way was she letting Hootch drive her home—she wasn't sure how to extricate herself from her predicament without embarrassing the man.

"Hootch. Hootch!" Maddie reached over and poked him in the arm. "I'm askin' the waitress to bring you some coffee."

He looked at her long and hard, like he was trying to place her. Then a frown settled across his face. "Don' wan' coffee," he said, batting at the waitress, who ignored him and poured him a cup anyway. Then he sighed, crashed his elbow onto the table hard enough to make the silverware jump, then leaned his cheek in his palm so that his left eye nearly closed. "You sure look pretty in that dress, Maddie."

It was one of the two she'd bought with the gift certificate Ryan had given her, a simple short sleeved jersey, purple with tiny white flowers. It was far too prissy for a place like this where the fashion statement ran more to fringe and cleavage. Since she had neither, this had been her only choice. She was about to say "thanks" when Hootch slurred, "But I bet you look a lot prettier out of it."

"Drink your coffee, Hootch."

"Don' wan'—"

Maddie leaned forward and said in a low, I-mean-*now* mother voice, "Either you drink that coffee or I'm outta here. Is that clear?"

He blinked several times with the effort to process her words, but eventually hand connected with cup and cup lifted to lips. Then she sighed. Land sakes, men were pathetic creatures. Next time, maybe she'd listen to the little voice. Except then a very unlittle voice cut through the music and the laughter, saying, "Maddie? You okay?"

Her heart nearly flew right out of her chest. She twisted around to see Ryan standing there like some avenging superhero, arms crossed over his chest, glowering so hard at Hootch she was surprised the man hadn't disintegrated on the spot. And Hootch, who was not so drunk that he couldn't sense an affront to his manhood, got shakily to his feet, fists clenched, and Maddie thought, *Oh, no.*

"Where the hell'd you come from?" Hootch said, right in

Ryan's face, which actually pretty much echoed Maddie's thoughts.

"Never mind about that. You're drunk."

"Am not," Hootch said, swaying indignantly.

"Come on, Maddie—I'll take you home and call Cal to come get Hootch—"

"No," she said.

Understandably enough, Ryan looked at her like she'd gone nuts. "You can't let *him* drive you home."

"I don't intend to! But I can take care of the situation—oh!"

Hootch had taken a wild swing at Ryan, missed, and gone crashing into the next table. Ryan grabbed him, apologized to the patrons, then hustled Hootch outside before he did any more damage.

"You can't jush barge in on my date!" Hootch said, wriggling in Ryan's grasp like Noah when Maddie tried to wash his ears. As soon as Ryan let go, the skinnier man stumbled, then reeled on Ryan, pointing unsteadily in his face. "She'sh mine! You gave her up! She'sh in love with you, but you're too stoo—" he belched "—pid to know a good thing when you shee it." In the silence that followed, Hootch's gaze wobbled between Maddie and Ryan.

Then he collapsed in a heap on the stairs outside the restaurant, bawling his eyes out.

"If the pattern holds," Ryan said, cutting the truck's engine in front of her house, "he won't remember any of what happened tonight."

"Too bad," Maddie said, her arms folded across her ribs.

Okay, so this wasn't going exactly the way he'd envisioned it.

He reached up, adjusted his hat. Let out a sigh. "Honey, I went to school with Hootch. He's just bad news. Always has been. So when I heard you were going out with him—"

"And just how did you find that out, anyway?"

"Hell, Hootch himself probably told half the town. And

before you ask, Blanche Scoggins—your barmaid?—tipped me off when the two of you came in."

"So you felt you had to come to my rescue."

His hand tightened around the steering wheel. "You don't understand—"

"Oh, but I think I do, Ryan Logan." Her eyes flashed like steel in the truck's dim interior. "But you know what? Maybe *some* of us don't plan on sittin' home for the rest of our lives, pining over the one that got away. Okay, so maybe Hootch wasn't the best choice, but I could have handled the situation myself. For the hundredth time, I don't need your *protection*—"

"Maddie—"

"—or a big brother, or a father figure, or whatever it is you think you can be to me without putting your butt on the line. So until you decide to do that, just stay the heck away from me. You got that?"

Then she bolted from the truck and slammed shut the door. Only then she turned around and said, "And by the way— seems to me that *stubbornness* isn't exactly a sign of maturity, either!"

His ears ringing, Ryan just sat there. How the hell was a man supposed to grovel when the woman wouldn't let him get a word in edgewise?

He could go after her, he supposed. Probably should go after her.

Then again, he decided, gunning the engine, maybe after a night spent stewing in her own juices, she'd be pliable enough to *listen*.

Maddie's heart fairly hopped right out of her chest at the sound of Ryan's truck outside her open front window the next afternoon.

He was already up to the steps when she got to the porch. With a bunch of flowers in his hand. Daffodils. From his own front yard, she imagined.

Nobody had ever brought her flowers before.

And for sure no man had ever looked at her before the way Ryan Logan was looking at her now.

Hope blazed through her. Mixed with a little triumph.

She crossed her arms, trying to keep a serious expression on her face. "You decided?"

His brows hitched, even as he leaned one hand on a support post and struck a relaxed pose, looking to her mind like a man who'd settled a few things in his. "Hell, Maddie, I'd decided before the business with Hootch. But you wouldn't shut up long enough for me to say my piece."

Her heart thunked once, twice, three times against her ribs. "Which is?"

A look of pure exasperation crossed his features. "Which is, that the thought of you with another man makes me crazy. But not near as crazy as the thought of trying to live without you. So here I am, heart in my hand and butt on the line. That good enough?"

She held out her hand. "It'll do," she said, her entire body singing with anticipation.

He didn't even ask if they'd be alone. He just followed.

Nobody said anything for a good two minutes, being far too preoccupied with kissing and trying to get up the stairs without killing themselves to bother with conversation. When they reached her bedroom, though, Ryan thought to ask where everybody was.

"All out," Maddie said, breaking contact only long enough to yank her T-shirt up over her head, tossing it across the room. Her hair, alive with static, glittered gold in the sunshine streaming through the open window. She went for his shirt buttons, since he apparently wasn't taking care of them fast enough to suit her. "Noah and Katie Grace had birthday parties, Ivy took Amy Rose away for a couple hours so—" she laughed "—I could get a nap or something."

"And Ned?" His shirt gone, he shivered at her hands on his chest.

"At Mildred's. Take off your pants."

He did, clumsily, feeling about sixteen. Only he'd never done this at sixteen.

She stood in front of him in a plain white cotton bra and panties, her lower lip caught between her teeth, her pale body awash in freckles and spidery, silvery stretch marks. Even with the twenty pounds she'd added to her frame since she'd had the baby, she seemed as delicate as a butterfly.

Only not.

He reached for her, capturing her face in his hands. "How long do we have?"

She grinned. "Long enough, I imagine." Her bra dropped to the floor. "Touch me," she whispered.

So he did.

The sheets were smooth and cool against his heated skin; outside, a robin trilled, seeking his mate. They couldn't seem to hold each other close enough, couldn't seem to kiss long enough or deeply enough or as much as they wanted. She smelled of lemons—"meringue pie", she whispered, smiling into his eyes—and tasted of spring.

He explored her body, unsure, patient, desperate to please, fingers dipping and tongue teasing. Buttercup yellow walls hissed echoes of her *yeses* and *pleases* until he took her up and over, and over again, with his touch, his mouth, because he figured it was damn time somebody did something for her and her alone.

Then, a cat-that-got-the-cream smile curving her lips, she straddled him, their hands linked by his shoulders. A sunbeam kissed her small, perfect breasts. Ryan followed suit.

"I love you, Maddie Mae," he whispered, and her smile softened, tears glittering in her eyes. When she leaned over to kiss him, he flipped her underneath him again, possessing her, thinking it was the middle of the afternoon, on a Saturday, and they were alone and he was here, in her bed, making love. Making peace with himself.

Claiming a gift he'd almost been too stupid to accept.

Her fingertips stroked his brow, his cheek, while her hair—longer again—fanned out in a thousand rays against the stark white pillow. She smiled again, a crooked smile, half innocence, half anything but.

"Now," she said.

"I didn't bring...I didn't expect..."

"Does it matter?"

He braced himself above her, eyes locked in understanding.

"You'll marry me, then?"

She grinned. Cocky. "Can I think about it?"

He backed away.

Laughing, she grabbed his backside. "Okay, okay...yes!"

"Even though," he said, slipping inside her, his heart nearly exploding as she arched her back, gasping through a smile, "I could break your heart?"

"I will marry you, Ryan Logan," she whispered, her eyes fixed on his as he began moving inside her, claiming his own right to happiness, "because clearly that is what I was led here to do."

Nobody said anything for a long time. Not because there wasn't a lot to say. There just wasn't any real hurry, now that they'd gotten the major things out of the way. Ryan tightened his arms around Maddie, skimming his lips over her forehead, and she thought she'd burst with joy. Then he said, "Sure is bright in here."

"I like bright."

His chuckle rumbled through his chest. "Think you can make the other house look like this?"

"Eventually," she said with a grin. Then she added, realizing, "No cell phone?"

"Nope."

Something in his voice made her shift to look in his eyes, but it still took her a minute to catch on. "Ryan! You joined the clinic?"

"I did. Signed on last week. I get every other night off and one full day a week."

She touched his face, frowning. "You sure this is what you want?"

"Yes." He pulled her head down to kiss her, hard, on the mouth. "I am."

"I'm glad, then. For you." She lay her head on his chest. "But it wouldn't've made a lick of difference to me."

"Even though my time was never my own?"

Maddie rubbed her cheek against his chest, then said, "When Jimmy'd walk out the door, I never knew when I'd see him again. Or even, there toward the end, *if* I'd see him again. That's what I couldn't deal with anymore, the not knowing. I've got no trouble sharing my man's heart as long as I know he's left part of it with me when he leaves. Long as I know he's coming back."

Ryan stroked her arm for a minute, then said, "You know, I finally got it through my thick head that it wasn't your sticking things out if they got rough that worried me. It was knowing there was no way you'd stay in a situation that would ultimately harm either you or the kids." He changed position so she had to look in his eyes. "I wasn't scared of trapping you. I was scared of *losing* you."

A breeze huffed through the open window, stirring her new sheer white curtains. Maddie stretched out on her side, her head propped in her hand. "Talk to me," she said softly. "Tell me about Suzanne."

Ryan mirrored her position, their hands linked on the bed between them. And he told her about how he and Suzanne had gone together for a long time, that she didn't want to sleep with him at first because of her religious scruples, but that after they got engaged, she changed her mind.

That she'd gotten pregnant.

Maddie frowned. Ryan had never mentioned a child.

"Suzie freaked," he went on, "petrified about what her parents would say when they found out. I told her, hang the damn big wedding, we'll just get married right away. Unfortunately the timing couldn't've been worse. Doc Patterson had just died, maybe a month before. I was so busy I couldn't see straight. It seemed like everytime we'd make plans, I'd have to cancel. She always said she understood. And I honestly believe she wanted to. Yet…she kept dragging her feet about getting married. Then one night, when I got back from a call that took me way the hell out to the boonies, I found Suzie waiting for me, huddled by the back door to the office and crying… ."

When the pause grew longer than Maddie thought it should, she said, softly, "She lost the baby?"

"Yeah," Ryan let out on a long breath. "She was only a few weeks along, so physically she was never in any danger. But emotionally, she was a mess. We both were. She never said so outright, but I'm sure she blamed herself, as if losing the baby was some sort of punishment. But she blamed me, too, finally admitting how much she hated that I was never around. That she couldn't count on me. Even though wasn't a damn thing I could have done to stop her miscarriage, even if I had been there, I realized our problems went way beyond that. There was no way I could ever make her happy, not unless I compromised the one thing I'd planned on doing since I was fourteen years old. So…" He let out a sigh. "She called off the wedding and basically walked out of my life. Married somebody else less than a year later."

"And that hurt," Maddie said gently.

Ryan brushed her hair out of her eyes, a half smile tilting his lips. "Like holy hell."

Maddie squeezed his hand. "Hey," she said. "I'm not Suzanne."

"Yeah. I know." Then he added, "I ran into her again, couple months back."

"You did?"

"Yep. She was here visiting her folks. She told me her marriage had dried up and that she was moving to California." He gave a mirthless chuckle. "Once again running instead of facing her problems right where she is. And I guess that's when it finally began to sink in that maybe I wasn't quite as responsible for her pain as I'd thought I was."

"Well, glory hallelujah," Maddie said. "And just for the record? I don't want you to *ever* feel responsible for my happiness, is that clear?"

"Oh, yeah?" In a lightning-quick move, he pinned her underneath him, his eyes soft with love and dark with wanting. Over her laughter, he said, "Hey. I'll make you happy if I damn well feel like it. And there's nothing you can do to stop me."

"Oh," she said. "Well, okay, if it means that much to you."

"You better believe it—"

The front door opened, sending a draft whooshing through the house.

"Hey, Maddie," Ivy called out. "I'm back with Little Bits! And I'm standing here yellin' like a dang fool because I'm not blind and I can see that Ryan's truck is out front and since I don't see the two of you down here, doesn't take a rocket scientist to figure out what's going on." Her laughter echoed up the stairs. "And don't hurry down on my account. I'll just make myself at home."

After a stunned couple of seconds, Maddie and Ryan looked at each other and burst out laughing.

Then they figured they might as well take the woman up on her offer, because heaven knew when they might get one that good again.

Epilogue

In typical male fashion, Ryan didn't see what the big deal was in putting together a wedding in a couple of weeks. But Maddie had said she'd been deprived of a real wedding the first time, so there was no way she was chintzing on this one, which meant she needed at least eight.

They compromised on six. And now that the day was here, Maddie had to admit, she didn't think she would've survived a minute longer. As she stood there in the small church dressing room, however, staring at her reflection, her stomach was chugging like a washing machine. Ivy, her matron of honor, had taken the kids off somewhere to give Maddie a few minutes alone with Grace, who was bouncing seven-month-old Amy Rose in her arms.

In a pretty yellow dress the color of the daffodils Ryan had brought Maddie that day, her foster mother shifted the baby—who was calmly chewing on the pink lace band that had been put back on her head no less than three times already—to one hip so she could reach up and fuss with one of the miniature pink rosebuds Luralene had worked into Maddie's upswept hair.

"He'll get here, don't worry," she said. "Grooms are notorious for getting to the church late. Lord, the organist had been holding forth for nearly ten minutes before George waltzed into the church on our wedding day. If I hadn't been so crazy in love with him, I would've killed him on the spot."

Maddie tried to laugh. "I know, but—"

Mildred burst in through the dressing room door, her tiny veiled hat askew. "It's okay, he's here, he's here. But I swear, if that old buzzard ever pulls anything like that on me again, he won't see his seventy-sixth birthday!"

Now Ivy stuck her head in. "Since all the grooms are present and accounted for, Reverend Meyerhauser says to get in place…it's showtime!"

The ladies exchanged a round of kisses and sniffles, then filed out into the lobby and then to the back of the church. Mildred—who had confided to Maddie that she'd heard J.T. one last time, right after Ned had declared his feelings, telling her it was time for both of them to move on—had resisted the idea of a double wedding at first, saying she didn't want to steal Ryan's and Maddie's thunder. Maddie had told her you couldn't have too much joy in a single day.

So down the aisle they trooped. The little ones went first, bumping into each other the whole way, Katie Grace stopping at one point to hike up her dress to scratch her leg; Grace followed next, a babbling Amy Rose in her arms; then Ivy in pale blue, her braids wound round and round her head; then Mildred in a fluttery pink chiffon dress and jacket, the hat now sitting straight on her head; and finally Maddie in Mary Logan's ivory lace wedding gown, her knees knocking, her bouquet trembling, but her smile as bright and sure as the May sun streaming through the stained glass windows. Then she took her place beside Ryan, who smiled at her and took her hand in his, holding it next to his heart, and the trembling stopped.

She glanced over at Ned, leaning not so heavily on a cane, who winked (he and Mildred had decided to live in the Emerson house so the kids would have someplace to visit where they could be spoiled without Maddie's and Ryan's knowledge or interference), and then at her son, who was grinning so hard she thought he'd push his ears right off his head, finally letting her gaze come home to roost in Ryan's gentle, loving eyes.

And after they exchanged their rings and said their "I dos" and both brides had been soundly kissed, the pastor shut his bible with a *whump,* pronounced them husbands and wives, then looked from Ned to Ryan, shaking his head. "And the Good Lord knows it's about damn time the two of you came to your senses!"

And the congregation shouted as one, *"Amen!"*

* * * * *